D0055635

THE LIBRARIAN
ALWAYS
RINGS TWICE

BERKLEY PRIME CRIME TITLES BY MARTY WINGATE

The Bodies in the Library
Murder Is a Must
The Librarian Always Rings Twice

The Librarian Always Rings Twice

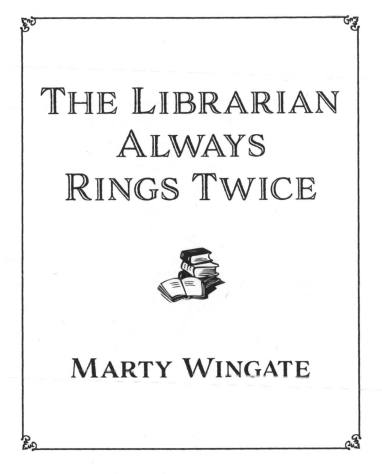

Marty Wingate

BERKLEY PRIME CRIME
NEW YORK

BERKLEY PRIME CRIME
Published by Berkley
An imprint of Penguin Random House LLC
penguinrandomhouse.com

Copyright © 2022 by Martha Wingate
Penguin Random House supports copyright. Copyright fuels creativity, encourages diverse
voices, promotes free speech, and creates a vibrant culture. Thank you for buying an authorized
edition of this book and for complying with copyright laws by not reproducing, scanning, or
distributing any part of it in any form without permission. You are supporting writers and
allowing Penguin Random House to continue to publish books for every reader.

BERKLEY and the BERKLEY & B colophon are registered trademarks and
BERKLEY PRIME CRIME is a trademark of Penguin Random House LLC.

Library of Congress Cataloging-in-Publication Data

Names: Wingate, Marty, author.
Title: The librarian always rings twice / Marty Wingate.
Description: First edition. | New York: Berkley Prime Crime, 2022. |
Series: First edition library mystery
Identifiers: LCCN 2021036498 (print) | LCCN 2021036499 (ebook) |
ISBN 9781984804167 (hardcover) | ISBN 9781984804181 (ebook)
Classification: LCC PS3623.I66225 L53 2022 (print) | LCC PS3623.I66225 (ebook) |
DDC 813/.6—dc23
LC record available at https://lccn.loc.gov/2021036498
LC ebook record available at https://lccn.loc.gov/2021036499

Printed in the United States of America
1   3   5   7   9   10   8   6   4   2

Book design by Laura K. Corless

This is a work of fiction. Names, characters, places, and incidents either are the product of
the author's imagination or are used fictitiously, and any resemblance to actual persons,
living or dead, business establishments, events, or locales is entirely coincidental.

To Leighton with love

THE LIBRARIAN
ALWAYS
RINGS TWICE

1

✧✦✧

"Shall I be Mother?"

Charles Henry Dill didn't wait for a response, but reached across the library table for the pot, the sleeve of his baby-blue linen jacket pulling up and exposing his hairy arm. He poured, managing to splash tea into the saucers and onto the highly polished walnut surface before, at last, hitting the cups.

Beside me, Mrs. Woolgar flinched and leapt up to get a towel— either that or she was about to go for his throat, a prospect I found not all that unappealing.

I stood. "No, let me."

Mrs. Woolgar sat down again as I retrieved a small towel from the trolley by the door. I mopped up the spill as Charles Henry distributed tea round the table, after which each of us poured the excess from the saucers back into the cups before adding milk. I noticed he had handed board member Maureen Frost, sitting next to him, a saucer with no spills.

"Well, now," Dill said, with a smirk of self-importance, "let me just say I'm ever so glad to be joining you here at Middlebank House and the First Edition Society, and I look forward with eager anticipation to working with our esteemed curator, Ms. Burke, in my new role as her assistant and, I daresay"—he chortled—"general dogsbody."

H ow had it come to this?

It had started on Monday. My boyfriend and I had returned from a week in Deal—a lovely seaside town in Kent—and I was ready and rested for the First Edition library's inaugural public open hours in two days' time. It was the logical next step to increasing the awareness of the Society, gaining new respect and members, and contributing to the overall knowledge base about those wonderful women writers from the Golden Age of Mystery.

But a library open to the public had been a shocking proposition— at least to the Society's secretary, Mrs. Glynis Woolgar. It took a fair bit of song and dance on my part to convince her that our founder, the late Lady Georgiana Fowling, had intended for her impressive collection of first editions—as well as rare and unusual printings—to be enjoyed, not hidden away. The secretary had agreed, but with reservations.

On my first day back at work, I had expected to find Mrs. Woolgar with her knickers in a twist about the launch of the Wednesday-afternoon opens, but instead, at our morning briefing, I had been met with an ashen face across the desk from me. Even before we had exchanged "good mornings," she made the pronouncement: "It's about Charles Henry."

Rarely was any news that involved Charles Henry Dill, Lady Fowling's lout of a nephew, good news, unless it was that he was out of the country. Because when he wasn't out of the country, he applied himself to his life's goal of trying to get more, more, more money out of his aunt's estate.

Mrs. Woolgar had told me his latest scheme was to become my assistant, and when I could find my voice again, I said, "But surely the board wouldn't allow it? Mr. Rennie wouldn't allow it?"

Duncan Rennie, the Society's solicitor, did his best to keep Dill and his machinations at bay. Sadly, as Mrs. Woolgar had pointed out, "Asking for a job isn't nefarious unto itself."

The board members' reasons for acquiescing had been another matter. The board comprised four dear old friends of her ladyship, plus a young one. Mrs. Audrey Moon and Mrs. Sylvia Moon—they had married brothers—and Jane Arbuthnot were in their eighties; Maureen Frost, in her early seventies; and my friend Adele Babbage, several decades younger than the others and ten years or so my junior.

Dill had worked his subterfuge quickly while I had been away, and he had kept under the radar of Mrs. Woolgar, aided and abetted by Maureen. First, he had worn down resistance from the Moons by "stopping in for a cuppa" every afternoon the week before. Under the guise of sharing stories of his aunt, he had revealed to them his wistful hope to be a part of the Society as a way of honoring her. Jane Arbuthnot had been easily swayed by Maureen. But I had been shocked to learn that Adele—the turncoat—had agreed to Dill's proposal, too.

The meeting had been arranged for Tuesday, the next afternoon.

When the attendees, including Mr. Rennie, had arrived, Mrs. Woolgar had taken them up to the library. I had stayed on the ground floor in the kitchenette to get the tea tray ready, and so when the front-door buzzer went off with the last in, Adele, I answered.

"Are you still speaking to me?" she asked, slapping a sweet smile on her face.

"Barely," I said.

Adele stepped in and stopped. "Is that his?"

A large white Panama hat hung on the hallstand.

"I'm afraid so. He's cut off that dreadful ponytail, probably so the hat would fit on his head. He must've taken scissors to it himself—it's all one length, and he has to tuck it behind his ears."

Adele wrinkled her nose. "Eww. Look, Hayley," she said, following me into the kitchenette, "I know hiring Charles Henry sounds dire, but the Moons as well as Jane have had to endure four years of his trickery in his attempt to get hold of Georgiana's fortune."

"And house," I had added as I arranged pastries on a tray.

"And house."

"What about Maureen?" I asked. "What does she see in him?"

"Yes," Adele said. "You'd think she'd have better judgment than this. Perhaps all those years ago, he wasn't quite so . . . Charles Henryish."

Nearly twenty years ago, Maureen, a local actress, and Charles Henry Dill had been involved. He had been in his forties and Maureen, married at the time, in her fifties. The affair had ended, and a few years later, Maureen's husband died, but it had been only in the four years since Lady Fowling's death that Dill and Maureen had picked things up again. Those were the only shreds of the story I could tease out of Mrs. Woolgar, who probably knew much more.

"And," Adele said, "it just seemed that a half day a week as your assistant would be a small price to pay to keep him quiet."

Possibly, but who would pay that price? Me.

I had handed Adele the tea service, taken the pastries, and headed upstairs to meet my doom.

It was done and dusted, and now Charles Henry reached out to nab the last black currant macaron, holding it aloft for a moment between a stubby finger and thumb. "I'm sure my dear aunt Georgiana would be so pleased to know that the *only living member of her family*"—he carried that description like a badge of courage—"is once more involved in her great undertaking."

Pairs of eyes darted round the table. No one attempted to contradict this outright lie. Even I, who had never met Lady Fowling in person, knew that *pleased* was not a word that would've described his aunt's reaction to the situation. Not after he had absconded with that set of eighteenth-century silver basting spoons. During her funeral reception. He had best watch his lies or the late Georgiana Fowling, founder of the First Edition Society and its library, might just rise from her grave and set her nephew straight.

"And now, Ms. Burke," Charles Henry said in his oleaginous fashion, "to the particulars of my employment. Shall we set our day and time now while we're all gathered? What about Monday mornings?"

"No," I said quickly, "I'm sorry, that won't suit." Did he think I wanted to spend my weekends dreading the start of the workweek?

"Friday mornings?" he offered with what he might've thought looked like a polite smile.

"Sadly"—*happily*—"that won't work with my schedule, either. I have a local adult-learning student starting on a special project Fridays."

"Well, then," Dill said, his voice practically gurgling with pleasure, "what is left but the middle of the week? Shall we say Wednesday afternoons?"

He had tricked me. He had wanted Wednesday afternoons all along so that he could be present during our public openings. What sort of devilry might Charles Henry get up to during those four hours when he could mingle with the public? Whose ear would he try to bend in the process—reporters, bloggers, academics—to support him in his desires? No, I would do everything I could to keep the proverbial bargepole between Dill and the public.

"You know," I said, "now that I think about it, Monday mornings just might work." There go my worry-free days off.

"Lovely," he said with some resignation. "Now, as to the particulars of my employment."

"No need to drag the board and Mr. Rennie through the details, Mr. Dill," I said, smiling innocently. "The two of us can sort all that out on your first morning. I'm sure the others need to be on their way."

They couldn't get out fast enough, offering quick good-byes along with weak congratulations to Charles Henry and quiet asides to me.

"*Arrivederci, mon amie!*" Adele whispered. "I'm stopping at the Minerva for Pauline. We have an evening class. We'll talk later."

"You're young," Jane Arbuthnot murmured as she left. "You'll survive."

"Dear Hayley," Mrs. Audrey Moon said, patting me on the arm. Mrs. Sylvia Moon added, "It's so good of you. I suppose we should've been stronger and not let him in, but he is Georgiana's only relative. Do let us know how you get on. Stop in for a sherry, why don't you?"

I noticed Dill had cornered Duncan Rennie before he could get out the door. Maureen Frost gave them a quick glance, leaned toward me and said, "He deserves a chance."

Mrs. Woolgar ushered the group, including my new assistant, downstairs to show them out. I remained in the library, propping my elbows on the table and sinking my head in my hands. She returned a few minutes later to find me unmoved—not an inch.

"Ms. Burke."

"Yes," I said, stretching my shoulders and then slumping back in my chair, "I know I must buck up. I'll tidy in here, and we can discuss this tomorrow at our morning briefing. You go on."

"Thank you. Mr. Rennie and I do have a few items to go over. But I want you to know that in no way will Charles Henry Dill be let loose to do as he pleases in Middlebank House. He remains as he always has been—not to be trusted. He will be watched."

The secretary left, and I followed her out as far as the landing, dragging one of the Chippendale chairs from the library behind me. She continued to the ground floor, but I stayed, placing the chair across from the full-length portrait of Lady Georgiana Fowling.

I sat down, heaved a great sigh, and said, "Well, now what?"

Even though I had never met her ladyship, I felt as if I knew her through this work of art. It had been painted in the 1960s, but in it she was dressed in retro fashion from the thirties in a burgundy satin evening dress with a halter top. The gown was cut on the bias and draped elegantly to the floor. She was turned slightly, revealing a low back, and had a hand on an empty chair—representing her late husband, Sir John.

I confess that on rare occasions I talk to the painting, but only in the sense that I use Lady Fowling's image as a sounding board. It isn't as if I thought she'd answer back—although the artist had done such a wonderful job of capturing the spirit of his subject that there were times when I felt as if her ladyship seemed about to reply. Needless to say, no one else knew I did this.

Today, she offered only her enigmatic smile, but I detected a steely glint in her look as if to say *beware*.

I lingered in case she had anything else to tell me. I stayed so still and quiet that when Bunter, Middlebank's tortoiseshell cat, padded up the stairs, he froze at the sight of me. I broke the moment with "Hello, cat," and he sauntered over and hopped up into my lap.

"What do you think of Charles Henry Dill?" I asked Bunter. "Will you lie in wait for him on the landing and pounce on his head when he passes?" I snorted, startling the cat. "Oof," I said as he used my tummy as a springboard and went flying down the stairs.

I returned the chair to its place as my phone, left on the library table, pinged with a message from my boyfriend, Val. At the end of our week at seaside, he had flown across the pond to visit one of his twin daughters, Bess, and her boyfriend, who had moved to the States a couple of months earlier to get involved in the theater scene. A good dad, his stay included helping them settle into their new flat.

Official now? You have a new employee?

Sad but true. How's the refurb?

Stripping wallpaper today. This evening Hamlet set in 1880s Tombstone.

Enjoy!

And you—the first open afternoon tomorrow. I'll expect a report.

Mrs. Woolgar and I started our Wednesday-morning briefing early. That was partly nerves, at least on my part, and mostly because we had short commutes to work. We both lived on-site—perks of our appointments. The secretary had the garden flat on the lower ground floor, which came with lots of sun as the land behind the terrace fell away. Her French doors opened onto the garden, which led to a gate that gave us access to the Gravel Walk that ran behind the entire terrace. My flat was on the second floor, above the library, and had brilliant views of the city on one side and out toward the Mendip Hills on the other.

"We've very little to do before this afternoon," I told her. "Everything is under control."

I thought it best to remain calm in front of the secretary, as I didn't feel as if she were yet one hundred percent behind the event. "I'll collect the brochures from the printers before lunch. That Edwardian inlaid occasional table you've chosen to use at the door is lovely. We have a new guest book for people to sign, and although it doesn't actually have a designated spot for email addresses, will you encourage people to leave theirs? Do you want a chair?"

"I don't need a chair, Ms. Burke," Mrs. Woolgar said. "I am perfectly capable of standing. I would prefer to greet our library patrons eye to eye."

The term *library patrons* gave me a thrill. "Is the sign ready?"

We had squabbled about this. Next to Middlebank's front door was a brass plaque that read *The First Edition Society*. When I had mentioned hanging a temporary sign on the door to announce the public hours, Mrs. Woolgar had balked.

"We are well identified already," she had said with a huff, "and a cheap-looking, computer-printed, plastic-covered notice stuck up on the door as if we're telling people the way to the beer garden has no place at Middlebank."

I had better taste than that, but there was no use pointing that out. Instead I had worked her round to the idea of a sign gradually, helped by a timely visit from our solicitor, Duncan Rennie. When I had put it to him, he commented that a proper notice might add to, instead of detract from, Middlebank's impressive presence. That's all the secretary had needed—an opinion from anyone other than me, but especially one from Mr. Rennie.

Now Mrs. Woolgar opened the bottom drawer of her desk and took out a heavy, ornate gold frame. The words, printed in bold, classic Garamond read:

The First Edition Library

Wednesday open hours

1 p.m. until 5 p.m.

Welcome

Please ring bell

"It looks lovely, Mrs. Woolgar, thanks so much for taking charge of it."

"You will keep an eye on them," she said, her brows furrowing above her eyeglass frames. "If they must take books off the shelf"— *In a library? God forbid*—"don't allow them to reshelve. They could tear a dust jacket or break a spine."

The most valuable books in the collection were under lock and key at the bank and would not be on display—at least not this first open day—but it wouldn't help to remind her of this.

"Yes, I'll watch them like a hawk. Did you check to see that our announcement appeared again today?"

Not that we expected a crowd. We had announced the new venture in the Society's newsletter, but much of our modest membership was outside of Bath and, indeed, scattered round the globe. That meant we needed to double our local efforts, so I had sent a notice to an online calendar called *Art! Books! Bath!* and contacted the local *Bath Live*. It had given us a brief mention.

"Yes, everything appeared as it should," Mrs. Woolgar said, and then she added, "I'm sure it will be a fine afternoon."

I took it as her way to calm my rising nerves, and I was ever so grateful. It's true that I was not the world's expert in the Golden Age of Mystery—I read Trollope at uni—but I was in the process of catching up. I continued to be surprised by what a long process it was.

Our briefing brief, I went back to my office. After I had faffed about for nearly an hour with no ability to concentrate on any one task, I was saved by a text from Val.

Is it possible to be over-Shakespeared?

Was it a bit much all in one day?

Fell asleep when Lear walked onto the gravediggers scene. Ready
for your afternoon?

As I ever will be. Wish me luck.

I love you. Good luck.

I left to collect the brochures, but walked straight past the printers on George Street and instead made my way down to the café on
the Pulteney Bridge for a rock cake and a cappuccino.

At twelve o'clock, I returned to Middlebank with the box of brochures, a bunch of roses, and caffeine-fueled nerves. Mrs. Woolgar's
office stood open and empty. While she was at her early lunch, I set
about getting ready for our afternoon. I moved the table in front of
the door, set out the guest book, located two short vases, and divided the roses between them. Leaving one on the table, I carried
the other vase up to the library, pausing in the doorway to look at
the room as if I were seeing it for the first time.

Floor-to-ceiling shelves of English oak lined almost every bit of
wall space. The long table took up the widest part of the room. On
the far side, two wingback chairs sat in front of the fireplace, which
was now filled with pine cones for summer. Pine cones and . . . I
looked closer and spied among the heap a manky catnip mouse,
which I quickly dispatched. The roses went into the powder room.
Brochures went everywhere, artfully arranged in fans.

Quarter to the hour, Mrs. Woolgar emerged from her flat below.
We ceremoniously hung out our shingle and retreated to our posts.
And waited.

Fifteen silent minutes went by, my tummy fluttering with antici-pation. At five past one, I looked down from the library landing to see Mrs. Woolgar standing at attention by the table. I looked again at eight past the hour to find her reading a brochure. At twenty past, I sat down by the fireplace and then leapt up. What if the sign had fallen off the door? I had made it to the landing when the buzzer sounded, nearly giving me a heart attack.

Mrs. Woolgar opened the door to two middle-aged women with rucksacks. We had a plan for large bags—to check them, much as you would at the British Library. The secretary explained this, and the women exchanged their rucksacks for tickets, signed the guest book, admired the entry, and headed up the stairs. The secretary took their packs to lock in her office.

"Hello," I greeted our visitors. That is, patrons. "Welcome to the First Edition library. Are you readers of mysteries?"

They hadn't read as much as they had watched on television, as it turned out, and so I found myself on more steady footing than I had expected.

"We are not a lending library," I explained, "but you're welcome to stay all afternoon if you like, reading a particular book or just perusing the titles. Please do let me know if you have any ques-tions."

"Is there a tearoom?" one of them asked.

It was the one thing Mrs. Woolgar and I had agreed on. "No, I'm sorry we don't have the space for a tearoom here at Middlebank."

They left after twenty minutes. I heard one of them say some-thing about the café at the Assembly Rooms. But the buzzer had sounded again, and so I greeted our next patron, an elderly man who quizzed me about poisons in mystery novels as if I were on *Mastermind*. When I failed the first round, he, too, asked if we had a tearoom. He was followed by two of Val's students from Bath College, who stayed barely long enough to come up to the library and say hello before they left. But I was left alone for only a moment.

A woman tiptoed in. Not an easy thing to do, as she was wearing a pair of the tallest espadrilles I'd ever seen. She had streaky blond hair and was dressed for summer in a short linen shift with a shapeless straw bag hitched over her shoulder.

She stood just inside and put a finger up to her lips in the universal library gesture, then waved at me—her nails flashing fuchsia—before taking in her surroundings.

"Hello, good afternoon," I said in a normal voice to put her at ease. "Welcome to the First Edition library."

She gazed at the shelves. "Would you look at that?" she said, in a hushed voice suitable for Durham Cathedral. "I've never seen such a thing. Are they yours?" She turned to me, squinting slightly, her eyes heavy with mascara and thick black liner.

"No, not actually mine. I'm Hayley Burke, curator of the library," I explained.

"Hayley, lovely to meet you. I'm Celia."

"Please do look round, Celia."

She went to the closest shelf and scanned the books, reading the titles aloud in a low voice, punctuated by tiny gasps.

"Are you on holiday?" I asked.

"I am," she said. "I don't half adore Bath. I adore all cities. My ex was always on about holidaying in the countryside. Not in a caravan park, mind you, where you could at least watch telly, but pitching a tent in the middle of nowhere and fishing and eating what he catches . . ." She looked over her shoulder and wrinkled her nose. "I don't like the countryside—it makes me nervous."

"Do you enjoy detective novels?" I asked.

"I'm mad about them. I started when I was fifteen. I came down with glandular fever and had to stay with my nan, and I almost drove the poor woman round the bend. One day she handed me *The Mysterious Affair at Styles* and said, 'Stop complaining and read this.' When my nan said to do something, you jolly well did it. The next day she asked if I liked it. Ah!" Celia put her hand to her chest and stumbled back. "Did I like it? *Did I like it?* I've read and reread them all more times than I can count—Christie, Sayers, the one from New Zealand, the one that died. Tell me, what's your favorite book?"

"It's so difficult to choose," I said, in perfect deflection. "What about you?"

"I love *Bertram's Hotel.* It's London, isn't it? And that Miss Marple, she's a one. But, if it isn't Christie, what about the story where the detective is laid up with a broken leg for the whole of the book? Wasn't that a clever bit?"

Celia continued to effuse about the Golden Age of Mystery, dropping the names of so many titles and characters that soon I was lost. Then she stopped abruptly and looked at me expectantly. Had she asked me a question?

"It's wonderful to be met with such enthusiasm," I said. "Did you notice we also have Daphne du Maurier on the shelf?"

"No! I love her and all, too."

We nattered on for half an hour about *Rebecca* and Laurence Olivier, until, at three o'clock, Celia said, "I'm gasping for a fag."

I was gasping for a cup of tea. She left for her cigarette, and, as there seemed to be a lull, I dashed into the loo, then down the stairs to the entry. "I'll just put the kettle on," I said as I hurried past Mrs. Woolgar to the kitchenette.

I ate a Hobnob, waiting for the kettle. As it was coming to a boil, the front door buzzed and I heard voices. But I stayed in the kitchenette long enough to pour up the tea in case I could come back down before it was stewed. When I went out to the entry, Mrs. Woolgar emerged from her office.

"Five. Three women, two men," she whispered. "Careful of the tall, thin woman with the brown hair, red highlights, rather beaky nose, and dark eyes. She's offered to start up and run a tearoom for us."

Five! I ran up the stairs, gave a breezy greeting to a man who stood gazing at Lady Fowling's portrait, and went in to meet the others.

Before I could finish my introductory words, the door buzzed again. Wasn't the foot traffic amazing? This time, a young woman came up the stairs holding a map of Bath in one hand and a well-thumbed paperback of *Das krumme Haus* in the other.

I listened more than I spoke as the group studied the shelves and chatted about their favorite settings. "Give me a village murder any day." "I do love the moors." "The Caribbean!"

Suddenly it was closing time. I followed the last group plus the German woman down the stairs at five minutes to five o'clock. The secretary retrieved their bags, and we bid them good afternoon. When the front door closed, I leaned against it.

"I'm knackered," I said. "That was a wonderful crowd, wasn't it? How many did we have all told?"

We counted up signatures in the guest book—eleven people.

"Eleven!" I exclaimed, although I felt as if I'd talked with fifty. Still, eleven was more than ten, which had been our top estimate.

"Have they all gone?" Mrs. Woolgar asked, glancing up the stairs. "I'm not sure I counted everyone out."

"I'll do a sweep."

On the landing, I gave Lady Fowling a smile and a nod before I looked into the empty library to find it wasn't empty after all. A man sat in one of the wingback chairs facing the cold fireplace. When I walked closer, he turned, noticed me, and stood. He looked about forty or perhaps a bit older—or younger—and he had dark blond hair that softly curled round his face and was just long enough to be gathered and tied into a short ponytail. He wore a loose white shirt tucked into tight black denims, and black boots.

"Hello," I said. "I hope you've enjoyed yourself this afternoon. I'm sorry to say we're closing now, but these are regular hours, so I hope we'll see you again next Wednesday." I noticed the book in his hand was one written by Lady Fowling and featuring her own detective. *Flambeaux and the Painted Night.* "Do you know Flambeaux?" I asked.

"Can we ever know all the man?" he replied with a smile, revealing a dimple on the left side of his mouth. "Flambeaux is a man of many parts. Do you agree?"

"Yes, certainly."

"His past is intriguingly vague," the man said. "We wonder, how did he come by his riches? From where does his sense of adventure arise? What of his ship? What is the connection between Brittany and Dorset? No, he speaks nothing of his past. Why did he turn to detecting? Flambeaux, the man of mystery."

Here we had a rare bird—a François Flambeaux superfan. I'm not sure I knew anyone else who had read the books, except for Mrs. Woolgar.

"Yes," I said with enthusiasm. At least he wasn't quizzing me on poisons or asking if we had a tearoom. "And mystery became his business, didn't it?"

"Perhaps taking it up to replace what he'd lost?"

"That's certainly one way of looking at it." The fine thing about a vague answer is that it gives you so many options.

"For the woman he loved, he put his early life behind. He never went back to it, even though she left him, which, naturally, broke his heart. But"—he paused for a long moment—"she left him with their child." The man looked down at the book in his hand and back up at me, and I saw his eyes were dark and troubled. "For the rest of his life, he carried with him both pain and love."

"You certainly know a great deal about her ladyship's sleuth," I said. None of this sounded familiar. I promised myself to start reading the Flambeaux books forthwith.

"Why wouldn't I know?" he asked. "I feel very close to Flambeaux, that is, to the man who inspired him. He was my grandfather. And my grandmother, the love of his life, was Lady Georgiana Fowling."

2

The man's words—*my grandmother, Lady Georgiana Fowling*—ricocheted round my empty head at such a speed I felt dizzy.

"I'm sorry," I said, "your grandmother? I'm afraid you're mistaken. Lady Fowling had no children."

"Yes, I understand she returned to England and lived her life without anyone knowing. Perhaps that is why she brought Flambeaux the detective to Dorset. But, wait now." The man smiled and held out his hand. "First, we must meet. I am John Aubrey." He pronounced his first name with an ever so slight softening of the *J*.

My eyes cut to the library door. If I called out, would Mrs. Woolgar hear? My mind worked quickly as I took his hand and said, "Lovely to meet you, Mr. Aubrey. I'm Hayley Burke, curator for the First Edition Society and its library. We're delighted you've visited today, but I believe there has been some sort of a mix-up."

"You are wary—this is to be expected."

Wary? Oh yes. Because either this was a scam or John Aubrey was a shilling short of a pound, and, as I was alone with him, I didn't much feel like finding out which.

"It's only that I think you must be working from misinformation inadvertently passed on to you." I strode confidently to the library door and nearly tripped over Bunter, who trotted in, leapt onto the long table, and sat down.

"Ms. Burke," Aubrey said, "I can see that I have delivered shocking news. You must be asking yourself why. Why would this grandson of Lady Georgiana Fowling walk into the story now?"

Yes, that was my question, and it was a bit disconcerting that he had asked it first. "Well, it does seem . . . out of the blue."

"You underestimate yourself. Word of the Society is spreading. I had determined to remain quiet about my grandmother—after all, am I not the recipient of the living she set up for her child—but your activities of late have brought memories flooding back."

"A . . . living?"

"And I confess to a longing to see the place that drew her, took her away from my grandfather and her child." He threw his arms wide as if taking in the library and more. "Only to see Middlebank, to experience it. I ask nothing else."

"Mr. Aubrey, I'm happy to help sort this matter out. Why don't we go downstairs and . . ." My voice failed me as I envisioned Mrs. Woolgar's face when she heard this claim. She might possibly attack the fellow with her handbag. It wouldn't be the first time she'd used it as a weapon. No, this would be better explained in private. "On second thought, as it's the end of the day, could I ask you to return tomorrow?"

"Tomorrow, tomorrow," he said, as if checking his internal calendar. "No, Ms. Burke, I am sorry, tomorrow is not possible."

Ah, there you are. Call his bluff and the scam artist is easily taken care of.

"But the next day," he said. "On Friday, I am happy to talk with you again. Shall we say, ten o'clock?"

He handed over the *Painted Night*, and said, "*François Paints the Night* is one of my favorites. The atmosphere of the old house, empty—or not? My grandmother had such a way with words."

I didn't bother to correct the title of the book, because when we walked out onto the landing, Aubrey paused at Lady Fowling's portrait.

"Did you know her?" he asked.

"No, I'm sorry to say, we never met."

His smile brought out a weak showing of his dimple. "But you feel her spirit, don't you? Especially here." I followed his gaze and thought I detected a hint of surprise in Georgiana Fowling's eyes.

Clutching Flambeaux to my chest, I followed Aubrey down the stairs to the empty entry and saw him out. When the door shut, I stood for a moment, rocking on my heels, ginning up my nerve. Then I turned to Mrs. Woolgar's closed office door, marched over, took a deep breath, and knocked. Nothing. I knocked again.

"Ms. Burke?"

I spun round. The secretary had come up from her flat in a fresh outfit. She wore a snug-fitting teal dress accented with a double lace collar. The 1930s style suited Mrs. Woolgar's pencil-like physique— it's no wonder she stuck with it.

When the front door buzzed, I flinched.

"That will be Mr. Rennie," she said, walking past me to let him in. "We're going to the theater this evening and have an early supper booked at the Garrick's Head." She paused. "Are you all right?"

Certainly not, but did I want to spoil her date?

"Yes, I'm fine."

"We can discuss how the afternoon went at our briefing in the morning." The secretary glanced down at the book in my hands. "Starting on Flambeaux?"

Gripping the leather binding, I kept my voice light. "Yes. Just a little bedtime reading."

I waved Mrs. Woolgar and Mr. Rennie off, went to the kitchenette, and poured out the cold tea while I considered my options.

Perhaps I wouldn't mention John Aubrey at our morning briefing— or ever. If he didn't appear on Friday, then no harm would've been done. On the other hand, if he did appear and I had said nothing . . . various scenes played out in my head as I walked up the two flights to my flat.

If John Aubrey's claim had upended me, what would it do to Mrs. Woolgar? The secretary acted as if she were the conduit of her ladyship's opinions on matters past or present. I was unclear how long Mrs. Woolgar had known Lady Fowling. Adele and I suspected it must be at least thirty years, which meant she had come on the scene decades after this purported early-1950s affair between Georgiana Fowling and François Flambeaux—that is, the man who was the inspiration for him—that had resulted in a baby. There was the crux of the matter. Would Lady Fowling have abandoned her child? Even I, who knew her only through the portrait, her notebooks, and other people's fond reminiscences, could not believe that.

My second-floor flat felt like a furnace. I opened windows at the front and back to invite a breeze, stripped off my work clothes, and sat at the open front window in knickers and bra with a cup of tea and two shortbread fingers. I looked unseeing out on the city, as I attempted to pull together what I knew.

Sir John had died in 1950, eighty years old, while Lady Fowling had been only thirty. By all accounts, even with the enormous age difference, they'd had a happy, albeit brief, marriage of ten years.

Her ladyship had remained at Middlebank the rest of her life, except for a period of time away just after her husband died. This absence from Bath was only ever mentioned in passing, as if it had been of no consequence. But how brief had that time been? Where did she go? When she returned, how did she seem? Was there anyone still alive who might remember?

I worked out a rough estimate of the years. A child born in, let's say, 1952 might become a parent in the early eighties, and today that resulting child would be somewhere round forty years old.

I shook these thoughts from my head. I needed a walk and I needed to shop—my cupboards were bare, and I couldn't exist on shortbread fingers alone. Off to Waitrose.

"What did he look like?" Val asked later that evening during our transatlantic chat. When he'd phoned and asked about the first public open day, I had started at the end of the afternoon, with meeting John Aubrey.

"He looked like a normal person," I said. "Possibly a few years younger than we are. Pleasant. He had curly blond hair. Soft curls." The enviable kind, I thought as I pulled the band from my ponytail and let my straight hair fall onto my shoulders. "It was tied back with a bit of ribbon. He was wearing a loose white shirt tucked into black denims, and he had tall black boots."

There was silence on the other end of the line, and then Val said, "Did he have a parrot on his shoulder?"

"That's it, he's a pirate!" But I stopped abruptly. "Wait now, he said something about Flambeaux . . . 'Where did he get his riches?' and something about adventures and carrying on the family business. And a ship! Does he think Flambeaux was a pirate?"

"Flambeaux is a fictional character," Val reminded me.

"Of course he is, but you've said yourself how often authors base fictional characters on real people. You told me Agatha Christie even put herself in her books."

"Hmm, Ariadne Oliver. So, do you think Flambeaux was real?"

"I don't know enough to say, but I will find out." I eyed my coffee table, where sat the first three Flambeaux books.

"Did you talk with Adele about it?"

Adele had been good friends with Lady Fowling for several years toward the end of her ladyship's life, and I believed she would take a more circumspect approach to Aubrey's claim than Mrs. Woolgar. When I got the chance to tell her.

"I would do," I told Val, "but at the moment it's difficult to find a slot in her schedule. She and Pauline are going on holiday next month—tent camping in France—and every evening one or both of them have a conversational French class."

We were quiet for a moment, allowing me time to fret. "I don't know what Mrs. Woolgar will do when I tell her."

Val, with a keen sense of when to change the subject, asked, "What do you hear from Dinah?"

"Good news," I said. "She's just passed the three-month mark in her new job."

My daughter might've been a slow starter—she took two gap years before going to uni—but when she hit her twenty-third birthday in the spring, she blossomed. She continued studying the history of everyday living at Sheffield, but now also had a job with a historical-homes group. She'd taken a driving course and paid half the upkeep on her housemate, Ginny's, car. She'd handled the responsibility so well, I didn't mind helping out with the insurance, seeing as how there was no hope in hell that her father would.

"Does this mean we are finished worrying about our daughters?" Val asked.

"Chance would be a fine thing," I said. "So, now, what is on your dad agenda for tomorrow?"

"Replacing window blinds. I'm running out of projects. And I miss you."

Such lovely words to hear. "I miss you, too."

We were silent, reluctant to end the connection, but eventually did, and soon after, I climbed into bed with *Flambeaux and the Painted Night.*

In the reverberating silence of the vast, empty house, a clutter of Queen Anne chairs, William and Mary walnut chests, and Georgian tables lay draped in enormous white sheets as if carrying on a secret confab of royal furniture. Surely in this place, no one had any business being alive or dead. Flambeaux listened with his enquiring ear flat to the wall, which had been papered with a gold brocade acanthus design quite popular in the early part of the last century, the flocking of which now

*tickled his auricle. He heard nothing, as he expected. But,
when the bedroom door flew open, Flambeaux's instincts took
charge of his limbs, and he leapt out the window as easily as he
had leapt off his ship's bow during that unfortunate encounter with the militia in Morocco, and onto the shallow, uneven
cornice of a false Elizabethan parapet, sadly tacked onto an
early-eighteenth-century-style Palladian manor. With the tips
of his fingers, Flambeaux clung to a stone griffin that stared
back at him, its hideous beak open and waiting.*

It was going to be a long night.

I didn't sleep well and awoke early with vague, unsettling scraps
of dreams about a ship. I pulled on old trousers and a shirt and
went out for a walk, hoping to clear my head. I had gone back and
forth, but in the end decided I would tell Mrs. Woolgar about John
Aubrey and his claim, on the off chance he showed up at our door on
Friday. I must prepare myself for her reaction, be ready to calm her,
make her see the sensible side of this. If there were one.

Back in my flat, I breakfasted on tea and toast and, although I
wasn't hungry, managed two slices with marmalade before readying
myself and heading downstairs to my office. I picked up a notebook
just to have something to hold and steeled myself for what was to
come. Mrs. Woolgar's office door stood open. I knocked.

She looked up from her computer. "Yes, Ms. Burke, come in. No
need to knock."

"Of course." It was as if my normal behavior had been preempted by this news, which continued to grow larger and of more portent by the second. I took my usual chair across the desk from her.

"I think we can count yesterday afternoon as a success," Mrs. Woolgar said, introducing what was to be the main topic of our meeting. "And even though I may have had a few misgivings to begin with, I admit now that your idea of opening the library to the public will be good for the Society. I believe her ladyship would've said the same thing."

So rare was it that Mrs. Woolgar let me win, I was heartily sorry I wasn't able to wallow in her concession speech. I needed to get this over with.

"Yes, a good start all round. Mrs. Woolgar, did you happen to notice the man in the white shirt and dark trousers? He came in with that big group, although I don't believe he was with them."

Mrs. Woolgar opened the guest book and ran her finger down the names. "Oh yes," she said, "he's the one who didn't sign. Some people are like that, loath to put down their name."

"It's John Aubrey." I cleared my throat. "Here's the thing."

I gave her as concise a recounting as possible, keeping my voice even and in control. When I reached the end—"and he said he wanted to see where she lived, that's all"—I kept my eyes on Mrs. Woolgar, ready for her outburst.

Closing the guest book, the secretary asked, "Where did he come from?"

"I . . . I don't think he said."

"Where did he say her ladyship spent this time away from Middlebank?"

"Brittany?"

"And the grandfather who was an inspiration for Flambeaux—what was his name?"

I shrugged. "The thing is, he seems quite familiar with Flambeaux. Perhaps he has the books?"

"Well, I don't know how that could be. Her ladyship had so few copies printed and gave them away only to her closest friends."

And family?

Mrs. Woolgar took off her glasses, pinched the bridge of her nose, and sighed. "Oh, Ms. Burke, I'm afraid you've been the victim of a prank. It wouldn't be the first time someone has tried to have us on. Several years before she died, her ladyship was approached by a woman claiming to be a psychic, who told her a Welsh dragon was buried under Sir John's tin factory in Sheffield and, for a fee, she would show us where. If she had been psychic, she would've known the factory had been pulled down in the 1960s and a housing estate built on the site. And there have been others. People get such strange ideas. I wouldn't let it worry you."

"He said he would be here tomorrow at ten to talk with us."

"Do you expect him to appear?"

The possibility grew fainter by the second. "Probably not."

"Why don't I ask Mr. Rennie to stop in tomorrow morning? Would that ease your mind?"

The presence of our solicitor might be just the thing to dampen John Aubrey's enthusiasm for lying. I exhaled and managed a smile. "Yes, Mr. Rennie has such a way about him. That would be perfect."

"There you are now, that's better," Mrs. Woolgar said, as if I were a child recovering from a tantrum.

"Mrs. Woolgar, if John Aubrey didn't put his name down, doesn't that mean we had a total of twelve patrons?"

* * *

O ur morning briefing ended, I embraced Mrs. Woolgar's com-
monsense reaction to the situation. I felt released from my
shackles and full of energy, so I wrote an article for the newsletter
about the success of the first afternoon open, after which I took myself out to lunch. I bought a cheese-and-pickle sandwich, sat in the
shade on a bench in the Parade Gardens, and listened to a brass
combo in the bandstand. Such a glorious summer's day in Bath.
Three children dashed past me, each with an ice cream. I looked
back at the kiosk near the edge of the lawn. Oh good, no queue.

As I stood waiting for my cone, I felt certain that tomorrow, Friday, John Aubrey would not show up. Mrs. Woolgar, Mr. Rennie,
and I would have coffee while Val's student worked on her special
project in the library. Then, on Saturday, I would take the train to
Liverpool to visit my mum, and on Sunday evening, Val would be
home. Although, not until quite late. He was to start teaching a summer short course Monday morning, and so, I wouldn't see him until
the afternoon. But still, the next few days were shaping up well.

F riday, Mrs. Woolgar and I dispensed with our briefing, doing
little more than exchanging "good mornings," before the front
door buzzed and our student arrived, a tall woman with short,
frosted brown hair and a receding chin.

"Frances, lovely to see you again."

"Hayley, thank you for allowing me into the collection."

Val's adult-learning classes at Bath College attracted all sorts of
people, but the average age skewed to older than your typical col-

lege student. The previous autumn, Frances Evers had turned forty, gone through a difficult divorce, sworn off men, and decided to change careers. I don't know what she had been like before, but these days Frances took life seriously. In the several times we'd met, I'd seen her smile once.

She and I had commiserated about exes and getting on with your life, even though it had been ten years since my divorce—wait, was it twelve?—and I had a grown daughter, whereas Frances had no children. Still, there was common ground, and it helped me accept her dour countenance.

"Come up," I said, and Frances followed me to the library. "I've gathered the paperbacks for you—we've nearly a hundred all told."

Frances picked up *The Regatta Mystery* by Christie from the top of a stack. The cover showed a woman with long blond hair and wearing a slinky dress being strangled. "I'm fascinated with how the paperback covers could reflect the time and trends," she said. "Women certainly didn't get treated well, did they?"

She had a working title for her paper: "The Bare Shoulder— Culture, World Events, and Murder." Frances hoped this would be of interest to a literary journal or a popular-fiction periodical, but had agreed to let us publish an excerpt first. With such attention, we could well become the international center for research into the Golden Age of Mystery.

Unpacking her laptop, notepad, and pencil, Frances said, "Well, I'd better get stuck in."

I returned to my office, but hadn't been there long before the front door buzzed. I glanced at the time—five minutes till ten o'clock—and I was reminded of the thing I should've been dreading but which had gone completely out of my head.

But it was the solicitor. Mrs. Woolgar got to the door first and opened it to Mr. Rennie, looking dapper as ever in his three-piece gray pin-striped suit. I greeted him, then stepped out and looked up and down the road. I saw nothing untoward and retreated indoors.

"Mr. Rennie, I hope I haven't wasted your time this morning."

"Nonsense, Ms. Burke. It's always better to be prepared. When this cowboy with his wild story doesn't show, we can always go over a few items of business. Perhaps we can help you think up tasks for Mr. Dill on Monday morning."

"I've got a few to offer," Mrs. Woolgar said under her breath.

"I may need them," I said. Mrs. Woolgar and I enjoyed a united front on the subject of Charles Henry Dill's working at the First Edition Society. "Anything innocuous and tedious. I'm hoping to bore him into quitting."

"You're very accommodating to take him on," Duncan said. "I know Sylvia and Audrey were quite relieved. And Maureen appreciates it, too."

"I'm willing to give him a chance," I said. But just the one.

We had remained in the entry, as if under an unspoken agreement, but now Duncan glanced at his watch. Five minutes past the hour.

"Well," the solicitor said, "I've been preparing the quarterly report, and if you'd like an early look—"

The front door buzzed, and the three of us froze.

"Shall I?" the solicitor asked.

"No," I said. "I'll answer."

John Aubrey stood on the pavement with hands on his hips, looking up at Middlebank and then to the left and right along the terrace. He appeared wholly unassuming. No pirate fancy dress today—instead, he wore a well-cut, casual summer suit, no tie, and his shirt collar unbuttoned. When he saw me, he smiled.

"Good morning, Ms. Burke."

"Mr. Aubrey, hello, good morning. Won't you come in?"

In the entry, Mrs. Woolgar and Mr. Rennie were the picture of suspicious minds. The secretary had her hands clasped at her waist and her chin thrust forward. The solicitor—not a tall man— appeared to have grown an inch or two. He held his arms at his sides, his fingers lightly drumming on his thighs. Neither smiled, neither frowned.

"Mr. Aubrey, let me introduce you to Mrs. Glynis Woolgar, who was a great friend of Lady Fowling's and is now secretary for the Society, and Mr. Duncan Rennie, her ladyship's solicitor who now manages the Society's business." I paused. "Mr. John Aubrey." No description available.

Aubrey offered his hand to Mrs. Woolgar, who paused only a second before her good manners took over and she accepted.

"So very pleased to meet you, Mrs. Woolgar. You are a direct link to my grandmother, and your presence is as if she herself were here."

"Yes, lovely to . . . meet you."

"Mr. Rennie," Aubrey said, extending his hand.

The solicitor took it and gave one firm shake. "Mr. Aubrey."

"Mrs. Woolgar and Mr. Rennie are here to help us sort out the situation," I said. "Shall we go to my office?"

Duncan shifted the wingback from near the door, and I pushed over my desk chair so that the four chairs formed a semicircle around the cold fireplace. We sat. I opened my mouth to begin, but Aubrey, adjusting his jacket, started first.

"Ms. Burke, I'm sorry to take you unawares on Wednesday afternoon. I repeat now what I told you then, for Mrs. Woolgar and Mr. Rennie to hear. I want nothing from you except for you to share your memories. We all want to understand our family, don't we? I've longed to see where my grandmother lived and to hear about her life and understand why she left her own child after so brief a time."

"Her ladyship never had a child." The statement burst out of Mrs. Woolgar as an accusation, her face reddening.

Mr. Rennie intervened. "You must admit, Mr. Aubrey, it is a far-fetched story, and without any details, how can we even begin to assess the validity of your claim?"

Aubrey nodded. "Yes. Of course, your mistrust is to be expected. But perhaps we can agree on the beginning. Lady Fowling was away from Middlebank for a period of time after her husband died, was she not?" No one answered, and he continued. "I can tell you that her time in Brittany, barely two years, was a happy time for her. True, she carried sadness for the loss of her husband, but grief takes many forms, doesn't it? And then love came upon her quickly. It was an escape for her from the sorrow and the constraints of her life—the expectations of others. But the happiness was not to last. She recognized her obligations to the memory of her husband and, of course, the morals of the time. And so she left, deciding, perhaps, that her child would be better off with his father."

Mrs. Woolgar's lips thinned to nothing as she clamped her mouth shut. Her hands gripped the arms of the chair, and her knuckles had turned white.

"What was your grandfather's name, Mr. Aubrey?" Duncan

asked. "And your father's name? Was this purported child a boy or a girl? You spoke to Ms. Burke of a living left by Lady Fowling, and I'm sure you realize that if such a thing existed, it would've been set up here, in Britain, and not in France."

"Your family's firm has a long history with the Fowlings," Aubrey said. "Your grandfather, Donald Rennie, was working when the child was born."

Duncan's face gave nothing away. "Yes, Donald was my grandfather. Now, about this child, Mr. Aubrey."

"My parents died when I was only a boy in a road traffic accident. My grandfather became a broken man. First he had suffered the loss of his Georgiana"—Mrs. Woolgar winced—"and then his only child. After that, he found life difficult and he sent me away, and I grew up in Dorset with relatives."

"Where in Dorset?"

"I am happy to provide you with details, Mr. Rennie. And in return, I ask of you only your memories, which cost nothing. It's true I have no memories of my own to share, but I do have this."

He reached into his jacket, pulled out a flat pocketbook, and opened it. Inside was an old black-and-white photo, the sort with scalloped edges. These were worn and dog-eared at the corners. Aubrey smiled at it and then handed it to Duncan, who examined the image before passing it to Mrs. Woolgar. She stared at the photo without blinking for so long that Duncan reached over, gently took it back from her, and gave it to me.

The photo had been taken at the seaside. A young woman wearing a modest one-piece bathing costume stood next to a rocky outcrop, while behind her, waves crashed onto the sandy shore. Her hair, shoulder length, had been caught by the wind, and she held it back with one hand as she smiled. Such a lovely smile—enigmatic, as if she had a secret to share. I knew that smile. Icy dread crept through my veins. I held the image up to the light to study her face more closely, and I noticed Duncan staring at the back of the photo.

I turned it over and read the words, "'With love, Georgiana.'"

3

Lady Fowling had kept personal notebooks, filling dozens and dozens of everyday school exercise books—the kind with marbled covers. For decades, she recorded everything from recipes and shopping lists to story ideas and random thoughts. I had found boxes of them the previous autumn and had read through most. I knew her handwriting, and I recognized it here.

"It was all my grandfather had left of her," Aubrey said quietly as he took the photo from me and put it back in his wallet.

"Mr. Aubrey," Duncan began, "about your documentation—your proof of this assertion."

Aubrey glanced at his watch. "My God, look at the time. I must be off. Please, Mr. Rennie, I will return with the facts and figures you require. Shall we say, Monday?"

"A phone number, Mr. Aubrey?" The solicitor persisted. "Your local address? Will you leave that with me?"

"I'll send it round, I promise you," Aubrey said, standing and moving toward the door. "I'm sorry to be under these ridiculous time constraints. Oh, to be on the open seas! Until Monday, Mrs. Woolgar, Ms. Burke, Mr. Rennie."

I followed him out, closing my office door on the way. In the entry, Aubrey paused, looking pained as he spoke in a low voice. "Thank you, Ms. Burke, for arranging this meeting. Again, I'm sorry this has come as such a shock to the people who thought they knew her so well. I hope you realize I hold my grandmother in the highest esteem and understand that life is not always easy and neat."

"No," I said, "no, it isn't. It's good of you to acknowledge that."

"Hayley?"

It was Frances from the library landing.

"Sorry—I don't mean to disturb you," she said.

"No, that's fine. Come down."

She tiptoed down the stairs. Aubrey stood on my left, and Frances, keeping a cautious eye on him, circled round to my right side.

Aubrey smiled at Frances and then turned to me with an expectant look.

I made the introductions, although I provided no details about Aubrey. "Frances is a student from Bath College working on a special project."

"Ms. Evers," Aubrey said. "It's a pleasure."

Not so much for Frances, whose receding chin disappeared even farther as she gave him a skeptical glance. "Yes, hello."

Aubrey's dimple appeared. "Are you by any chance including the François Flambeaux stories in your study?"

"Who?" Frances asked.

"No, she's focusing only on paperback editions," I explained. "Frances, did you want to ask me something?"

Frances looked at me blankly, then at Aubrey, who continued to smile at her. Her cheeks took on a neon-pink glow. "Yes, I did. It's . . . I'm sorry, it seems to have slipped my mind. Perhaps later."

She hurried up the stairs. Aubrey called after her, "Lovely to meet you, Frances." He nodded to me. "Ms. Burke, until next time."

When he'd gone, I returned to my office, where I found Mr. Rennie holding Mrs. Woolgar's hand, murmuring, "There are a thousand reasons he might have a photo—you know how things are sold on these days. Ephemera is highly collectible."

When Mrs. Woolgar noticed me, she slipped her hand away from his.

"This is preposterous," she said, but her voice was weak.

"He seems so sincere," I said. "Could any part of what he's saying be true?"

"Which part?" the secretary shot back.

"No parts." I replied quickly. "I don't know why I said that."

"I don't know what his game is, but we'll call his bluff," the solicitor said. "He'll need to provide us with names, dates, and places. Hard facts will prove him wrong. Whatever it is he wants, it won't work."

"He says he doesn't want money," I reminded them.

"Probably only trying to put us at our ease," Mr. Rennie said.

"Her ladyship would never have abandoned her child," Mrs. Woolgar said. "The very thought. I don't care if she was a young girl."

But she hadn't been a young girl. In John Aubrey's tale, Lady Fowling would've been in her early thirties.

"He could be a thief," Mrs. Woolgar said as we shifted the chairs back to their places. "We'd better change the password on the alarm system."

"I don't want either of you to worry about this," Duncan said. "He has nothing."

He had a photo of Lady Fowling, but now that Mrs. Woolgar had recovered her spirits, I didn't think it wise to point that out.

"But," the solicitor added, "let's keep this to ourselves at the moment—shall we?"

I arrived back in Bath Sunday evening after a weekend with my mum. The time had gone by in a flash, as usual. I had taken the train Saturday morning, and, wanting to use the time wisely but having abandoned the *Painted Night*, I opened up *Flambeaux and Murder at the Crossroads*.

> *The gas streetlight, erected just before electricity caught on, and which remained a working beacon as a sign of the village's past and its connection to Lord Bagshot, who had given money for the illumination after the dreadful occurrence at the crossroads, and who had personally unveiled the structure with its glass enclosure set atop a molded metal stand in the style of Inigo Jones with the Bagshot coat of arms proudly displayed on all four sides of its base, flickered warmly.*

Although I loved Lady Fowling's detective, and her enthusiasm for writing was beyond compare, I could take only a bit of Flambeaux at a time. After a few pages, I had set the book aside and bought tea and a slice of lemon drizzle from the trolley.

On my return journey Sunday evening, I had given myself a break from Flambeaux. I must've had pirates on my mind, because I'd brought along a copy of Daphne du Maurier's *Frenchman's Creek* I'd come across in a charity shop. I didn't get far there, either. Dona was still rattling along in the carriage on the way to Cornwall when Val rang, and I happily turned my attention to my own romance.

The train pulled into the station at quarter past ten and, as it was still quite light, I strolled up Manvers and along the Grand Parade and eventually up to our terrace, swinging my weekend bag at my side. There was still a fair amount of both foot and car traffic, common for a summer evening. I had passed the entrance to Hedgemead Park when, up ahead, I saw a man standing at Middlebank's doorstep.

This had been one of Mrs. Woolgar's arguments against publicizing open times at the library—she worried that every manjack would appear at all hours thinking he could get in. I saw this fellow's hand reach out as if he were about to press the buzzer, and I flashed on the image of the secretary plodding up the stairs from her flat late on a Sunday night. I broke into a trot, calling, "Hello, can I help you?"

The man stepped back, giving me the chance to insinuate myself between him and the door. I held the key in my hand, just to let him know I belonged there. He was about my height with sparse hair, a face that narrowed to a point, and round, gold-framed glasses, giving him the appearance of a baby owl.

"I'm looking for Milo," he said, blinking slowly.

"Sorry, there's no one here by that name."

"Milo Overton," he said.

"No. You have the wrong house."

"Are you sure?"

"Yes," I said, rather snappishly, "I'm quite sure. There is no Milo Overton here."

He shrugged, turned, and walked away, but over his shoulder said, "When he does get here, say Jelley was looking for him."

I clicked my tongue at his retreating figure and stuck the key in the lock.

Inside, I switched off the alarm and turned to Bunter, who had appeared from nowhere, as cats do, and sat waiting silently at my heels. Reaching in my bag, I pulled out a catnip mouse, dangled it above his nose, and said, "Do I look like a messenger service for this Milo Overton? Or for someone named Jelley? No, I do not."

The cat, showing great interest in his new toy but none in my chatter, walked in a circle while keeping his nose in the same place, eyes on the prize. I tossed the mouse high in the air, and it sailed past the staircase and into the far corner near my office. Bunter sprang into action, and the chase was on.

Reality set in early the next morning when, not long after four as the sky began to lighten, my eyes popped open. Monday had come. Today, the First Edition Society gained a new employee, and I an albatross round my neck: Charles Henry Dill.

This business with John Aubrey had distracted me, but Aubrey was nothing compared with Dill, who needed only to set foot over the threshold of Middlebank to put my hackles up. And now he would be my assistant.

Go back to sleep. But my eyes refused to stay shut. After an hour of fighting it, I flung back the bedcovers and pulled on my clothes. Perhaps I could walk off my anger at Dill's worming his way into the Society for his own devious purposes. I took my usual route, striding briskly down Bennett Street toward the Circus and over to the Crescent before circling back through Victoria Park.

It had just gone six o'clock when I passed the entrance to Hedge-mead Park. Traffic was thickening as I puffed my way up this last rise. Almost home. I had paused to catch my breath and push a sweaty hank of hair off my face when I saw a man standing at the door of Middlebank. This man, I knew.

"Mr. Aubrey?"

But when he turned, I saw it wasn't Aubrey at all. He was the same height and build and coloring, but when I came closer, I saw that his hair, although also dark blond and long enough for a short ponytail, had waves, not curls.

"I'm so sorry," I said, "I thought you were—"

"You thought I was John," the man said, smiling. Now I could see clearly that he looked nothing like Aubrey. He had no dimple. The man ran his hand through his hair. "You aren't the first. I should have a cut, and that would put shed to the mistake of identity."

"You know John Aubrey?" I asked. "I'm Hayley Burke, curator here at the First Edition Society. Are you looking for him?"

"You're Hayley? Good. I was just about to put this through the letter box," he said, holding out a brown envelope addressed to me. "John asked me to drop it off."

"Oh, thank you. Are you his . . . brother?"

The man laughed. "No, John doesn't have a brother. Look, he

said to tell you he'll be round as soon as he can, it's only that he can't stay in one place too long, not at this time of year. Well, good day."

He walked off, but I said, "Wait. Who are you?"

"Sorry," he said, and came back toward me. "I'm Milo Overton."

"Milo?" I repeated. "Milo Overton? There was a fellow here last night asking for you."

He frowned. "Was there? Who?"

"He said his name was Jelley."

"Jelley? What was he doing here?"

"I wondered the same thing."

Overton shook his head and laughed. "I'm sorry he disturbed you. I'll catch him up later and make sure it won't happen again."

He turned to go, but I said, "Mr. Overton, wait. Do you work for Mr. Aubrey?"

"In a manner of speaking."

"Do you know why he came to Middlebank?"

Milo's eyes narrowed and he looked guarded. "It's to do with his family."

"Do you know where he is? You see, I have no way of getting in touch with him."

"Well, won't it be in there?" Overton asked, nodding toward the brown envelope in my hand.

He must've seen the dubious look I gave the envelope, because he shook his head. "Ah, John. Here, let me give you my mobile number, and you can let me know what else you need."

I fumbled in my pocket for my phone, afraid he would vanish before I could get this one concrete piece of information.

"Right, I'm ready."

He rattled off his number. I tapped it in and sent a text.

I heard a single *clang* like a ship's bell. Overton patted his jacket pocket and said, "There you are."

I left the letter on my desk and went up to my flat, where I stretched out on my bed just for a moment's rest. I awoke two and a half hours later, still sticky with sweat. I leapt into the shower and managed to make it downstairs with five minutes to spare before the morning briefing, my damp hair hanging loose. I'd had no breakfast—not even a cup of tea—and so dashed into the kitchenette and rifled through the biscuit tin, eating the last three chocolate digestives as I waited for the kettle to boil. At precisely nine, I sank into a chair in Mrs. Woolgar's office, the tea bag still floating in my mug. I jumped up again.

"Sorry—hang on." I retrieved the brown envelope from my office and returned to Mrs. Woolgar, laying it on the corner of her desk as I told her the story of Milo Overton's early-morning hand delivery.

"Have you opened it?" the secretary asked, eyeing the envelope as if it were an adder about to strike.

"No," I said, "I thought I should wait for . . . I will do it now." I stuck my finger under the flap, but Mrs. Woolgar put a hand up and instead held out her letter opener as if it were a scalpel. I took it, performed the operation, and pulled out a single sheet of paper. A sticky note slapped to it read, *Dear Ms. Burke, For your records. Regards, John Aubrey.* Below his name were a few marks that suggested birds in flight. The page beneath the sticky note was a photocopy of a yearly statement from Smythe Investments Ltd., with a London address.

"A living?" I said, looking at the amount of money in the account. "What sort of living would this buy you?"

I passed it to the secretary, who scanned the information. "I can't see that he could get even ten pounds a year. And what sort of proof is it?" She scoffed, but I heard an edge to her voice. "Where has this money originated? What has been paid out and when? He provided no details about himself apart from a postbox number. We have no way to contact him."

"But I have Milo's mobile number, and he works for Aubrey."

"Doing what?" Mrs. Woolgar demanded.

I shrugged. "Assistant. Business partner? Maybe he's a valet?"

"Really, Ms. Burke? That's a bit old-fashioned, don't you think?"

"Yes. I suppose so."

"We'll let Mr. Rennie look into this 'living' and see how far that gets Mr. Aubrey."

"Good. That's a relief, because I already have an unpleasant task ahead of me this morning."

Mrs. Woolgar made a sympathetic noise. "Yes, Charles Henry."

Just get through these few hours, I told myself. After that, the rest of the day held great promise. Val had both a morning and evening class, but free time between, and I expected him to be here around lunchtime. I should mention to Mrs. Woolgar I would be taking the afternoon off.

"I asked Mr. Dill to arrive at nine thirty." I checked the time. Ten more minutes of peace.

"I've made a list of tasks you might assign to him," the secretary said, handing over a paper. I read the first: *Take stock of tea, coffee, and biscuit supplies in kitchenette.*

I snorted, happy to be back on an even keel with Mrs. Woolgar in our joint disregard for Charles Henry. I moved cautiously into troubled waters. "Mrs. Woolgar. I'm reading the Flambeaux books, in case John Aubrey is gleaning information from them to use on us."

Even behind her glasses, I saw the anger flare in her eyes.

I held up the leather-bound *Flambeaux and the Painted Night* and asked, "Didn't George Bayntun do a lovely job?"

The fire went out and Mrs. Woolgar smiled as she reached for the book. "Her ladyship was so proud to see her books in print and on the shelves of the library among those authors she admired the most."

George Bayntun, a dealer in rare and collectible books in Bath, also carried out repair and rebinding. The business had been round forever, and as the owner had been a friend of Lady Fowling's, he had acted as publisher for her.

The secretary handed the book back. "I don't see how what John Aubrey is saying would have any relation to her ladyship's books. All the sets are accounted for, and so I'm not sure how he would've got hold of a set."

"Were there other Flambeaux stories besides the published books?"

"Not to my knowledge. Lady Fowling had stopped writing her books before I came on."

François Flambeaux had been part of Lady Fowling's past, but not part of her secretary's. Here was a clue to Mrs. Woolgar's history, which I knew next to nothing about. "Had you known her ladyship long before you took the post as her personal assistant?"

The secretary turned her head slightly, and the reflection of the computer screen in her glasses as usual did a fine job of deflection. "Did she make mention of Flambeaux in her notebooks?"

"Now and then, as I recall. But, couldn't there be unfinished manuscripts lying hidden somewhere?"

"If there are, Ms. Burke, I don't know where you would begin to search for those."

But I knew.

The front-door buzzer heralded the arrival of my new assistant. As I walked out to the entry, I scraped back my hair and secured it in its band before opening the door to Charles Henry Dill, the jacket of his baby-blue linen suit barely able to be buttoned round his middle, looking ever so pleased with himself.

He swept the Panama hat off his thick black-and-silver hair and said, "Good morning, boss."

I winced. "Mr. Dill, good morning. Come through."

I led him to my office and sat down at my desk, gesturing to the chair opposite. "Well, here we are, your first morning. We may as well get stuck in, don't you think? First, to the particulars of your employment. Monday mornings, nine thirty until one. After one month's time, you'll have a performance review, and—"

"Performance review? I don't see that's necessary after only a month."

"You are new to the job, Mr. Dill, and as your employer, we—the Society—cannot overlook our responsibilities."

"Is that so," he muttered, but then brightened. "I say, Ms. Burke, aren't you coming up to your one-year anniversary as curator? That must mean you'll be having your own performance review quite soon."

Would I? That hadn't occurred to me. I wonder if it had occurred to the board.

"Do you by any chance have experience as an indexer, Mr. Dill?"

"A what?"

"Indexer. A person who creates the index at the end of a book or periodicals. An indexer sorts through text, calling out and categorizing topics, names, titles, and then compiles an alphabetical list. We have no index for the Society's newsletter, and one is desperately needed in order to better serve our growing membership and help with individual research opportunities."

Dill's face fell. Not the glamour job he'd hoped for?

"Oh. Well, how hard can it be?"

I smiled indulgently. "I wouldn't let a member of the Society of Indexers hear you ask that. To be an indexer is to be able to organize the world. Fortunately, for this project, you may just get by with an online short course that I have found for you. Who knows, perhaps this will lead you to a profession?" *Because I don't recall you've ever had one in the past.* "This should take you three hours, which makes it perfect for your first morning. Next week, you'll begin on the newsletters."

"Pfft," Dill said. "Hardly seems a task to occupy me for long."

"Oh, I should tell you Lady Fowling started the newsletter as an occasional mailing about forty years ago, but only the last five have been digitized, so you'll be working from photocopies for the most part."

Dill sighed.

"You brought your laptop?" I asked.

He brightened. "Yes. I thought it would be best for me to have access to the records and such of the Society. Perhaps you'll provide me with the pass codes?"

"I don't think that will be necessary."

"It would allow me to help you update the *About* page on the website. I would think you'd want to add me as a member of staff and point out I am Lady Georgiana's only living family member."

Are you? We'll see about that. The thought popped into my head, but I immediately corrected myself. Of course he's Lady Fowling's only living relative, because John Aubrey is not her grandson.

"Why don't we set you up at the table in the library, where you can begin your instruction?"

He was a reluctant student, was Charles Henry Dill. Twice, he managed to bumble logging on to the website, and it took him three tries to sign up for the class. When it came to filling out his personal information, he asked if he shouldn't need to use the Society's credit card number to pay.

"It's already paid for," I said, pointing to his screen and the box that read *Paid*. I would not let him annoy me, I would not. "I'll check back with you in an hour."

"Wouldn't be a cup of tea going, would there?" he said as I walked out.

"In an hour, Mr. Dill."

True to my word, at eleven o'clock, I took him up his tea and rewarded him with a plate of Maries, my least favorite biscuit and so no great loss. He looked at the plate and asked, "You wouldn't have any custard creams?"

"No, we wouldn't."

I returned to my desk and, with a cup of tea and custard creams at hand, read newsletters from five other historical literary societies, hoping to get ideas. I forgot all about Charles Henry Dill until about twelve thirty, when Mrs. Woolgar came to my door and mentioned how quiet he'd been.

"Yes," I said, going out to the entry, "I'd better check."

Bzzzzz.

At the sound of the buzzer, I held my breath. Then I asked myself how it had come to be that the arrival of someone at the front door of Middlebank was such a frightening event?

I marched to the door and flung it opened to John Aubrey, once again in his pirate fancy dress.

"Good morning, Ms. Burke," he said. "A lovely day in Bath, but continued warm. I don't know how you look so fresh."

"Mr. Aubrey," I said, stepping back to let him in. I couldn't help smiling in return with his dimple winking at me.

Mrs. Woolgar had shot into her office at the sound of the buzzer, but now emerged.

"Good morning, Mrs. Woolgar," Aubrey said.

She had her handbag under her arm and held fast to the brown envelope. "Good morning, Mr. Aubrey," she said, looking as if she wished him anything but. "We received your financial information, and I'm just about to take it over to Mr. Rennie."

"Ah," Aubrey said, "my man Milo made his delivery. Excellent. Please give Mr. Rennie my regards. And let me say, Mrs. Woolgar, that with your efficiency and competent manner, I can see how Lady Fowling relied on you."

Even the secretary couldn't object to that statement. "Yes, of course," she replied faintly. "That is, thank you." She reached the door and added, "Ms. Burke, I'll return after lunch."

"I'm taking an hour or so off after lunch," I said, glad for the opening, "but I'll check with you before the end of the day."

Once Mrs. Woolgar was out the door, I turned back to John Aubrey, who stood looking as if he had nowhere to go and was quite happy about it. What was I to do with him?

Charles Henry appeared on the library landing.

"Did I hear someone mention my auntie Georgiana's name?"

4

We looked up to see Dill pausing for a moment at the top of the stairs before marching down and holding out his hand. "Hello, sir. I am Charles Henry Dill, Lady Fowling's nephew."

It was like watching a car crash in slow motion, and I stood frozen, helpless to stop it. I tried but got only as far as opening my mouth as Aubrey took Dill's hand in both of his, gave it a hearty shake, and said, "You are her nephew? Is this true? What a wonderful meeting, for that makes us cousins, you and I! We are first cousins . . . or are we removed? I am unclear on these designations. Still, it's very good to meet you, Charles Henry Dill. I am John Aubrey, Lady Fowling's grandson."

I ticked off Charles Henry's facial expressions one by one as he looked from Aubrey to me and back. Shock, confusion, disbelief, anger—all in the span of a moment—as his jaw dropped lower and lower. Finally, he began to sputter.

"You . . . I . . . sorry, did you say . . ."

"Mr. Dill," I cut in, "Mr. Aubrey has acquired some perhaps misleading information about his family's history and how it relates to the Fowlings, and I don't believe this is the time or place to go into it, so I would like you to go back to the library and finish today's assignment."

Dill's voice shot into soprano range. "Her grandson?" He turned to me, his face like a beetroot. "Is that what he said?"

"Go up to the library, Mr. Dill, and we'll discuss this later."

"Yes, Mr. Dill," Aubrey said, his brow furrowed and his face full of concern. "I'm sorry this has taken you unawares, it's only that—"

I put a hand up. "Please, Mr. Aubrey, I'll take care of this."

Dill jabbed his finger into Aubrey's chest. "I'll have you know, sir, my aunt had no children."

"Mr. Dill!"

I pushed my way between them and batted his hand away. He drew back.

"Go to the library," I said. "Now. I will follow."

Charles Henry huffed and puffed. His eyes glowed red. He was like a boiler about to explode. That might've caused some people to back off, but I stood my ground. If I could weather my daughter's shrieking outrage at age sixteen when I told her she couldn't go off with a group of friends to Amsterdam for the weekend, I could survive this.

Dill narrowed his eyes at Aubrey before pivoting and stomping up the stairs, disturbing Bunter, who had been napping on the chair beside Lady Fowling's portrait. The cat streaked down to the entry and disappeared into the secretary's office.

"Mr. Aubrey," I said, already weary of the day, "would you like a cup of tea?"

"Yes, Ms. Burke, a cup of tea is what we need." Aubrey glanced up the stairs after Charles Henry, then back at me. "This was a shock for my cousin. I'm sorry to be the cause of such unhappiness."

"Why don't you wait for me in the kitchenette? It's just there, round the back of the staircase and across from my office."

Aubrey gave an abbreviated bow, turned, and went off. I took a deep breath and headed to the library.

Charles Henry sat at one end of the long table, laptop closed and arms crossed. He looked up at me, sharp and wary.

"Where did he come from? Why are you letting him perpetrate this fraud on my aunt's estate? He's a rogue and a liar. You can see that, can't you? He's trying to lay claim to property and wealth that aren't rightfully his."

Typical. It wasn't about Georgiana Fowling's life and her loves, it was all about what Charles Henry Dill thought was due him.

"He isn't asking for money."

Dill spat out a laugh. "Pull the other one, why don't you."

"This is all being sorted, and there's no need for you to be concerned." Although, if he and Aubrey were family, then . . . no, better not to think about that. "Now, are you going to finish your work today, or shall we call this whole enterprise off?"

He threw his shoulders back. "Of course I'll finish my work."

"Good. Then I'll leave you to it and go downstairs to Mr. Aubrey and—"

"Send him packing, I hope," Dill muttered.

In the kitchenette, the kettle was coming to a boil, the tea bags lay on the counter, and the pot was warming. John Aubrey sat, his hands folded on the table.

"I thought it too presumptuous of me to look in the biscuit tin."

I laughed and handed it over. "See what you can find." I poured up the tea, set the pot on the table, and said, "Mr. Aubrey."

He looked up from a packet of Hobnobs. "Please, will you call me John?"

"Yes, fine."

"And I may call you Hayley?"

"Of course you may." I took the milk jug out of the fridge and sat down. Perhaps if I started on the fringes of his story, I could learn something useful. "Tell me, John, what work do you do?"

He shrugged one shoulder. "I have ideas."

"Ideas about what sort of work you'd like to do?"

"No, only ideas."

At about forty, shouldn't he have had some sort of job? I gave up on starting at the edge and cut to the chase. "Tell me about your grandfather. What do you remember about him?"

Aubrey's face lit up. "Ah, such a man! He was a man whose life was full and exciting and who would take chances and be bold. He was kind, but at the same time did not mind making the fool look like a fool. It was something they shared, you know—he and Georgiana. Mocking the rich and lazy. There was such a man who lived near them, and once, she said to my grandfather, for a joke, 'Why don't you steal his . . .'" John patted his head.

"His hat?" I offered.

"No, no," John said. "The man was vain—his hairpiece! And grandfather did it, just for her. They had such a laugh about it after."

At that moment, I wished I could've seen Lady Fowling as a carefree young woman.

"Sometimes, they would go off together during the day," John said, "escaping the world, to a small stream nearby and fish and cook their food. Such a life."

"This was in Brittany?"

A shadow passed over his face. "Is it true that she told no one of that time?"

"I don't know. And it was so long ago, I'm not sure anyone . . . wait, now, I wonder if the Moons would remember."

"The moon?"

"Mrs. Sylvia Moon and Mrs. Audrey Moon are the oldest friends of Lady Fowling's I can think of. I'll ask."

It did not escape me that I was sitting down with the enemy—at least as far as Mrs. Woolgar was concerned—and I had just offered to aid him in his search for memories. But how else were we going to find out what he wanted?

"Is the tea ready?" John asked.

I filled our cups, took a bite of a Hobnob, and prodded further.

"You grew up in Dorset? Where?"

"Do you know Lyme Regis?" John asked.

"Oh yes." I didn't even try to stop the smile that spread over my face. "Val, my boyfriend, took me there for our first actual date."

"Then you know the beauty and wild nature along that part of the coast. The tall cliffs, little coves, creeks almost hidden by growth, leading up to . . . where?"

"And your grandfather moved to Dorset?"

"Flambeaux the detective. He could not put his own life in order, so he did so for others. I remember his story of the sad, tender parting with Georgiana. They sat on a spit of sand at the beach in the early hours of a morning, knowing they had little time left. After she had come back to England, he abandoned his ship." John sighed. "Left it to the wild. It's probably still in the small creek where he would hide it, but now a mere skeleton of its former glory."

But if Flambeaux moved to England, too, why didn't he try to contact—I caught myself. These stories John wove had gaping holes in them, I knew they did. It was only that the image of Georgiana, a young woman, turning her back on love and . . .

I jumped when the door buzzer went off. But I was happy about this arrival, because after all, weren't my biggest problems already inside Middlebank? Plus, I had checked the time.

It had been only eight days since Val and I last saw each other, but we were not even a year into our relationship, and any length of separation still resulted in a romantic reunion. When I opened the door, he stayed on the threshold for a moment, and we took each other in.

"There you are now," he said, his voice low and husky.

"Hayley," Aubrey said, practically at my elbow, "I've just noticed the time. I should be on my way."

I took Val's hand, drew him in, and introduced the men.

"Mr. Moffatt, very pleased to meet you."

"Val teaches at Bath College," I explained. "The college collaborates with the Society on many of its events."

Aubrey showed us his dimple. "I sense more than a professional relationship here."

Val gave my hand a squeeze.

"Mr. Aubrey," I said, "that is, John, I feel that there are still things we need to sort out."

"Do not worry, Hayley," he said, heading out the door. "I will return. Tomorrow? I'm uncertain. My time is not my own these days, and just as my grandfather could not leave *La Mouette* for long, so must I be away."

"How can we reach you?" I asked, pursuing him onto the pavement.

"Try this," he said, and rattled off a number.

I patted the empty pockets of my trousers. "Wait, I need to—"

I turned to see Val with phone in hand. "Got it," he said.

John went on his way, and I stepped back in and closed the door. I stretched my arms round Val's neck and said, "Thank you for not being a pirate."

He pulled me close and regarded me for a moment before replying, "You're welcome."

I brushed his lips with mine and then gave him a proper kiss. "And you are welcome—home. I have the afternoon off, and lunch awaits us in my flat."

I kept hold of his hand as we walked up the stairs.

"What was Aubrey talking about?" Val asked. "His time is not his own?"

"I have no idea."

When I reached the first-floor landing, I remembered I was not off work quite yet. "Hang on," I said to Val, and dragged myself into the library.

Charles Henry was hunkered over his laptop, typing furiously.

"All finished with your course?" I asked.

He muttered something, but didn't look up. When I walked to his end of the table, he slapped the lid closed and said, "Yes, Ms. Burke, indexing course successfully completed, exam taken, Bob's your uncle. Hello, Mr. Moffatt."

"Mr. Dill," Val said.

I glanced at the closed laptop and said, "I may have forgotten to mention that I set myself up as your administrator, and so I will get the results of your final exam."

Dill's face went blank. "Yes, well . . . it's possible I didn't get to the very end of the exam, but I will do so before next Monday. Now, Ms. Burke, about this bounder making these outrageous claims—"

"I'll see you next week, Mr. Dill. By then, I'm sure all will be settled."

I made certain Charles Henry was out of Middlebank before Val and I continued to my flat, where we quite successfully put John Aubrey, Dill, and Lady Fowling's past out of our minds. Eventually, we stood in the shower together letting the cool water do its best to refresh us, and finally we got round to lunch of cold chicken and salads. I poured out glasses of chilled, fizzy elderflower water, and we began to catch up on the week apart.

"The New York visit went well? Bess and Adam sound happy," I said.

"They're so busy they don't have time to be unhappy," Val said. "I wish she wasn't so far away. Becky's going over in September."

"The twins reunited," I said. "Adam had better beware."

"You've been busy here at Middlebank. How was Frances on her first Friday?"

"Organized, focused, serious."

Val stretched his legs out under the table. "She'll own her own publishing company before we know it, she's that driven. And she won't be any trouble to you. Good thing—sounds as if you'll have your hands full with Dill and now John Aubrey."

There's a pair. "He's a disconcerting man, John Aubrey," I said. "He's affable, but never answers a question directly. Mum says if he doesn't want money, we have to ask ourselves, what is it he does want."

"Lenore has a way of getting to the heart of it, doesn't she?" Val asked, pulling out his mobile. "Do you want his number?"

Val read it off, and I tapped it into my phone. When I tried to save it in my contacts as John Aubrey, I discovered the number already there, but belonging to someone else.

"He gave me Milo Overton's mobile number!"

"The fellow you found on the doorstep this morning?"

"Was that only this morning? Perhaps this is what Milo gets paid for—fielding questions about John. He'd better prepare himself."

Nearly five o'clock, Val left for his class. On my own way downstairs, I lingered on the library landing and finally faced Lady Fowling's portrait—something I'd been avoiding since Wednesday when John Aubrey had made his declaration.

She had a formidable look about her today, just the response I would've expected from a cheeky question about her love life. That's why I hadn't asked. I didn't ask now, but studied her face and finally saw in it the young woman on the beach all those years ago.

"You looked happy," I said.

There it was—her smile.

I continued downstairs and looked in on Mrs. Woolgar.

"Maureen Frost rang," the secretary said. "She wanted news on how Charles Henry's first day at work went."

"Can't she ask him herself?"

"I believe she's looking for a more evenhanded report," Mrs. Woolgar said.

"I'm not sure where she'll get that. He was fine, I suppose. Until he met John Aubrey."

Mrs. Woolgar went silent for a moment. "Did Aubrey tell his tale again?"

"In a way. I introduced them, and John greeted him as a long-lost relative. That didn't go over well. Now Charles Henry will tell Maureen, and we'll need to explain to the rest of the board."

"He cannot be allowed to get away with this," Mrs. Woolgar said, and I knew she wasn't talking about the nephew.

"The thing is, Mrs. Woolgar, I'm not sure John is breaking a law."

"Libel," she snapped. "Or is it slander? Duncan will know."

"What about the dragon psychic and the others? What happened to them? Did Mr. Rennie have to warn them off?"

Mrs. Woolgar frowned. "No, not as I recall. They seemed to just go away of their own accord."

"Well, then, perhaps that's what John Aubrey will do."

I spent the evening in Cornwall. *Frenchman's Creek* is a cracking story full of swashbuckling and romance. But even as I enjoyed the daring escapades of Dona and her pirate, an odd feeling crept over me. Had I read the book before and forgotten? Was there a film version?

After nine, I got up from the sofa, stretched, and went to the kitchen for a glass of wine. "Dona was a woman in desperate need of an adventure," I said to Bunter, who had come up to visit for the evening. The cat made no comment, but jumped down from the window seat, stretched, and walked to the door of my flat.

"I'd say Lady Fowling had needed an adventure, too, after Sir John died. She certainly deserved a little lightness in her life. If she had met a pirate named—"

I froze with the glass halfway to my lips. In *Frenchman's Creek*, Dona had met a pirate named Jean Benoit-Aubéry. And now, arrived here on our doorstep at Middlebank, was John Aubrey.

"*La Mouette,*" I whispered. "John said his grandfather's ship had that name. Did he actually believe his grandfather was the pirate from Daphne du Maurier's *Frenchman's Creek*? And that this same pirate was the inspiration for François Flambeaux? He's mixing his centuries, first off, and honestly, if he were looking for a load of codswallop to feed us, couldn't he have come up with something more original?"

Bunter, still at the door, stretched up to the handle and batted it. I let him out and went back to the book.

5

At eight the next morning, I awoke on the sofa with my face stuck on the paperback cover of *Frenchman's Creek*. I'd finished, but hadn't done it justice and would need to reread the ending, the beginning, and then the entire book. It was that good. After a quick shower, I dressed, took a sip of tea to clear my head, and rang Milo Overton.

". . . and it's extremely important I see John, so please tell me how to get in touch with him."

"I'll let him know he's needed," Overton said, "but until then, perhaps you and I can have a word? I'm not too far from Middlebank. I could be there in twenty minutes."

Just enough time for a slice of toast before dashing down to the entry, where I turned the alarm off, unlocked the door, and paced. It was just before nine. Mrs. Woolgar was due up from her flat at any moment, and it would be easier to talk with Milo without her glowering presence. When the buzzer sounded, I pounced on the door.

Milo Overton looked the picture of sensibility, even if he did resemble John. And now that I had this second, closer look at him, were they really all that much alike?

"So, this is Middlebank," Milo said, admiring his surroundings.

"Are you familiar with it?"

"John hasn't stopped talking about the place."

"Milo, I don't quite understand what he is hoping to accomplish here."

Milo offered a pleasant smile, but, of course, without the dimple.

"I'm not sure he knows himself. When John gets taken with an idea, he's in his own world."

"But why Lady Fowling?"

"Well, he does know a great deal about the family, and he gave me to believe that . . . regardless, John means no harm. You shouldn't worry, I'll keep an eye on him."

In my mind, Milo transformed from a business associate to a handler. I'd better get this straight.

"But he seems to be confusing an old book with this idea that—"

"Mr. Aubrey!"

I looked over Milo's shoulder and across the entry to Mrs. Woolgar standing at the top of the stairs from her flat.

"Mr. Aubrey," she continued, stalking across the space, "unless you have actual proof to show us, I don't—"

Milo turned round to face her, and the secretary stopped abruptly. She leaned forward, peered at him, then straightened and pushed her glasses up the bridge of her nose.

"I'm terribly sorry, sir. I mistook you for someone else."

"Mrs. Woolgar," I said, "this is Milo Overton, an associate of Mr. Aubrey's."

Milo gave her a slight bow and said, "John has spoken of you, Mrs. Woolgar. Hayley, I won't disturb you any longer. Let me know if you need anything else."

I needed a great deal more than what he had offered—I needed details. But Mrs. Woolgar was too emotional about this, and I wouldn't ask in front of her.

Milo left and I followed the secretary into her office and told her what he'd said.

"If this Aubrey believes what he's spouting," she said, "then it's a doctor we'll need, not a lawyer."

"Has Mr. Rennie discovered anything about this 'living'?"

Mrs. Woolgar shook her head. "Very little. Fifteen years ago, this current investment firm acquired a company that was a subsidiary of a previous firm that had changed its name sometime in the 1970s. That's as far as he's managed."

"Mrs. Woolgar, have you read *Frenchman's Creek*?"

She looked up at this abrupt change of subject. "Yes, of course, but it was years ago. Why do you ask?"

Why . . . why had I asked? "I thought I might create a few themed displays in the library for tomorrow afternoon. Perhaps author groupings."

"Quite appropriate—du Maurier was a favorite of her ladyship's. We don't have anything else to discuss this morning, do we, Ms. Burke? I have an appointment with Ms. Frost, who wanted to discuss a few—"

"Yes, I believe we're finished."

Perhaps Maureen and Mrs. Woolgar liked to share a good natter about their men. Fine with me, because it meant leaving the briefing on a pleasant note. Later, I would mention John Aubrey's appropriation of *Frenchman's Creek* for his own purposes. The news should be a relief to her, but I often had trouble guessing what Mrs. Woolgar's reactions would be. Now I took myself to Waitrose to replenish our biscuit supply.

I made short work of it and soon I stood in the queue to pay, my handbasket piled with digestives, ginger nuts, shortbread fingers, custard creams, and, for Charles Henry, Maries. While I waited, I occupied myself as usual by observing what other people were buying. A woman waiting at the next till had a trolley with enough orange squash and enormous bags of crisps to feed a very hungry troop of Scouts. The fellow in front of me had a package of reduced-price sausages, two large cans of lager, a disposable barbecue grill, and . . . then he caught me peeking.

I smiled innocently, looked away, and then back. "Oh, hello," I said. "You're . . . it's Jelley, isn't it?"

"S'right. You're at Middlebank."

"Did Milo catch you up?" I asked.

Jelley gave me an owlish blink. "Thought you didn't know Milo."

"I didn't then, but I do now. It's only that—"

"Next!" the woman at the till called out, and Jelley took his turn.

Having one successful Wednesday public opening under our belts, Mrs. Woolgar and I were quite at ease the next day. We discussed whether we should expect more or fewer patrons, and eventually settled on the same number as the first week. She admired my displays in the library. I'd arranged two small tables in out-of-the-way spots—one with books of Margery Allingham's earliest Campion and another with Patricia Wentworth's Miss Silver. I mixed the editions and included a few vintage paperbacks, because Frances had said she might stop in.

Promptly at one o'clock the buzzer sounded to signal we were on our way. Our first visitor was Milo Overton.

Mrs. Woolgar watched as I led him to the library, where he gave a brief glance about and complimented me on the collection before telling me that he and John had had a disagreement.

"These stories he tells, Hayley, I didn't realize how far he'd gone without giving you an explanation. If you knew his background, you would understand he isn't lying, but , ,John doesn't see it that way. I don't want him to waste your time."

If John wasn't such an affable fellow, I might complain. "Is Lady Fowling his grandmother?" I felt a traitor for even asking the question.

Milo exhaled. "Look, I know where you can hear the entire story. John doesn't want me to share this information, but it isn't as if I'm breaking a trust. I realize you'll be busy this afternoon, but perhaps we could talk tomorrow."

"Yes, that would be fine." And an enormous relief.

When four proper visitors came trooping up the stairs followed close on by three more, Milo left. I spoke with each one. Twenty minutes later, I heard more voices and thought I might need reinforcements before Val was to arrive at three.

"Hayley!"

Celia waved her fuchsia-pink nails at me from the doorway. I waved in return, and, while I told the woman next to me that Middlebank had no tearoom, a happy thought came to me. *Celia is a repeat patron.* Yes, the First Edition library demands more than just a onetime visit.

"Welcome back, Celia," I said when I reached her.

"Yeah, thanks," she said, her head swiveling left and right as she squinted at the crowd.

"Are you looking for someone?" Perhaps she'd asked a friend to meet her. I hoped so, because word of mouth is the best sort of advertising.

"No," she said, focusing on me, her eyes as wide as the mascara would allow.

"You're having a good long holiday in Bath, aren't you?" I asked.

"Yeah, I've got a first-floor flat just by the Abbey for the month. It's lovely to be right in the middle of the city, innit?"

The view below her window would be of a sea of day-trippers who would change to a crowd of noisy drinkers spilling out of the pubs late at night. And on Sundays, the Abbey bells would sound as if they were in your front room.

"Lovely," I agreed.

Something large and round and baby blue caught my eye, and I turned in time to see Charles Henry Dill make his entrance.

Puffed up and hands in his jacket pockets, he paused in the library doorway and surveyed his surroundings as if he were lord of the manor. He began greeting people as he walked in, and when he came close enough, I heard him say, "And of course, my aunt Georgiana often asked my advice about which mystery novel to read next."

"Mr. Dill," I said. "Welcome to the First Edition library. How nice of you to *visit*. Please do let me know if you have any questions about the Golden Age of Mystery."

He frowned at me and I frowned back. I shouldn't leave him alone, or soon he'd be telling people the First Edition Society had been his own idea. But if I policed him, how would I talk with the real library patrons? Then I saw Maureen Frost. Good, his keeper. I waved her over and left the two of them together.

A few people left, but more arrived, among them Frances.

"I'm so pleased to see you," I said.

"I wanted to support the effort."

We were swimming in support. Look now, here were Mrs. Moon and Mrs. Moon, their eyes wide at the crowd. They saw me across the room and silently clapped

"Well done!" Audrey said, when I'd reached them.

"It's so good of you to come," I said.

"Is he here?" Sylvia whispered to me, scanning the crowd. "That young man. The one who says he's . . . you know."

Oh, so that's why they had come—they wanted to meet John Aubrey.

Sylvia leaned closer. "There wouldn't be a bit of sherry going, would there?"

"There's always a bit of sherry for you," I murmured. "When there's a break, we'll nip down to my office."

The Moons settled at the table and struck up a conversation with a young man who was looking through a Spanish edition of *Death on the Nile*. I noticed Jane Arbuthnot slip into the room. The only board member not in attendance was Adele, but she taught school and would still be with her students. I'd caught her up on the John Aubrey situation over the phone and asked for her advice. She had grown thoughtful, but then told me not to worry about any rumors flying round, because Georgiana wouldn't have. Then she had said something in French and promised we'd meet soon.

I took a moment to look round and was pleased to see everyone having a fine time—except for Frances. She had taken up a lonely post near one of my display tables. I went over to chat and looked at the Patricia Wentworth paperback in her hands. It showed a young woman sprawled on the ground with a menacing figure in the background. The woman had a shift on that was so sheer you could practically see her—

"Is that Miss Silver? I thought she was an old lady," I said.

Just then, Val came up beside us. "Hiya," he said. "This is amazing."

"It is," I agreed. "If only they'd stop asking for tea. The Moons are expecting sherry, of course, so I thought I'd take them down to my office. Will you keep an eye on things? I'll bring more brochures back."

I escorted Audrey and Sylvia downstairs, and as we passed, Mrs. Woolgar reported the astonishing number of twenty-three. "But down to fourteen now."

In my office, I settled the Moons in the wingback chairs by the fireplace, retrieved the sherry and glasses from the kitchenette, and poured them each a tot. "Look now," I said, nodding to the mantel, where Bunter sat next to a set of brass candlesticks doing his impression of a ceramic cat. "We have company."

"Poor dear," Sylvia said to me, "you're exhausted. Can't you stay and rest?"

"Well, why not? Just for a moment." I poured a sherry for myself and sat on the footstool between them. "Actually, I did want to ask you two—"

"About that young man?" Audrey asked.

But Mrs. Woolgar knocked and looked in. When I saw her pursed lips and granitelike face, I stood. "I'd better get back to work. We'll do this later. You two stay here and enjoy yourselves." I swallowed my sherry and followed the secretary to the entry.

"It's John, isn't it?"

I didn't wait for an answer, but raced up the stairs, catching myself at the library door. So what if John Aubrey were here? We're open to the public, after all. Where was the harm in it? I spied him across the room calmly looking at books. I worked my way over.

"Hayley," he said when I reached him. "Look at the people you've brought together. Wouldn't my grandmother be proud?"

That gave me pause. She would, wouldn't she? I'd ask her later when everyone had gone.

"People love a good mystery," I said.

"And I see you attract not only the aficionado, but also the scholar, for here is Frances."

Frances hadn't moved an inch from the table display nearby, but looked up at her name.

"It's lovely to see you again, Frances," John said, drawing nearer to her.

She pulled her chin in and gave him a fierce look as if she might bite his head off. I stepped closer.

"Frances, you remember—"

"Mr. Aubrey," she filled in. "Of course. Well, Hayley, are you pleased with the turnout?"

"I certainly am," I said, casting an eye over the room and noting that Celia had stayed. She stood near the door, squinting at us.

"Frances," John said, "I would be interested in hearing your opinion of my grandmother's own stories. I believe you would see the passion behind the words, and—"

"You, sir!"

The voice reverberated in the room. Ambient chatter ceased and all eyes flew to the speaker, Charles Henry Dill, who stood in front of the fireplace with Maureen. He pointed an accusatory finger at John as he advanced across the room, people parting to let him through.

"My cousin is not happy," John whispered.

Dill's voice grew louder, if that was possible. "Do you actually believe you can take advantage of a woman's reputation when she is not alive to defend herself?"

"Charles Henry!" Maureen called after him.

"Mr. Dill," I said, "this is neither the time nor the place—"

John put a hand on my shoulder, "No, Hayley, I understand—"

"Using a woman as a shield?" Dill shouted, raising a clenched fist. "Coward!"

I saw Val pushing his way through the crowd, but it was tough going, because people had closed in, as if to watch a fight on the school grounds.

"Stop this now," I demanded.

John stretched his arms out toward Charles Henry, as if in supplication. "Please, let us sit down and talk about what we have in common."

I stepped between the men, but Dill shoved me out of the way. I caught myself against the table, but I couldn't stop Charles Henry's fist making contact with John's nose. I heard the crunching impact of skin and cartilage. It knocked John into one of the small displays, overturning the table and sending the lamp and books crashing to the floor.

There was an eruption of gasps and shouts, and the crowd broke into what seemed like a thousand movements. Val grabbed me. Many people recoiled, but several jumped on Charles Henry, struggling to hold him back as he shouted in a garbled voice, "I won't let you do this!"

Someone shrieked, "John!"

It was Frances. She dropped to the floor beside Aubrey, who had landed against the bookshelves, his hand covering his nose.

"A handkerchief!" she shouted. "Who has a handkerchief?"

Dozens of hands began patting jacket and trouser pockets, but it was John who pulled one out first. Blood was already dripping onto his shirt. Frances gently moved his hand away, put the folded handkerchief against his nose, and replaced his hand. "Lean forward a bit," she said quietly, "and rest there."

"Are you all right?" Val asked me.

"Yes." But my nerves were taut with anger and shock. "Would you keep an eye on Charles Henry?"

"I'll do more than that," Val said, and stormed over to the fireplace. Dill caught sight of him and retreated behind Maureen.

The room quieted, the only sound a general murmur that rose and fell like an ocean current. People milled about, looking lost. I drew a deep breath and said, "Thank you for attending our library open hours today. I'm afraid we'll need to close early, so please make your way down to the entry." This could be the last we would ever see of the public. The thought made my eyes prick with tears.

As if on cue, Mrs. Woolgar was at the door.

"This way, please," she said. Patrons filed out, but many came to me first and said, "I'm happy to be called as a witness." "Do you want my details for the police?" "That fellow did nothing to provoke the attack."

Such kindness almost undid me, but I managed to thank each one and suggest they make a mark beside their names in the guest book downstairs, in case they were needed.

The library emptied and we were left alone—a subdued Charles Henry Dill, rubbing his knuckles, with Maureen at his side and Val standing guard; John, still on the floor with Frances in attendance; and me.

"John?" I asked.

"Yes, Hayley," he said in a nasal tone. "I am all right." He put his clean hand over his nurse's. "Because of you."

Frances glanced up at me and stood, backing away a step. "I've had Red Cross training," she said.

"Well," I said, narrowing my eyes at Dill across the room, "I'll need to phone the police."

Dill erupted. "The police? What for?"

"Assault," Val snapped. "On Hayley as well as Aubrey."

"What?" Dill's face drained of color. "It isn't as if I—"

Maureen grabbed his arm, and even from across the room I could see Dill wince at her grip.

"No police," John said. He clambered up from the floor and took the bloody handkerchief away from his nose, testing with the back of his hand to make sure the flow had stopped. "That is not necessary—not for me. I'm fine. This is an emotional time, and I do not blame my . . . I will not blame Mr. Dill for his action."

Charles Henry's face turned puce at this kindness, his mouth working as if filled with too many replies jockeying to get out of the gate.

"Thank you, Mr. Aubrey," Maureen said. "It won't happen again."

Dill made a choking noise and then went silent. Maureen gave him a nudge and, his head high, he stalked out of the library. She followed.

And then we were four.

"Hayley," John said, "are you all right?" I nodded. He exhaled. "I feel quite like Flambeaux, captured, put under guard, and forced to await a plan of rescue thought up by his love. She visited him dressed as a boy, you know," he said to Frances. "And they discussed his escape in code. She saved him."

Yes, she did—that is how Dona saved Jean Benoit-Aubéry in *Frenchman's Creek*. But that wasn't the scene in which she dressed as a boy. You've slipped up, John Aubrey.

Frances was at the library door in a twinkling, turning only long enough to say, "I'll see you on Friday morning, Hayley. Bye now."

John watched her, a slight frown on his brow. "There is a sadness in her," he said.

"She's gone through a rough patch this last year," I told him, "and she doesn't need to be messed about with."

"No," John replied, "I would never . . . ah well. I, too, must leave. Until next time."

I let him see himself out, hoping Mrs. Woolgar wasn't lying in wait. Val was last to go—he had a departmental meeting.

"I'll ring and beg off," he offered, cupping my face in his hands. "No, you go. I'll see you later."

I stood in the middle of the library. Apart from the overturned table display, the room looked none the worse for wear. But I knew damage had been done. Word would get out of the punch-up at the First Edition Society, and in the library, no less. I didn't believe that old saying that any publicity was good publicity. Our mission was to spread the word about the women authors of the Golden Age of Mystery, not act out scenes of violence.

Downstairs, Mrs. Woolgar had put the entry in order and left her office door ajar.

"No damage to the library," I said, looking in. "You saw what happened?"

The secretary stood behind her desk, where she kept stacks of ledgers dating from the Iron Age. "Yes. I went up when I heard the shout."

"John didn't want the police called in."

"Just as well. Charles Henry was provoked."

It took me a moment to reply, because I couldn't actually believe what I'd heard. "Are you taking Dill's side?" I asked.

The secretary whirled round. "No, I . . . of course, I would never . . ." She drew her arms in as if besieged by a swarm of nipping corgis. "It's this Aubrey. I will not have some delusional stranger come into Middlebank specifically to cause trouble."

"What trouble?"

"He's attempting to drag the Fowling name into the gutter. Lady

Fowling in particular, besmirching her legacy by telling lies about her past."

Besmirch, what a silly-sounding word.

"I doubt if—"

"You've been taken in by this charlatan!" Mrs. Woolgar shouted at me, and then put a hand to her chest, as if shocked at her own outburst. "But, of course, you never knew her ladyship, so I suppose it's easy for you to believe his lies."

First, a fight in the library and now this. The secretary wasn't the only one who'd had enough.

"I have not been taken in," I retorted, and Mrs. Woolgar stepped back at my heat. "And I'm not saying I believe his words, but he is a mystery, and I think we should learn more about him before we dismiss him out of hand."

"What happened this afternoon will be all over the internet," the secretary said.

The words were an accusation, but tinged with the impression of an apology for her behavior—a particular talent of Mrs. Woolgar's. I reminded myself that even if Lady Fowling were not here to suffer direct damage to her character, her aide-de-camp would certainly take the hit.

"No, I don't think we'll see much about it. To anyone else, it looked like nothing more than a disagreement. We've had worse."

Mrs. Woolgar conceded the point with a nod, but said, "Something needs to be done about this John Aubrey."

"Yes," I said. "I'll get right on that tomorrow. I have a lead."

Or, at least Milo had something to show me that would explain. Explain what, I wasn't sure.

Finished with work for the day, I went to my flat and began making a list of the stories John had told about his grandmother and the pirate that he'd lifted from *Frenchman's Creek*. To start with, the name Jean Benoit-Aubéry. Was John Aubrey his real name or had he assumed it? He had taken the story of stealing the wig from the head of slow and stupid Godolphin and switched it to a toupee snatched off the head of another fool. There was the bit whereby Dona conveys the rescue plan to her pirate lover—but there, he had combined elements from two different parts. The last scene, on that spit of sand at the beach early in the morning, he'd left mostly untouched.

Just gone seven, I walked out of Middlebank House and was hit by a wave of heat—a summer evening in Bath. The stone buildings, having soaked up the sun during the day, now radiated their warmth into the early-evening air. I needed to clear my head and took a circuitous route to meet Val for dinner, passing tourists sprawled under the huge plane trees at the Circus and, farther along, strewn about the grass in Victoria Gardens across from the Royal Crescent.

With my head clear, I made my way back to the ASK Italian on Broad Street, and by the time I arrived, Val already had a table for us against a wall, and a bottle of wine open. I scooted in next to him. At first we talked of nothing more important than tagliatelle with ragù. It was only after we'd ordered that the topic for the evening, John Aubrey, came up.

"It's an odd story to cobble together," Val said. "Selections from du Maurier with a dash of Lady Fowling reality. Did he really think he'd be believed?"

"He has her photo," I said. "That was a shock for Mrs. Woolgar, I can tell you."

"He didn't provoke Dill today."

"Only by his presence," I said. "John gets up Charles Henry's nose, that's for certain. He's in a panic at the thought of someone else laying claim to Lady Fowling's fortune, even if he's never to get it."

"When did Aubrey meet Frances?"

"On Friday. He'd better watch himself there—she doesn't seem to be one to put up with unwanted advances. Although," I admitted, "she did seem a bit emotional. And she was first to him after the punch."

" 'Red Cross training,' " Val said. "Although, it was a bloody nose, not a heart attack."

At the end of the evening, Val and I walked back hand in hand, quiet and drowsy from the wine and an overload of pasta. Half past ten and long summer evenings meant there was still a bit of light in the sky.

We paused at the corner before the terrace as I wondered if the ice cream shop down on Walcot was still open.

"Look," Val said.

Not far ahead, a man stood at the entrance to Hedgemead Park. He had his back to us, and it looked as if he were holding on to the side of the wrought-iron gate.

"Is that Aubrey?"

"John?" I called. The figure sank slowly, as if folding in on itself. "John!"

We ran, reaching him as he landed on the ground. I saw a spot about the size of a ten-pence piece on the right side of his back, like a small tear in his shirt.

One hand slipped off the gate, and his body slumped sideways, turning toward us.

"Milo!" I said.

Not John Aubrey, but Milo Overton, with a dazed and surprised look on his face.

"Val," I said, but he was already on the phone to 999. "Milo, tell me what's wrong. Are you ill?"

Milo's mouth moved.

"What?" I asked. "What is it?"

"I said . . ." Milo whispered, ". . . I said I am not . . . I am not . . ."

6

Milo was alive when the ambulance arrived. While we waited, I tried to keep him talking, asking him what had happened, but he was in and out of consciousness. Val put his phone on speaker, and the woman at emergency services kept us on the line gathering more information—who, where, what.

Not ten minutes later the EMTs were at work. "Mr. Overton? Milo?" one asked in a loud voice. "Can you tell me what has happened?"

We stood back from the flurry of activity, along with a few other passersby who had stopped to watch.

As the wheeled stretcher carrying Milo was loaded into the ambulance, two police cars pulled up to the curb, their blue-and-yellow-checkered Battenberg paint and flashing blue lights bright against the failing light. Uniformed police constables emptied out of each and spoke to the EMTs, who nodded to us and then pulled away.

We told the PCs all we could. Yes, we knew who the man was.

That is, I did—Val had never met him. We saw nothing and no one, and came across him only as he collapsed. Yes, we were local. Extremely local, as Middlebank's door was only a bit farther up the road. We didn't know his next of kin, but we knew someone Milo worked with, although we had no way of contacting him.

Nearly twelve o'clock and now well and truly dark, two officers escorted us up the road and saw us safely in the door at Middlebank. I reset the alarm and locked up as Bunter, whose bed was in a corner of Mrs. Woolgar's office, came out, yawned, stretched, and went off to the kitchenette, where his food dish was kept.

"I think I'll ring the hospital," I said to Val as we went up to my flat, "even though they'll tell us nothing."

The hospital told us nothing, but they were nice about it. After that, Val and I sat at the kitchen table and talked over the event.

"They look very much alike, don't they?" Val asked. "Aubrey and Milo."

"Yes, at first."

"Had he seemed ill to you?"

"No," I said, "but I only met him twice. Three times—he was here yesterday afternoon. Probably, something came on him suddenly. Heart attack or . . . I don't know. How will they find John?" I rubbed my face. It seemed that the day had held twice as many hours as it should, and most of them stressful. My head felt as if it were stuffed with cotton wool.

I put my hand over Val's. "I'm knackered. Let's go to bed."

I opened my eyes the next morning and saw Val awake and watching me. He pulled me close and I tucked my head into the crook of his arm and we lay there, quiet. We'd had a few practical discussions about living together, each time coming to the conclusion that he should keep his house and I should keep my flat. And so, we went along, sharing many nights and sleeping alone others. Still, these mornings were the best.

After breakfast, we arrived downstairs at quarter to nine. The second my foot touched the ground floor, the front-door buzzer sounded. I stopped and gave Val a backward glance before turning off the alarm and opening the door.

"Ms. Burke, Mr. Moffatt, good morning."

Detective Sergeant Ronald Hopgood, he of the gray push-broom mustache and caterpillar eyebrows. I spared a thought for police everywhere—when was their unexpected appearance at your door ever a welcome sight?

"Is he dead?" I asked.

"You're asking about Milo Overton, I take it," Hopgood said. "I'm sorry to say he is."

"Oh, how sad," I said. Both for Milo and for the thought of what might lie ahead—an enquiry. The sun beat down on Hopgood, who wore his usual dark suit, although I hoped for his sake it was a summer weight. "Come through, Sergeant. Tea?"

"A cup of tea never goes amiss."

I glanced out at the pavement before closing the door. "Is Detective Constable Pye not with you?"

"Pye is down the way at Hedgemead Park with a team, examining the area."

"Sergeant Hopgood," Val said, "I have a class at ten."

"Ah, you've an hour or so to spare, then, Mr. Moffatt? Good, because I would like you to be included in this chat."

The Chat. I'm sorry to say that I was all too familiar with it.

In the kitchenette, I put the kettle on and reached for a packet of digestive biscuits. How canny of me to replenish our supply.

"Tell me what happened last evening," Hopgood said, "just as you remember it."

The story we presented was short and lacking in detail.

"The only words he spoke were, 'I said I am not . . .'" I looked at Val. "Is that right?"

Val nodded. "He repeated it and tried to say more, but we couldn't make it out."

"Does either of you know what he meant by that?"

We didn't.

"How did he die?" Val asked.

"He was stabbed, Mr. Moffatt," Hopgood said.

"Stabbed?" I asked. "There was no blood. Did you see any blood?" I asked Val.

"There was little blood to be seen," Hopgood said. "A very thin knife went into his back, and the bleeding was internal. We'll know more after the postmortem report is filed."

Murder. Well, why else would the police come calling? I reached for the cups and saucers, and they rattled in my hands as I remembered the dark spot I saw on the back of Milo's shirt.

"Had it just happened?" I asked. "Right there at the entrance to the park?"

"Did either of you see anyone else before you came upon him?" Hopgood countered.

We had been walking back hand in hand on a dusky summer evening from a lovely dinner, why would we be aware of anyone else in the world? Val and I looked at each other and shrugged.

"There must've been people about, but I couldn't tell you for certain," Val said.

"A car speeding away?" Hopgood asked, his eyebrows lifted in hope.

"But you will have CCTV, won't you?" I asked.

"Being gathered as we speak, Ms. Burke, but they are not our only way of gathering information. I've got uniforms out there now doorstepping. Anything else about Milo Overton you can tell me?"

About a man I'd met only two or three times? I searched my memory for even a mention of . . . "Oh, a fellow came here looking for him. A friend, I think."

Both Hopgood and Val raised their eyebrows at that. "His name is Jelley." I proceeded to brief them on my two meetings with the owl-faced man. "Milo sort of laughed when I mentioned him."

Out the corner of my eye, I saw movement.

"Mrs. Woolgar?"

She came to the door. The stairs down to her flat were only a few feet away, and I realized she could've been listening for several minutes.

"Detective Sergeant Hopgood," the secretary said when he stood. "Good morning. I thought I heard your voice."

"The sergeant has come to tell us Milo Overton has died," I told her.

"Oh, I'm sorry," she said. "But, who is Milo Overton?"

"You met him a few days ago when he stopped by," I said, "but you mistook him for John Aubrey."

A flicker of something— a reaction I couldn't read—crossed her face. "Yes, of course. But I didn't realize you knew him well enough that you would be notified of his death."

"Val and I came across him last evening out on the pavement. He had collapsed, and we contacted 999."

"It happened here, at Middlebank?"

I explained, and all the while Hopgood listened and watched. Then the buzzer sounded.

"Shall I?" Mrs. Woolgar asked.

"No, please, let me." I hurried past her. What if it was John? Did he know about Milo?

"'Morning, Hayley. My guv'nor here?"

"Hello, Kenny."

Detective Constable Kenny Pye stood in contrast to his superior in several ways—younger, with dark skin and shiny black hair, an occasional twinkle in his eye, and an approachable manner. He made a good foil to the brusque Hopgood. I knew two sides of Kenny. Not only was he a police detective, but also a writer. And unattached, as far as I knew. I clung to the distant hope that one day I could introduce him to my daughter, Dinah, but the opportunity had yet to present itself.

"Your guv'nor is having a cuppa," I said. "Go through."

Val came out of the kitchenette, squeezing past Mrs. Woolgar, who had remained in the doorway. "I've been released and need to get to class," he said to me, and then turned to DC Pye and added quietly, "See you this afternoon."

Val was Kenny's writing coach—a fact that DS Hopgood was entirely aware of, although it was never discussed openly. This was most likely because Pye wrote a series of stories set in 1920s London featuring a detective named Alehouse.

"It's only a first draft," Kenny said in a low voice.

"So you'll be ready for the second draft. Now the fun begins," Val replied, and turned to me. "Later, love," he said, gave me a kiss, and left.

"Pye," Hopgood said, "any joy?"

"Nothing yet, boss," Kenny said. "'Morning, Mrs. Woolgar."

"Hello, Detective Constable," she replied. "Would you like a cup of tea?"

"I'll put the kettle on," I offered.

"No, thank you, Ms. Burke, we'll be on our way," Hopgood said. I noticed Kenny give the teapot a longing look. "But first, tell me, who is John Aubrey?"

That seemed to be Mrs. Woolgar's cue to leave. "Ms. Burke, I'll be in my office."

"John and Milo work together," I explained to the DS.

"Where?"

"I'm not entirely sure. We've met them only recently. John attended our first two public open afternoons."

"And they are followers of detective fiction? Members of your Golden Age of Mystery society?"

Hopgood's brows floated above his eyes, innocent, enquiring.

"Yes, well, John is a fan of the genre."

Was that vague enough? Did Hopgood see through me? John's story was too long and too complicated and lacked so many facts that there was no way I could begin to explain who John Aubrey was. Or thought he was. And what did it have to do with Milo?

The sergeant's brows settled into a noncommittal pose, but I saw a sharp look in his eyes, and I knew there would be more questions later. After all, he knew where to find me.

"We need John Aubrey's contact information," Hopgood said.

Get in the queue. "I don't have it—but I have Milo's number. Perhaps you could start there." I read it off my phone to Kenny.

"Pye, you'll need to get on that. Ms. Burke, if you think of anything else . . . well, I'm sure we'll be in touch." He stood and brushed biscuit crumbs from his lapel. "In any case, I'll expect you both at the station in the morning to sign your statements."

I saw them out, went to my office, then came out again and went to Mrs. Woolgar's.

"I'm sure it's distressing for you," she said first thing. "To have the police here about this man's death. But it doesn't actually concern you, does it?"

She asked it in an even voice, and perhaps she didn't intend for it to have any other meaning, but I heard her words as *Nothing to do with the Society, I hope?*

"No concern of mine that I can see, except that I'd met Milo. I'm sure it has nothing to do with John."

"You said they worked together?"

"Yes, they do. Did."

"Where is Mr. Aubrey?"

"I don't know. Perhaps he's left Bath for good." That flicker of an eyelid told me Mrs. Woolgar didn't believe it. I didn't, either. "I need to go out this morning, but I'll be back by lunch."

I didn't offer a reason and she didn't ask for one. "Take your time, Ms. Burke, we have no pressing business."

I set out down the terrace and onto Bennett Street, passing the Assembly Rooms and scanning the faces of the people round me. Why? Did I think I would run into John by chance? I walked past the

Jane Austen Centre and glanced over into Queen Square. The population of Bath must increase by thousands on any summer's day, and so I don't know what made me think I could accidentally encounter the one particular person I wanted to find. I got a coffee at the kiosk in Victoria Park, sat in the shade, and kept an eye on the crowd as I asked myself questions.

Who would want to kill Milo? Did it have something to do with his work? How would John find out? I should've told the police of our connection. I would tell them. Yes, I would tell them now. I sprang off the bench, tossed my cup in the nearest bin, and set off to the Avon and Somerset Police Station on Manvers.

I had reached the bottom of Union Street when my phone rang. I pulled out of the crowd that flowed toward the Roman Baths and looked at the screen. I didn't recognize the number.

"Hello?"

"Hayley? I can't reach Milo. Have you seen him this morning?"

"John?"

His call answered one question and posed another. Yes, John Aubrey did have his own mobile, but why did he think I would know anything about Milo?

"John, can we meet? Where are you?"

"Is Milo with you? Are you at Middlebank?"

"No, he . . . I would rather discuss this in person, but away from Middlebank." I cringed at how awkward I sounded, but I wouldn't give him this news over the phone.

John was silent for a moment. "I'm coming in now. Where shall I meet you?" His voice was tentative, serious.

Coming in from where? "How about the Parade Gardens, that's fairly central? At the bottom of the steps."

I arrived fifteen minutes later and found John already there. He looked less like a pirate today, dressed in denims and a madras shirt. I noticed his nose was still a bit swollen from Charles Henry's punch.

"Why couldn't we meet at Middlebank?" he asked. "Is there a problem?"

A woman ran a pushchair over my foot as she dragged a toddler along. Just behind her came a quartet of young men, their voices raised in high spirits. I realized telling John about Milo in public wasn't the best idea, but I couldn't change course now.

I led him to a quiet spot. "I didn't know how to get in touch with you. No one did."

"Milo knows how to reach me."

"That's just it, John. Milo has died."

He looked puzzled. "Milo? Milo is dead? When? How? Was it an accident?"

"It happened last night. He was attacked." I told the story quickly and simply, and ended with, "The police came to see us this morning with questions. Where did Milo live? Does he have a family? But there was little we could tell them."

John looked out across the Parade Gardens as if searching for something he'd lost. "Why? Why Milo? And now what will I do?"

"The police want to talk with you," I said, "but we couldn't tell them how to reach you. Or where you're staying."

He didn't move. Would I need to give him a push?

"Hayley, would you like a cup of tea?"

When you've delivered bad news of this magnitude, you had to give the recipient some leeway, didn't you? "Yes, of course."

We left the gardens. I let John lead, and when we turned onto the bridge, I thought we'd stop in the café. But we passed it and contin-

ued in silence down Great Pulteney Street with all its Georgian ti-
diness. It wasn't really the time for small talk, but when we reached
Sydney Gardens, I asked, "Where are we going?"

John turned and, with a weak showing of his dimple, said, "It isn't
far."

I followed him to the towpath along the Kennet and Avon Canal.
A lovely day for a walk, I thought, sidestepping couples and families
carrying picnic hampers. It had been ages since I'd come this way. I
remembered dragging a protesting teenage Dinah along here and up
to a lovely view of the city from Bathwick Fields. Were we going
that far today?

We passed narrow boats parked along the side of the canal. No,
parked wasn't the proper word. *Moored*, that was it. They were
moored. Although fifty or so feet long, they were only about seven
feet wide, and so could line up along the canal edge and still give
room in the center for boats on the move.

A large family came between us, and I didn't realize John had
stopped until he called my name. He'd stepped off the towpath and
stood with one foot on board a narrow boat painted blue with red
trim. Its name stood out in white script: *La Mouette 2.*

"Welcome to my home," he said, putting out a hand to help me
aboard.

"You live on a narrow boat?"

I stepped in and blinked at the sun reflecting off the water. I
looked back at the walkers only a couple of feet away along the tree-
lined towpath, marveling at how different the world looked from
this vantage.

"Would you like a tour?" John asked. He unlocked a door and
nodded down a couple of steps into the cabin.

I hesitated for only a moment.

"Yes, sure," I said, followed him down into the cabin, and waited while he put the kettle on. "I can run off one of the batteries for many hours," he explained, "but at a proper moorage, there are electrics available."

He showed me the tiller bar in the back and waved toward the berth in the front. He pointed out the raised lip at the edge of shelves—a "fiddle," he called it—to keep things from sliding off. Over our heads was a pigeon box, a tiny, pointed roof structure. On a narrow boat, John said, everything had its place. "There is more storage than a person might think," he added, opening a cupboard door to reveal a surprising abundance of space. Then he patted the seat of the settee. "Inside here is my treasure chest."

"It's lovely and cozy," I said, glancing out a window at the side to see the passing parade of feet.

"You and Val must come for dinner one evening."

"Did Milo live here, too?"

John laughed. "Milo on the water? No, he prefers"—his smile disappeared—"preferred to keep his feet on land. He was staying in a hotel."

Once we were seated with tea, John opened a packet of jammy dodgers and dumped them onto a plate. We were quiet as he stared off into space. Until now, I had seen him as young and full of insubstantial stories with no real grounding, but now he looked older and weary.

"How fortuitous of you to come upon Milo," John said, "because it means, at the end, he saw a friendly face, someone he knew."

"Did you talk with him yesterday evening?"

"No," John said, his forehead wrinkled. "And that was my fault.

But he said he had some business that needed his attention. You say Milo spoke to you. What was it he said?"

I took a sip of tea. "His words were, 'I said I am not . . .' but he wasn't able to finish."

"Stabbed," John said.

"We didn't know that at the time. I thought he'd had a heart attack. But it was late, the pubs were emptying, so whatever fight he got into might've been on purpose or a mistake or . . ." I was rather hoping John would choose an option or come up with another, but he kept silent, staring into his mug. "You and Milo worked together—or did he work for you? Do you know anyone who would want to hurt him?"

"Milo had a good eye. He was the kind of man who could look at a situation and see what was needed. He did that not only for me, but also for others. But his help, even when requested, wasn't always accepted. That's what he told me once."

"What sort of work did Milo do for you?" I asked.

"Whatever was needed. He was ballast, Hayley, keeping the world stable."

"So, he was like William?" I asked. Yes, Jean Benoit-Aubéry and *Frenchman's Creek*. At that moment, it seemed kinder to go along with things.

John gave me a puzzled look. "Have I met William?" Then he shook his head. "I will miss Milo. We had a professional relationship, but we had become friends, you see. It's what happens when you work with someone closely, isn't it? Like you and Mrs. Woolgar."

Mrs. Woolgar and I had only brief flashes of working together, and I couldn't say we were any sort of friends, but I understood what he meant.

"What would Flambeaux do, Hayley? Would he give up when faced with such a terrible situation, or would he be bold?"

"Flambeaux sensed the possibilities, don't you think? And he was bold enough to leave his jar of tobacco in the bedside table of a woman he knew only from her portrait."

John cocked his head. "Tobacco? My grandfather didn't smoke." The dimple appeared. "But he did leave a rose at her bedside—a red rose, fresh cut, its perfume heavy in the air."

It seemed that du Maurier's pirate and Georgiana Fowling's François Flambeaux had parted company again.

A glance at his watch, and John stood. "I'm sorry, Hayley, I'm afraid I must move on. Moorage times are strictly enforced. It's unfortunate that I don't have the little creek in which Flambeaux could hide his ship from those who wished him harm."

Moorage time limits—a rather prosaic reason for always needing to dash off. You see, I told myself, there's a logical explanation for everything.

"But you will talk with the police," I said. "Ask for Detective Sergeant Hopgood or Detective Constable Kenny Pye."

"Yes, I will as soon as I am moored again." As we climbed out of the cabin, John said, "Hayley, when I rang Milo this morning, there was nothing. Do the police have his mobile?"

"They didn't tell me. You should ask them." Just don't expect an answer.

I stepped up and out of the boat, and John nodded to the rope at the front. "Can you help? See how the rope is looped through the ring on the bank?"

With a bit of instruction and watching John do the same at the back of the boat, I successfully unmoored one end of *La Mouette 2*. I tossed the rope onto the boat, and as John started the engine and prepared to leave, I said, "Have you read *Frenchman's Creek* by Daphne du Maurier?"

"No, I haven't," he said. "Do you recommend it?"

7

There now—I'd found John, told him the terrible news, and learned that his narrow boat was the reason for his quirky behavior. At least, part of the reason. I'd also told him to go to the police. Now I could move on to my next project. I walked back to Middlebank, buying a sandwich at the newsagent on my way.

As I neared Hedgemead Park, I could see the blue-and-white police tape that cordoned off one side of the entrance, the place where Milo fell. I walked through the gates and stood at the top of the lazy zigzag path that led down to where Guinea Lane met the Paragon—the lower entrance. The small park was heavily treed, and I felt the temperature drop several degrees when I reached the shade. I peered down into the dim landscape, but could see nothing other than a few walkers on their way up or down. Police must've finished their search.

Inside Middlebank, I looked in on Mrs. Woolgar, at her computer.

"I've set myself a task for the afternoon," I said. "A search for any unpublished Flambeaux stories Lady Fowling might've left lying about. And so, after I eat my lunch, I'm going to the cellar."

The secretary looked up. "Thank you for that notice. I hope you'll remember your mobile."

I suppose this could be Mrs. Woolgar's version of a running joke. And all because of that one time when I'd gone down without my phone and locked myself in and no one knew where I was.

"Will do. And I'll keep the door open."

After my sandwich, I pulled on a jumper—the cellar was always a bit chilly—and descended to the lower ground floor. The door on my right was to Mrs. Woolgar's flat. I turned left and walked down a short corridor.

I had learned early on in my tenure as curator at the First Edition Society that Middlebank's cellar held secrets. Vast secrets, I liked to say, because it sounded more mysterious. I had discovered a couple of them, and I hoped that Lady Fowling might have at least one more waiting for me. I would admit only to myself that I thought of the cellar as a refuge, too—a good place to get away from the world's chaos.

As soon as I'd unlocked and opened the door, Bunter shot past me and disappeared into the furniture jungle. I, on the other hand, stood on the threshold and considered my options. The room was larger than it appeared, because at the far end the space widened, taking in the former coal bin. The contents of the cellar spanned well over a century of Fowlings at Middlebank, but to get in, I faced dismantling an intricate maze of coatracks, commodes, chairs, occasional tables, and more. I had done this twice before and each time had tried my best to put everything back as it had been, but I'd never been good at puzzles.

Taking a deep breath, I began dragging pieces out into the corridor one by one. After an hour, I had made a narrow and convoluted path for myself, like a woodworm eating its way through the leg of a Georgian lowboy. As I worked my way in, I opened any drawer I could reach, feeling all the way to the back and knocking on the wood in case there was a secret panel.

I came up with a framed picture of the queen, circa 1960s; a sixpence and a half crown—old money, and so dating from before 1971; and a war bond. I stood amid a sea of furniture and asked, "Well, now where?"

A scrabbling noise came from behind an Art Nouveau carved fire surround, followed by Bunter's head popping up from behind it like a jack-in-the-box.

"That way, is it? Right, coming."

The cat disappeared, but I forged ahead, because I'd spotted a sideboard with drawers. I had to hold my breath to squeeze between a glass panel display cabinet and a towering wardrobe, then discovered my access blocked by a dining table long enough to seat an army. Lucky me, there was space below, and so I crawled under and resurfaced just as I heard a *thunk* and a scraping sound.

"Bunter," I called out, "that had better be you."

"Ms. Burke?"

"Back here, Mrs. Woolgar."

There was the rattle of a cup, and in a minute, Mrs. Woolgar appeared from round the corner with tea in one hand and a plate of shortbread fingers in the other. She looked about her. "Can you advise on a route?"

"If you circle round that dressing table, there's enough room to . . . hang on, I'm coming."

Back under the table and with a bit of squirming, Mrs. Woolgar and I met over what might've been one of the earliest television cabinets in existence. I reached out and took the tea and shortbread.

"Thank you," I said. "This is just what I needed."

"Have you come across anything useful?" she asked.

"Not yet."

Mrs. Woolgar took a lace-edged handkerchief from her sleeve and dusted the corner of a carved walnut cabinet next to her. "My, I don't recognize many of the pieces back in this corner. Sir John's, I suppose. Well, I'll leave you to it."

I worked my way back and perched on the long table while I had my tea, watching Bunter spring from one piece of furniture to another, making a circuit of the entire cellar in short order. Cats were ace at parkour. Finished with my tea break, I tackled the sideboard and came up with nothing, not even an overlooked tarnished silver teaspoon.

Then I noticed behind the sideboard, hidden under an upturned needlepoint piano bench, was a trunk. It took me another half hour of furniture shifting to have enough room to open it, telling myself all the while it was probably full of old bed linens.

"Even so," I said to Bunter, who sat atop a long-case clock, "I will not give up. I'll burrow my way out along another path and continue the search, because I sense something. I'm close." I could hear the cat purr.

"Here we go," I said, and opened the trunk. Nestled among yellowing bed linen lay a smaller box, this one dark mahogany with mother-of-pearl inlay. A tea chest, I thought. It might be two hundred years old, from a time when tea was a valuable commodity. Fortunately, the key was in the lock. I took the chest out, set it on the table, and opened it.

The box held paper—old-fashioned, crinkly onionskin. I leaned in and read the typewritten top sheet:

"François Flambeaux: How It All Began"

by

Georgiana Fowling

Below, she'd signed her name with a blue fountain pen. I put my hand out to touch it and then looked round the cellar, needing to share the news.

The cat hopped down and sniffed the corner of the tea chest. "Look, Bunter," I whispered to him. "Look what we've found."

The manuscript had been tied with twine, and when I pulled it out, I found that it was only about twenty pages, and another bundle lay beneath with the title "François and the Adder's Holiday," and below that, "François Pockets the Clue." And there were more.

A treasure chest of short stories, the most important of which I held in my hand: "How It All Began." This had to be François Flambeaux's origin story. I closed the lid on the trunk, sat down on it, slipped the twine off the sheaf, and read.

The river runs higher today that it did then, swelling peacefully to fill the banks and covering the roots of willow and thickets of reed. The creek that runs off it, hidden by a tangle of growth, now served only as a graveyard for boats, relics of years past. Yet each had its own story to tell. Listen. On a quiet night, you might hear the creaks and moans as the tide lifts the boats, and you might mistake those sounds for a nightjar. Or perhaps not. Perhaps instead you hear an echo of the past. Listen—is that his voice? Low and close, he tells her to come aboard, that all is ready.

By the time I reached the last scene on that spit of sand—the place where they parted and François considered what to do with the rest of his life—I could barely see the words for my tears. I whisked them away, wiped my nose on the sleeve of my jumper, and reached out to the cat, who had settled comfortably with all four legs tucked under. "Oh, Bunter, how sad."

His eyes were slits, but sprang open when my phone pinged with a message from Val.

Good day?

I'm in the cellar.

And you remembered your phone. Dinner?

I was shocked to see that it had gone six o'clock. I replied:

Here. Pizza.

Will stop for wine.

I love you.

A little sob escaped as I hit send.

After a moment, he responded:

I love you, too. See you soon.

I'd better get upstairs, because apart from wanting to see Val, I desperately needed the loo.

My attempts to erase all signs of crying hadn't worked, apparently, because when Val arrived at my flat and looked into my eyes, he took me in his arms. We stayed that way for a minute, but at last, when I'd soaked up enough comfort, I said, "I'm all right."

Val held me at arm's length. "Is it Milo's murder? This business with John?"

"Both, I suppose," I said, "but mostly, it's that." I nodded to the coffee table and the typewritten manuscript of "How It All Began."

"Bloody hell," Val said, handing me the bottle of wine. "How did you ever find it?"

Lady Fowling, through Bunter, had guided me, of course. I didn't say it aloud, but I'd felt it to be the case on a few earlier occasions, and I believe Val knew it.

"May I?"

"Have at it," I said, and went to open the bottle as he started to read.

I ordered pizza and poured myself a glass of wine. Val would need to wait, because it wouldn't do to spill red wine on the only copy of a priceless manuscript. He read the first several pages, then skimmed to the end. He looked up at me.

"This is amazing," he said. "It's remarkable. Her writing was much simpler, but you can see glimpses of where she was headed."

I smiled—the writing instructor at work. "But you see what it is, don't you?" I asked. "Fan fiction. She took *Frenchman's Creek*, changed a few bits, added her own parts, and came up with François. And, there are more stories. I found them in there," I said, nodding to the tea chest I'd set at the end of the sofa.

The front door buzzed, and Val went down to collect our dinner. Over the meal, we put Flambeaux aside, and I caught him up on locating John.

"He lives on a narrow boat?" Val asked, and I saw a glint in his green eyes.

"Have you been on one?" I asked.

"Once. A day trip for the girls' twelfth birthday. They invited friends and my mum did the food, so all I had to do was drive the boat. We went almost as far as Devizes—there are twenty-nine locks that start there. I'd've done it gladly, but the girls wanted to get back for a film. Still, it was fantastic cruising along the canal with the countryside drifting by you."

"Twenty-nine locks?"

"It isn't difficult once you . . ." He shook his head. "Right. Now, back to Flambeaux. What do we know?"

"Flambeaux did indeed start out a pirate."

Val poured us more wine. "He fell in love, and they had an adventure or two."

"But then she left him, and he gave up his swashbuckling ways and used his wiles to solve crimes—he became Flambeaux the detective."

"He never needed money," Val said, "because of all that pirate treasure he'd amassed."

"He vowed to always keep her memory in his heart," I said. "The woman who had left him."

"But was that woman Georgiana Fowling?" Val asked.

I picked at a bit of cheese that had oozed into the cardboard box. "The thing is, the differences between Flambeaux's origin story and *Frenchman's Creek*—John knows Lady Fowling's version."

"What does that mean?" Val asked. "Did John Aubrey read this story?"

"How could he—it's typewritten. And probably at least sixty years old. But just to make sure, I'll check with George Bayntun. They published the Flambeaux books, they might know something about the stories."

"You don't want to ask Glynis first?"

"No, I don't," I said. "This story creates a bond between Lady Fowling and John Aubrey that excludes her. I'm not sure how she would take it."

"Perhaps the real Flambeaux received copies of the stories. Was his name Aubrey?"

"Does this mean John really is Lady Fowling's grandson?" There, I'd said it aloud.

"He'd have to take a DNA test."

"Why?" I asked. "He's not making any claims to the estate. He doesn't seem to be announcing to the world that he's related or wouldn't we have heard about it? It looks as if he's told only those of us inside Middlebank—Mrs. Woolgar, Duncan, me, you. Is that it?"

"You forget Charles Henry Dill."

8

The next morning, Val stayed only long enough for a quick a cup of tea.

"See you in a bit," I said. "At the police station."

"Mmm," Val replied as he left. "My favorite place for a rendezvous."

Mrs. Woolgar and I offered "good mornings" as we passed in the entry, she to her office, I to mine. It was Friday, and Frances was expected, so there would be no morning briefing.

When Frances arrived, I walked up to the library with her. "I'm delighted you came to the afternoon open."

She turned to me, her eyes shining. "It was quite an afternoon, wasn't it? You never know, do you, what may be on the horizon?"

This was more animated than I'd ever seen her, and I could guess to what she referred.

"True. I'm sorry about the . . . trouble."

Frances busied herself with straightening stacks of paperback books and checking that her pen was in working order, and as she did so, she asked, "Who was that man?"

"The one who punched John? Charles Henry Dill. He's Lady Fowling's nephew. He's her only surviving relative."

"Is he?"

Was that a question or a comment? Had I told her about John's claim? "As far as we know he is," I said. Unable to recall how much Frances knew, I wondered if I should tell her about Milo. Then common sense took hold.

"Well," I said, "I'll leave you to it."

I put my head in Mrs. Woolgar's office. "Frances is set for the morning, and now I need to nip down to the police station."

"How was your cellar expedition?"

Easy, now, Hayley, don't frighten her.

"Oh, the cellar. I do have something to show you, but it can wait until later."

"That's fine, Ms. Burke. I'll spend the afternoon working on the international correspondence."

Val and I met on the pavement in front of the Avon and Somerset Police Station at half past ten. Inside, the desk sergeant—a woman, and new since I'd last stopped in—told us DS Hopgood and DC Pye were not on the premises, but our statements were ready. Just as well they weren't around, because how was I to explain the connection— possible connection—John had with Lady Fowling when my mind was in such a muddle? As I read and signed mine, I wondered if John had been in yet, but I couldn't find a way to introduce the subject before Val and I found ourselves out on the pavement again.

After coffee and an almond croissant at the Bertinet by the rail station, I dusted powdered sugar off my chest, Val returned to his work, and I walked up Manvers to the George Bayntun bookshop. A bell tinkled when I opened the door, and I paused just inside to breathe in the fragrance of old books combined with the smell of leather and glue from the binding workshop.

On the other side of a high counter covered with trays of note cards, pencils, and erasers sat a woman with a bun high atop her head from which frizzled wisps of gray had escaped. She had a stack of books at each elbow and her eye on the computer screen in front of her. Her hand hovered over the mouse.

"There you are, you little bugger," she exclaimed, clicked the mouse, and flung herself against the back of her chair.

"Hello, good morning," she said. "Can I help you?"

I'd had little to do with the bookshop thus far in my tenure at the First Edition Society, because Mrs. Woolgar preferred to deal with any person, place, or thing that still had Lady Fowling's personal touch on it, so I started at the beginning and introduced myself.

"Very pleased to meet you, I'm sure, Hayley," she said. "I'm Teresa Wells. May I say we still miss Lady Fowling? Up until those last months, she would often come in for a browse and a cup of tea. Such a spirit she had."

"Yes, she did," I said, and then added, "At least, that's what I hear. I'm sorry that I never met her. Everyone admires the Flambeaux series, too. You did such a fine job of printing and binding."

"It was a joy," she said. "Lady Fowling left us with a complete set, as I'm sure you know." She gestured to the back wall, where, behind the glass of one of the bookcases, I recognized the Flambeaux spines.

"Not for sale, of course. We would've been happy to print more and list them in our catalog, but she preferred to retain all other copies and give them as gifts."

I edged my way over to take a look. "Can you tell me, apart from the complete set of novels, do you by any chance have a collection of short stories?"

Teresa had followed me over. "Flambeaux short stories? No, I've never seen them. Are you looking to publish? We'd be very interested."

"I'm not sure how finished she left them or how many there are, but I will mention your offer to the board." As soon as I explain to them that the stories had been found. I counted the Flambeaux books behind the glass and found no more or less than what should be there.

"So, Lady Fowling took all the sets, apart from this one," I said. "She didn't have you ship a set to anyone? I'm only asking for the sake of the Society's history."

"We might've put something in the post for her. Is this a mystery for the Golden Age of Mystery library?" Teresa asked, her eyes gleaming. "I tell you what—we've decades of business transactions in storage upstairs. I'll have a shufti."

My next task took careful handling. I wanted others to read the stories I'd found in the tea chest, but the origin story was the most important, because it seemed to hold clues to John's life. I wasn't about to pass round the onionskin sheets of "How It All Began," and so I now headed for the quick-print shop. I made a copy by laying each onionskin sheet on the flat glass scanner—there was no way I was putting sixty-odd-year-old paper through the feeder. Once I checked the quality, I emailed the file to myself and printed out six copies from the copy. The rest of the François stories would keep until next week. Then I stopped for lunch, and over a spinach pasta salad at the Waitrose café, I texted Adele about dinner.

Raven?

A few minutes later, she replied, sounding as if she were channeling Hercule Poirot.

Bonjour, mon amie! News about the pirate?

On so many fronts. See you at 7?

À tout à l'heure

I took a wild stab that meant "yes."

That evening, I arrived at the Raven before Adele and secured our corner table upstairs, where the windows on either side were open and a breeze stirred the air. I started on the bottle of wine —a small congratulations to myself for avoiding Mrs. Woolgar that afternoon. I hadn't wanted to slip up and mention the stories I'd found before getting some advice on how best to proceed. Mrs. Woolgar didn't seem to know about them, and for the secretary to not know something about Lady Fowling might not sit well.

Adele appeared at the top of the stairs, holding up her mass of red curls with one hand and fanning the back of her neck with the other.

"Where's Val?" she asked as I poured her glass.

"He'll be along."

"Right, then, catch me up."

I fleshed out the few details I'd given her about John, told her that Milo had been murdered, but then needed to go back to the beginning and explain who he was, and by the time I finished, the stories had slopped over into each other and Adele was on her second glass of wine.

"Well," she said, "even if John and Milo worked together, at least the murder doesn't have anything to do with Middlebank, so you won't be involved in the enquiry."

She caught my eye, and I realized she expected an answer. "Yes," I said. "I mean, no. We had to sign our statements, of course."

"Do the police know about Aubrey's connection to the Society?"

"Don't let Mrs. Woolgar hear you say John has a connection," I said. "I suppose they must know by now, because he was to go in today to tell them what he knew about Milo." I sipped my wine and added, "They looked a bit alike."

"Aubrey and Milo? Are . . . were they related?"

"No," I said. "At least, I don't believe so. And it was only at a first quick glance that they could be mistaken. Once you look them in the face, they're quite different."

"Why do you think John Aubrey chose *Frenchman's Creek* for the basis of his myth about Flambeaux?" Adele asked.

I held up a forefinger. "I've found an answer to that question, although it brings up a host of others. You see, I made a visit to the cellar yesterday."

"You and that cellar," Adele said. "Or should I say, you, Georgiana, and that cellar. Does she talk to you down there?"

I ignored her comment. "Here's what I found." I handed her a copy of Flambeaux's origin story.

She looked at the title and her mouth dropped open. "Oh my God."

"That's yours for the keeping. Take a look, and I'll order our food."

Val came up the stairs and met me at the bar. "Hiya," he said, putting a hand on my waist. He glanced back to Adele. "Another bottle, do you think?"

"I'd say so."

Adele did a quick read of the entire story and had reached the last page by the time our food arrived. "Listen to this," she said.

The sun edged its way above the horizon, a thin line but a fiery show of grief and loss as he watched her leave, climbing the rocks up from that spit of sand and careful to hold her muslin skirt, the delicate fabric of which had been sent to her from India by a great-uncle only two years previous. At the top of the path, her eyes were drawn back down to the shore, where he stood and cast a last farewell.

Adele pressed the photocopied story to her chest and, eyes sparkling with tears, said, "It's as if I can hear her voice."

It was the best authentication I could hope for apart from Mrs. Woolgar's.

Val reached for the brown sauce and applied a liberal amount to his sausage and chips. "You can see how she played with descriptions, can't you?" he asked. "And how it led to her later works, where she really let go."

He and Adele discussed how an author's writing style can grow over time, while I ate my chicken-and-mushroom pie. When they were finished, I brought them back to the topic at hand. "Lady Fowling changed a few things from *Frenchman's Creek* to suit her own purposes."

"That happens in fan fiction, doesn't it?" Adele directed this question to Val.

"Some writers are sticklers for keeping to the original, but for others, it's a jumping-off point."

"This is Flambeaux's backstory," I said, "before he started detecting. And there's more. I found a stack of other François stories in the same chest. I haven't read them yet, but they seem to predate the books. They could be ideas that she expanded into full-length novels or they could stand on their own. They are all typewritten and never published, as far as we know."

"And so," Val pointed out, "how does John Aubrey know these things?"

"Exactly," I said. "When I said that the pirate had left his jar of tobacco in the woman's bedside table, which is what happened in *Frenchman's Creek*, John corrected me. He said his grandfather didn't smoke, and he had actually left a red rose. The red-rose version is in here." I tapped the François story.

"Georgiana didn't smoke, and she never liked being around it," Adele said.

"And here's another," I said. "Stealing Godolphin's wig in du Maurier became stealing a toupee from . . . some foolish man."

"So, he hasn't made it all up," Adele said as she reached for the second bottle of wine and divided the remainder among our glasses.

"Did Hayley tell you he lives on a narrow boat?" Val asked. "He's invited us out."

"What, no pirate ship?" Adele said.

"John's named his narrow boat *La Mouette 2*," I told her.

"There's a bit of cheek," Adele said. "I want to talk with him."

"Good," I said. "He's away now, searching for moorage, I think, but as soon as he's back, I'll let you know."

"Did Lady Fowling ever mention to you that she went away after Sir John died?" Val asked.

Adele stared off into space. "She might've, but if she did, it was only in passing."

I fiddled with the last carrot on my plate. "Do you think it's possible? Do you believe she might have . . ."

"What, 'strayed'?" Adele asked. "Georgiana was a widow, couldn't she have done as she bloody well pleased? Or is that the point—she couldn't. You haven't shown this to Glynis yet, have you?"

I shook my head. "The photo was enough of a blow. She hasn't heard these stories of John's—that is, of Lady Fowling's. I plan to leave a copy of the story on her desk this evening before I go to bed."

Val grinned. "And then hightail it out of town to your mum's first thing in the morning?"

"Yes." I laughed, but sobered up immediately. "Mrs. Woolgar may make the connection between Flambeaux and *Frenchman's Creek*, but I suppose I'll be the one to explain the rest."

Adele sat back against the bench and crossed her arms. "Think of what Georgiana was faced with. A widow at thirty, a vast fortune to oversee, and all alone. It isn't easy making decisions when you think you've no one on your side."

I caught a wistful tone in Adele's voice and thought she might be talking not only about Lady Fowling, but also herself and the struggles she'd had as a young gay woman getting up the courage to tell her mother.

"When you had no one, Georgiana was your champion, wasn't she?"

"She was that," Adele agreed. "I remember she said when a woman had to make a difficult decision, she would always wonder what might've happened if she'd taken the other road."

It came to me that John had said much the same thing.

G ive Lenore my love," Val had said when he'd given me a kiss and left me on the doorstep at Middlebank. "And good luck Monday morning."

I had taken a copy of "How It All Began" and placed it on the secretary's desk along with a note about where I'd found it. I added nothing further. The next morning, I was safely on an early train to see my mum and didn't have to face Mrs. Woolgar for two more days.

I arrived at Liverpool Lime Street just past eleven on Saturday morning. I had two changes on the journey, but still, I preferred the train to a car—especially as I didn't drive. I walked up from the station to Mum's flat, a building designed for independent pensioners, and after a coffee, we set out for a day of shopping and lunch. It was a bit of a celebration, this, because it was Mum's first excursion using only a cane to get round after a surgery two months earlier had put her game leg to rights.

We took a taxi in and nosed around a few shops, before we sat down to lunch and ordered the set three-course meal with a glass of prosecco.

While we ate, I caught her up on events. "It sounds a mess, I know," I said, stabbing a Jersey potato and pushing it round in the hollandaise sauce, "but I can't seem to get through it in any proper sort of order. But I've brought a copy of Flambeaux's origin story for you to read."

"John doesn't want money," Mum said.

"He hasn't asked for any. If he tried that, I'm certain Duncan would be on him in an instant about taking a DNA test."

"He hasn't gone to the newspapers with his story?"

"No. He didn't even want the police called when Charles Henry punched him."

"And speaking of," Mum said, pushing the last flakes of salmon into a heap on her plate, "if your solicitor did ask for a DNA sample from John, who would it be compared with?"

Lady Fowling's only living relative. "But, if Charles Henry is so certain John is a liar, why hasn't he demanded the test be done?"

"And what does Lady Fowling say about John Aubrey and his claim?" Mum asked.

That made three—Mum, Val, and Adele—who had cottoned on to my occasional habit of checking in with her ladyship.

"Well, I can tell you this much," I said, "I don't believe she's at all angry about it."

After lunch, we managed one more shop before taking a taxi

home, where Mum lay in her reclining chair and I stretched out on the sofa. When I woke, she was reading "How It All Began."

"Now," Mum said, "I need to read *Frenchman's Creek* so that I can compare the two."

I stretched and yawned and got up to switch the kettle on. "I'm surprised you haven't already."

"No, I've read *Rebecca*, of course, and *My Cousin Rachel* and *Jamaica Inn*. She certainly knew how to put her female characters in peril. Physically and emotionally."

The kettle switched off, I poured up the tea, and had a nose round in the biscuit tin, coming across an unopened packet of dark-chocolate-dipped shortbread. By the time we were sitting over our brew, I was licking chocolate off my fingers. My phone rang—my daughter on a video call—and I chased the biscuit with a sip of tea before I answered.

"Dinah, sweetie," I said, "how lovely to see you. Here's your gran."

We shared the call, the three of us chatting about nothing and everything, laughing, and having a right old time.

"Mum," Dinah said, "did Gran tell you that I think we three should have a weekend holiday? Ginny says it's fine whenever I want the car, and so I could drive. Wouldn't it be fun? We could go to Scotland or Cornwall or the Lake District."

That my twenty-three-year-old daughter wanted to spend time with her mum and grandmother warmed my heart.

"Sweetie, this is a fantastic idea, but don't you think you need a bit more experience driving short journeys first?"

"Ah, now, Mum, you know you want to. Just think, the three Burke women take to the road!"

She knew her way round her mother, I'll say that for my daughter. We were not, at least on paper, the three Burke women. I'd taken back my maiden name when I divorced Roger, but she had been Tamworth for the first eleven years of her life and remained so. Still, since she'd turned twenty-one, Dinah had made a few comments about changing her name by deed poll. I had tried to conceal my delight.

My mum chimed in. "I'm all for a holiday!"

How did I become the responsible adult? "Right, you two, we'll give it a think."

If I had been any more chirpy at Monday morning's briefing with Mrs. Woolgar, I could've flown up to the curtain rod and perched there.

"Hello, good morning, and how was your weekend?" I sat on the edge of the chair, mug of tea in hand, hoping a good attitude would help put a positive outlook on the day. I could see the photocopy of Flambeaux's origin story on the secretary's desk. *Get it over with, Hayley.*

"So"—I nodded to the story—"what did you think?"

"Remarkable," Mrs. Woolgar said, and the constriction round my heart loosened. "What a clever mind her ladyship had. When I read this story, I realized what her inspiration was, of course—*Frenchman's Creek* by du Maurier—and so I reread the book over the weekend. I could see she had chosen the elements she wanted and wove them into Flambeaux's backstory. Interesting what she picked to retain and what she altered to make the story her own."

Now is the time for me to join up the dots for her, but still I hesitated. How would Mrs. Woolgar react when she learned that John Aubrey knew something about Lady Fowling that she had only just learned?

"You say there are more stories?" the secretary asked. "I suppose it's common for a writer to put early works aside, but I do wish her ladyship had shared this with her readers." The secretary patted the stack of pages. "She had a great fondness for a good romance."

The front-door buzzer went off, sounding a reprieve for me. I stood, but hesitated. "Mrs. Woolgar, perhaps we could talk more about this later? And, I'll bring down the other stories, too—before the end of the day."

But now I had other fish to fry.

"Good morning, Ms. Burke." My assistant stood on the doorstep, Panama hat held against his chest with both hands in what could pass for a meek attitude. He offered a polite smile.

"Good morning, Mr. Dill," I said. I moved out of the way, but he didn't shift from the doorstep until I said, "Come through."

What a remarkable change. Not only in his attire—still a linen suit, but this one a mint green—but also in demeanor. Charles Henry Dill minus his smug look and general swagger appeared a diminished being. A mere shadow of his former self.

"Before we go further, Ms. Burke, I have a small confession to make."

I put my hand against the closed door to steady myself. What was it—he'd got in another punch-up with John Aubrey? He'd tried to get a loan using the Fowling fortune as collateral?

"Yes?"

"As I'm sure you are already aware, I did not yet complete the exam for the online indexing course. I humbly beg your forgiveness, but the last few questions brought up, in my mind, questions of their own, and I preferred to discuss the issues with you first." He hung his head as his fingers toyed with the brim of his hat.

Did he actually have more questions, or was he waffling? Did it matter? I'd had more important issues on my mind than checking up on his exam, and so I would call us even.

"Thank you for explaining. I'd be happy to talk you through the end of the exam. After all, the point is that you learn."

We went to the library, and once we were settled, Dill cleared his throat and said, "It was when I considered one of the aims of indexing that questions arose for me, Ms. Burke. We are to 'anticipate the needs of the user' when choosing what is significant information, but who are our users?"

Who indeed? It was a question I'd brought up with Mrs. Woolgar at one of our early briefings, hoping to identify whom the Society attracts and therefore look for ways to attract more of the same. That Charles Henry now brought up the same question threw me into a quandary—brush this off as his usual blag or treat it seriously?

"The Society attracts a broad"—although shallow—"audience of scholars, readers, and writers. Social historians, too. Why don't you come up with a list of categories you think apply, and we'll take a look?"

He seemed satisfied with my answer, and so I left him to it, promising tea at eleven.

In my office, I tackled two boxes of newsletters from the earliest days of the First Edition Society. Those issues were charming Lady Fowling creations. She had written her own thoughts on Golden Age of Mystery books, reviewed contemporary literary journals, and decorated the margins with illustrations of books and cats.

There had appeared the occasional article by some knowledgeable Society member, and a regular feature called "Mystery at Middlebank" in which Bunter the cat—perhaps Bunter III or IV—had taken up pen to write about his feline exploits. Her ladyship had shared bits of news about members and published their letters. One asked after a particular flower in Miss Marple's garden and another about the type of paint Troy used. Whoever this Troy was.

When Bunter, who had been keeping me company in the wingback chair by the door, jumped down and stretched, I checked the time. Nearly eleven.

I, too, stretched. I went into the kitchenette, put the kettle on, and opened a new packet of Marie biscuits. The front door buzzed. *John*, I thought, as if he had become a regular at Middlebank. I wasn't up for an Aubrey-Dill rematch and would stash him in my office and out of Charles Henry's way. But when I opened the door, I found instead our local constabulary.

"Sergeant Hopgood," I said, stepping back in surprise.

"Ms. Burke, good morning. I was hoping to have a word with you. Is this a bad time?"

I didn't think you were meant to turn away the police. "No, of course not. Come through. Cup of tea?"

"No tea, thank you," Hopgood said. "I was nearby and stopped to ask if you've spoken to this John Aubrey."

The secretary came to her office door.

"Good morning, Mrs. Woolgar," Hopgood greeted her.

"Sergeant," she replied with a nod.

"Yes," I said, "I told John you needed to speak with him. He hasn't been in?"

"I say, Ms. Burke, is there a cup of tea going?"

Charles Henry had come out onto the library landing, but he stopped short the moment he saw Hopgood. Had he truly been looking for tea? I doubted it. He'd heard John Aubrey's name mentioned and couldn't help putting his nose in.

Sergeant Hopgood stood gazing up to the landing as his eyebrows slowly levitated.

"Mr. Charles Henry Dill, is it?" he asked.

Dill looked back. "Yes. It's . . . you are . . ."

"Detective Sergeant Hopgood," I reminded him.

"I know that," Dill said to me. "Hello, sir."

The sergeant studied Charles Henry. "Tell me, Mr. Dill," he asked in a friendly tone, "are you still at the same address? Grove Street, was it?"

He remembered that from the previous October? I knew it as Maureen's flat, although I'd never been inside.

Charles Henry put a hand on the railing. "Yes, that's correct."

The DS turned back to me. "Well, Ms. Burke, I'll be on my way. Thank you."

I saw him out and turned round. Charles Henry remained on the landing, Mrs. Woolgar in her doorway, and I with my back to the door. Had Sergeant Hopgood gotten what he'd come for? I glanced up at Dill, who looked away. Then the kettle began to whistle, and, without a word, we three went our separate ways.

9

When I arrived with Charles Henry's tea and a stack of photo-copied newsletters, he stuck out his bottom lip. "You said you wouldn't notify the police," he complained.

"John was the one who said not to phone the police," I said, setting his cup and saucer on the table. "You remember him, don't you—the man you punched?" Dill pulled his tea closer and didn't answer. "DS Hopgood wasn't at Middlebank about you. A man was attacked near here late on Wednesday evening, and he died."

"What has that to do with you or this Aubrey?"

"Val and I came across the fellow. He'd collapsed at the gate to Hedgemead Park. His name was Milo Overton. He worked for John."

Charles Henry narrowed his eyes. "And?" he asked.

"And nothing," I said.

Except for this: DS Hopgood had arrived with a question about

John Aubrey, but had taken away with him information on Charles Henry.

I texted Val and we arranged to meet for a late lunch between his classes, leaving me the early part of the afternoon for work. Off-site. At one o'clock, I went upstairs to see Charles Henry off.

"Would you mind, Ms. Burke, if I take these newsletter copies with me? I'm sure Maureen would love to see them."

That gave me pause, because I don't believe I'd ever heard anything so considerate come out of his mouth.

"Yes, of course you may," I said. "Bring them back with you next week."

He tucked them in his satchel, and we walked down to the entry together. At the door, I asked, "Maureen must've been involved quite early in the days of the Society. Do you know when she and Lady Fowling first met?"

"Maureen's mother and Aunt Georgiana were friends," he said. "They had met through some charity to help poor readers. It was the seventies. Maureen lived in London at the time, but she met Auntie on one of her visits home."

Had Maureen heard stories about Lady Fowling's time away after Sir John died? I should talk with her. I *should* do, but Maureen always seemed a bit daunting to me, and so, I preferred my information secondhand.

I shut the door and went to the secretary's office. "Mrs. Woolgar, I'll be out for a while. I want to check in with George Bayntun. I'll fetch the rest of Lady Fowling's stories when I return." But first, I would try a fishing expedition. "Before he left, Charles Henry was telling me about Maureen, her mother, and her ladyship and how they became friends. That's a long association with Middlebank." There it was—a perfect opening for Mrs. Woolgar to share a bit of her own past.

"Yes, it was a good many years ago now," the secretary said, "but some memories never fade."

I waited just in case she might offer more. She didn't.

L unch was a fair bit off yet, so I stopped at the Minerva for an orange squash and a packet of crisps. I stood against the wall at the end of the short bar, chatting with Pauline about her upcoming trip to France while she took drink orders and pulled pints.

"I don't know," she said, "we're probably too old to learn another language. Adele's having trouble with verb conjugation, and I'm stumbling over all those damned silent letters. If they don't need them, why are they there?"

"You'll have a lovely holiday," I said. "Buying your food from a local farmer, cooking over an open fire—really getting away from it all." I was happy for them, but even happier that it was Adele and Pauline who would be tent camping in the French countryside, and not me.

Pauline set an overflowing pint of bitter on the bar and giggled. "You should've seen Adele's face when I said we'd catch our own fish. I was only half kidding, because my dad used to do the very thing on our holidays. For bait, he'd buy any old meat that had been re-duced for quick sale, and we'd cut it up in bits. With a sharp fillet knife, I can clean and gut a perch fresh out of the river quicker than you can sing 'God Save the Queen.'"

Give me my haddock already battered and fried and with a mound of chips, thank you very much. I downed the remainder of my drink, bade Pauline "adieu," and struck out, heading down to the narrow boats on the canal.

On my way, I rang John, and he answered.

"Hayley?" he asked.

"John, where are you? You haven't been in to see the police yet."

"I've had a devil of a time finding a spot—summer and all the closest moorage is booked. I've been to Bathampton and past Saltford, back and forth. But at last I've found a spot, quite near where I was on Thursday."

Quite near where I was at that moment. I shaded my eyes and peered down the canal. I spotted him and waved.

"Come aboard," he said when I reached *La Mouette 2*.

"Why don't you come ashore?" I replied. "We'll meet Val for lunch." *Then escort you to the police station, where my responsibilities will be finished.*

We walked back down the towpath and through Sydney Gardens, and met Val at the Pulteney Bridge. The Boater, the nearest pub to hand, had garden seating overlooking the weir, and we found a table under an umbrella and settled with our drinks. Although I knew I should ask John how he had learned of Flambeaux's origin story—details that had never been published—at that moment, I didn't have the energy, and so when Val brought up the subject of narrow boats, I sat back, ate my fish-and-chips, and listened to John talk, as any other man might, about boats and such. The fantasy world of Flambeaux made nary an appearance.

Eventually, the conversation turned to Milo.

"He has a sister," John said. "She lives in Canada. I believe his ex-wife returned to Gothenburg a few years ago. The company will have his details better than I."

"Did you work there?" Val asked.

"Me? No, not exactly, but it's where I first encountered Milo when they wanted my idea." John looked into his pint glass, almost empty, a frown on his brow and lines round his mouth. "I will tell the police all I know, but that seems a paltry effort. I must do more." He looked up at Val and then at me, and I saw a fire in his eyes. "I will help find out who did this to him."

"That's the job of the police," Val said, channeling Sergeant Hopgood.

"Yes, of course it is, but what else can I do? Perhaps it will help me more than them—help me keep my feet on the ground. Milo would want that. And don't I have it in my blood?" he asked. "When my grandfather—that is, Flambeaux—offered his help to the police in finding the white peacock, he was met with resistance, but he persisted."

John seemed so earnest that I didn't have the heart to tell him what sort of reaction he would get from his offer. We finished our lunches and made our way to Manvers Street, where the desk sergeant greeted me cautiously, until I laid blame elsewhere.

"Good afternoon," I said. "Detective Sergeant Hopgood and Detective Constable Pye are expecting us." One of us, at any rate. "Could you tell them John Aubrey is here?"

We three stood off to the side in the lobby, Val and John in deep discussion about something called a *windlass* on a narrow boat. I kept my eye on the locked door across the room. It didn't take long before Sergeant Hopgood emerged. When he saw us, he stopped and studied John from the back. John turned, and Hopgood's eyebrows slammed together and then broke apart, one of them shooting up at an acute angle.

"Mr. Aubrey?" he asked.

"This is Detective Sergeant Hopgood," I said.

John approached the DS with his hand out. "Hello, Sergeant, I'm happy to meet you, although grieved at the circumstances. What can I do to help?"

"Well, Mr. Aubrey, good of you to come in," Hopgood said. "I have only a few questions. Come through and we'll have a chat. Thank you, Ms. Burke, Mr. Moffatt."

We watched them disappear into the inner workings of the station. Perhaps they were headed for Interview #1, my old haunt.

"He noticed, didn't he?" Val asked. "The resemblance?"

"I'd say he did."

"At lunch, John seemed more . . . I don't know how to describe it."

"Stable?" I offered. "Perhaps Milo's death has brought him back down to earth."

"Except for the bit about the white peacock," Val said. "There's no peacock mentioned in *Frenchman's Creek*, is there?"

"Nor in Flambeaux's origin story." I gave Val a kiss. "I'll ring you later."

He went off to class, and I crossed the road to look in at George Bayntun's.

"Hello, Hayley," Teresa said, pulling out an oversized ledger from underneath a mountain of papers. "I've located the years we published Lady Fowling's books, but I don't see a collection of short stories mentioned. But here"—she tapped a finger on the page—"is a note that we delivered the complete sets of Flambeaux books to Middlebank on this date. All the sets apart from one."

"What does that say?" I asked, pointing to a note in pencil too small for me to read.

"It's a notation about postal charges for one set. It says, 'to family.'"

"Does it say what family?" I asked. "Dill, perhaps? That was Lady Fowling's younger sister." *Or was it Aubrey?*

I could ask Mrs. Woolgar for a list of everyone who received a set of Flambeaux—I'm certain the records must exist. But until we learned more, I'd thought it best to avoid the whole prickly subject of John Aubrey.

"I'll need to dig out our postal ledgers next," Teresa said. "Cross-reference, you know. Isn't it fun what sort of investigations you curators get up to?"

I walked out of the bookshop as John emerged from the police station. He crossed the road to meet me.

"How did it go with Sergeant Hopgood?" I asked.

"I told them what I could," John said, but he looked exasperated. "They told me they do not need my help in the matter of Milo's murder. But I can't let that deter me. I must do this, I feel compelled . . . how can I explain?"

He didn't need to explain.

We turned and walked up Pierrepont Street toward the Parade Gardens. "Flambeaux knew so much, perhaps the answer lies with him. Was it a moonless night—one of those dark moments when evil awaited?" John asked. "Or an accident on the adder's holiday? Perhaps Milo, as François did, pocketed the clue himself. What do you think?"

Peacocks, adders, clues—I really did need to read the rest of the François stories.

"I'm sure the police are following several lines of enquiry."

"Then they should welcome my assistance. I have it in my blood, you understand. Because of Flambeaux." He checked the time. "I'd best be off."

"But you're in a forty-eight-hour moorage," I reminded him.

"Yes, and good thing," he said with a smile. "I have an appointment."

John continued on his way, but I stopped and leaned on the stone balustrade, looking down into the Parade Gardens. It had gone six, too late to ring or text Mrs. Woolgar to explain why I'd been absent the rest of the day. We didn't have that sort of "after-hours" relationship. Val was in class, Adele learning French, and I would spend the evening with Flambeaux.

I turned to go, but had taken only one step when someone grabbed my arm and wheezed in my ear.

"You didn't hear me calling, did you?"

Celia. She let go my arm and leaned over, hands on her thighs and her streaky blond hair hanging down as she caught her breath.

"No, I didn't hear you," I said. "Sorry."

"S'all right," she said with a laugh and a cough. "I've got to cut down on the fags. Look, Hayley, are you off somewhere? I could just do with a drink. Come along?"

"Oh, why not," I said. What's one drink? And didn't we need to treat our library patrons with care? "Where would you like to go?"

"Anywhere you like."

"Well, let's see, we're not too far from the—"

"Abbey Green's near my flat," Celia said. "The place with the massive plane tree—there's a pub there. It's become my local, actually, since I've been here."

And close by. We sat in the garden at the Crystal Palace pub, up against a tall divider of fake ivy, Celia with a gin and tonic and a cigarette, and I with a glass of red wine. She deposited her straw bag on the table, scooted herself back from our table, and exhaled. She waved at the smoke, successfully spreading it round.

"So, Celia, you've a good long holiday in Bath. Enjoying yourself?"

"I am," she said, squinting at me, her eyes nearly disappearing behind the load of mascara and kohl. "It's just nice to have a break from your job and all that."

"What do you do?"

"Me?" she asked. "Nothing special. I work at a place near Plymouth."

"Are you from Cornwall?" I asked.

"Oh yeah. Well, no, not originally. London. Slough, actually."

"That was quite a move, wasn't it?" I asked.

"I suppose." Celia took a gulp of her drink. She crossed her legs, and her dangling espadrilled foot bobbed up and down, beating a quick time only she could hear. "Anything to get away from my ex—although they keep trying to suck you back in, don't they?"

I suppose it was true for some, but beyond Roger's perfunctory apology of "It didn't mean anything"—a reference to me catching him in bed with the woman from the fish-and-chips stand, and a line he had repeated ad nauseam—he'd let me do what I want. Any delay in leaving was on me, but I had at last made the break, and I could still feel the exhilaration the day Dinah and I had moved from Swindon to Bath. The sense of freedom—and the panic.

"Leaving London worked out better than I could ever have imagined," Celia said. "Because that's how I met my boyfriend." She finished off her drink. "Say, I'll just pop into the bar and get us another round, shall I?"

I didn't need another glass of wine, but didn't have the chance to decline before she disappeared. When she returned with the drinks, she said, "I ordered us a plate of chips, thought we might need something in our tummies."

"Yes, good, thanks. So, your boyfriend works in Plymouth."

"Yeah," she said, "he's lovely. He's doing a bit of work here in Bath at the moment, and we're meeting up. He's the nicest fellow, and he really knows how to listen, because . . ." She lowered her eyelids, and I wondered how much energy it would take to lift them again. Then she looked up, squinting at the nearby tables. "Oh, I might as well tell you. You see, my ex was not a very nice person. I knew that, my friends knew that, only it took me a while to do anything about it."

Our food arrived, and the fragrance of the greasy chips nearly overwhelmed me. Celia kept talking, occasionally waving a chip round as she told me the story of her marriage and divorce.

"Well, I was in a right state, wasn't I? I knew I had to get away, because of how he had been so awful, and so I left—moved to Plymouth for this job. But even after things died down, I just wasn't myself, you know? And so, I did what everyone says you should do—I decided to see a therapist."

Celia moved into chapter two of her story, about how she found a therapist through the company. What sort of company it was, she didn't say. Or perhaps she did. Not that she wasn't entertaining, but

I was making a business of eating and was well on my way to finishing the chips by the time she arrived at her happy ending.

"We talked about things. You know as you do with a therapist. But then"—she squeezed her shoulders together—"we fell in love! I know it isn't supposed to happen. Therapist and client, you know. But it did. You just can't stop something like that, can you?"

"And this is the fellow you're to meet?" I asked.

"Yeah," she said, scanning the drinkers at the other tables. "Yeah. It's only that we haven't quite managed it yet." Her second G-and-T had vanished. "Say, that was a bit of a set-to at your library last week, wasn't it?"

"I'm sorry about that." I had forgotten Celia had still been there, but now recalled her across the room, squinting at John, Frances, and me. "I hope it won't discourage you from visiting again." I had not brought up the subject of the next afternoon open with Mrs. Woolgar, hoping that if I didn't, she wouldn't try to stop it.

"Not a bit of it, it's still a lovely place." Celia swirled her glass as if it still contained liquid. "That man, the one who got the punch, who is he?"

"John Aubrey. He's a . . . great fan of Lady Fowling, the Society founder. It's her library. She was a champion of the women authors of the Golden Age of Mystery."

"And the fellow who punched him was somebody named Dill?"

"It was a misunderstanding, that's all," I said, popping out of my chair and grabbing our glasses. "My shout. Same again?"

Another G-and-T for Celia, but my third drink was an orange squash with fizzy water. I did order a second plate of chips.

We ended the evening with a one-sided discussion of some Poirot story I'd never heard of in which no one could figure out how the murderer got in or out of the house without being seen. Apparently, at the end, everything had been explained.

"Look here, I'll show you how he did it," Celia said. "See, this vinegar bottle is the victim, and he was here. Now, the brown sauce is the murderer and he's over there." She picked up the pot of Colman's. "And here comes Colonel Mustard, the nosy parker!" She hooted with laughter. "You know, Colonel Mustard, like in Cluedo!"

We walked out of the pub and stopped for a moment to get our bearings. A stream of people flowed through Abbey Green chatting and laughing. When Celia took off, I followed, but I stopped at the corner before we left the square and looked back. Someone in the crowd had caught my eye—someone had been looking at me. Us. It had been so fleeting my mind couldn't even assign an identity, and I was left with only a hint of recognition. Was it a person I knew or merely a passing face from our literary salons or exhibition? Perhaps a library patron?

"Hayley!" Celia called. "You coming this way?"

"Yes, coming."

Celia's holiday flat was on the first floor above a shop.

"You see," she said, "truly the city center. Brilliant, innit?"

"Lucky you," I said. "Hope to see you Wednesday at the afternoon open. 'Night now." I left her at the door and continued to Middlebank, where I climbed into bed.

While I slept, my brain assembled a Picasso-like picture puzzle of my day. Squares showing unrelated faces and things bumped up against one another. Celia squinting at me from across the library next to Mrs. Woolgar scheming with Charles Henry. Pauline demonstrating how to bait a fishing line and Adele translating into French—or what sounded like it. Val in a pirate outfit standing on the bow of a narrow boat. Hmm, I rather liked that last one.

I awoke early, dressed, and downed half a cup of tea before going out and straight to the quick-copy shop with the rest of the Flambeaux stories in a satchel tucked under my arm. I wanted Mrs. Woolgar to know I wasn't skiving off work by missing our morning briefing, and so I put a sticky note on her door saying I was out on an errand and would return soon.

I copied the stories, first laying each onionskin page on the glass, then checked for quality before I ran off copies. When I'd finished, I felt a bit light-headed, and so continued on to the café on the Pulteney Bridge for a rock cake and a proper pot of tea.

Nearly eleven when I returned.

"I'll just pop up and change my clothes," I said to Mrs. Woolgar, who stood in the kitchenette making her own tea. "I have copies of all the stories for you, let me just sort them out." I turned to go and added, without looking at her, "About tomorrow afternoon. We will open to the public as usual." Silence. "Don't you think?"

"Will we need to hire a bouncer?" she asked, and I could only hope this was a rare display of wit.

"Not if Charles Henry stays away," I said.

"Not if John Aubrey stays away, you mean."

And with that standoff, I went upstairs. In my flat, I set out the stories across the sofa and coffee table, originals on their own, and then piles that contained one of each story. Among them were "François and the Adder's Holiday," "François Pockets the Clue," and "François and the Purloined Peacock."

I sat down to read this last one. After a few pages, Bunter slipped through my open door, hopped up onto the coffee table, and sat on "François on the Boards."

"John was right," I said to the cat. "It is a white peacock. Listen to this."

> *Only François, with his incomparable skill for seeing patterns where none existed, spotted the eyes that looked out at him from between the branches of a box hedge, unkempt from years of neglect by the head gardener, who did not care for its scent and therefore left it to grow into its own shape with elegantly arched branches and yet sparse limbs. Filling each leafless gap and forming the shape of a massive fan that would've suited a giant exotic dancer, enormous feathery white eyes quivered, but did not blink.*

I laughed aloud. Bunter hopped down and skittered out the door.

"But she meant this one to be funny," I said to his vanishing tortoiseshell tail. "Don't you think?"

Perhaps it was the voices downstairs that had startled the cat, or maybe he had noticed the time. I'd taken longer than I should've and needed to get back to work. I grabbed one set of the stories and skipped down to the entry. Low conversation came from the secretary's office. I shouldn't interrupt, and so went to my own desk, but hadn't had the chance to sit down before I heard Mrs. Woolgar say, "Of course she'll take care of it."

In a moment, the secretary appeared at my door and behind her, Maureen Frost, her face ashen.

"It's Charles Henry," Maureen said. "The police have taken him in for questioning."

10

❧❦❧

"Why are the police questioning Charles Henry?" I asked. "It can't be about punching John, because no one has told them."

"I'm not sure," Maureen said, looking away as she answered. "The detective sergeant said they wanted only to have a chat."

The Chat. That certainly gave me pause.

"I'm sure there's no cause for alarm," I said.

"They have . . ." Maureen's mouth worked, but no sound came out.

"They have taken his suit," Mrs. Woolgar finished. "The one he was wearing last Wednesday."

Dear God—last Wednesday, Charles Henry punched John. Last Wednesday, Milo was murdered.

"I told Maureen you would go to the station," Mrs. Woolgar said, "because the police know you."

There's a ringing endorsement—I'm known to the police. Isn't that what they say about repeat offenders?

"I don't know how I can help," I said. "If he needs legal advice, shouldn't you ask Mr. Rennie?"

"Duncan is ready to step in if it's appropriate," Mrs. Woolgar said, "although criminal law"—her eyes flitted to Maureen—"is not his area of expertise. And apart from that, how would it look to send a solicitor if one isn't needed?"

And so, send in the curator? I was ready to call this a fool's errand until I looked at the two women before me. Mrs. Woolgar clenching her hands at her waist. Maureen—I'd never seen her look anything but in control, down to her steel-gray pageboy, but at the moment I wasn't sure if she'd even combed her hair.

I threw my phone in my bag and slung the strap over my shoulder. "All right, I'm off."

The desk sergeant lifted an eyebrow at me as if to say, *Here again, are you? I know your type. Like to bother my officers when they ought to be doing their jobs, do you?*

"Hello, I'm Hayley Burke." The eyebrow stayed up. "May I please see Detective Sergeant Hopgood?" I asked. "Or DC Pye?"

"I'm sorry, love, the detectives are not at everyone's beck and call. Now, if there's something one of our PCs can do for you—"

Her phone rang and she put up a finger to pause our conversation. I leaned over to catch a bit of air from the tiny fan she had pointed at her face, but she gave me a look and I backed away again.

"Sir," she answered. Her eyes darted to me and then away. "I won't need to, sir, she's standing right here." A pause. "Yes, sir." She put down the receiver and offered a conciliatory smile, and I felt myself being shifted to the approved list. "Won't you sit down? Someone will be out."

I sat in a molded plastic chair. The lobby was warm and the air heavy, and my mind, seeking some pleasant diversion, wandered away from Charles Henry to thoughts of ice cream. A Magnum would be nice right about now. Or a 99. Even a tiny tub of vanilla flecked with strawberry.

"All right there?" Kenny Pye asked.

He stood at the door that led to the inner workings of the station.

"I'm not sure," I said.

"Come through." The detective constable held the door, and I passed into an air-conditioned corridor. I sighed.

He led me past Interview #1—already occupied by Charles Henry?—and into Interview #2.

"Tea?" Kenny asked.

"No, thank you," I said. He grinned. I believe he knew my opinion of the police station brew.

"Boss'll be in soon."

When the DC had gone, I pulled out my phone, but couldn't decide who I should text and what I should say. I put the phone back just as Sergeant Hopgood came in, file folder under his arm.

"Why am I here?" I asked.

Hopgood sat down at the table across from me. His caterpillars quivered. "I was given to understand you arrived at the station before I had a chance to request your presence."

"Yes, all right. *I* know why I am here. I thought I could be of some help to you with . . . about . . . concerning Charles Henry Dill. But I don't know why *you* want me here."

"I certainly hope you can be of some help," Hopgood replied. "By the way, I appreciate you escorting Mr. Aubrey to the station yesterday."

"Did John tell you all you needed to know about Milo? Did he have any idea who might've murdered him?"

"Early days, yet, Ms. Burke."

I translated that as the usual police response of *Mind your own business.*

Hopgood opened his file folder. "You were a witness to an altercation Wednesday afternoon of last week?"

"Did John tell you that?"

"No, it was Mr. Dill who told us. I'd like to hear it from you."

Perhaps Charles Henry should've had a solicitor with him after all.

"It was Wednesday afternoon," I explained. "The library is open to the public every Wednesday from one until five. We've just started this, and last week was only the second time. Charles Henry was a bit upset at seeing John."

"Did you think John Aubrey provoked Mr. Dill in any way?"

"No, it's only that . . . I'm sure Charles Henry told you this. John thinks that Lady Fowling is his grandmother."

"Is she?"

I lifted my hands in the air, palms up. "There's no firm evidence. But it irks Charles Henry, who has always made all he can out of the fact that he is Lady Fowling's only living relative."

"He called Aubrey an impostor who is attempting a fraud on his grandmother's estate."

"I don't know about the impostor bit, but John isn't attempting fraud," I said. "It seems he only wants to be a part of the family. But Charles Henry's hitting John has nothing to do with Milo."

Hopgood grew thoughtful and silent.

"Does it?" I asked.

Kenny came in and nodded to the DS.

Hopgood rose. "We have a bit of CCTV I'd like you to see, Ms. Burke."

I followed the two of them down the corridor and into a room with television monitors. Hopgood stood nearby, indicating where I should sit, and Kenny worked the keyboard.

"We've got this from down at the bottom of Hedgemead Park," Pye told me.

"This is about Milo? But wasn't he stabbed at the top entrance, where Val and I found him?"

"Not necessarily," Kenny said. "The ME says it was a long, thin blade that went in from the back into his upper abdomen and punctured the liver. There was a great deal of bleeding, but all internal—barely a spot on the surface of the skin. With that wound, he could've remained upright, walking and talking for several minutes. Possibly up to three quarters of an hour although he may have been disoriented by the end."

I sank into the chair and swallowed hard.

"So it hadn't just happened," I said.

"Watch now," Kenny said.

The black-and-white image on the screen jumped with a regular beat—one picture per second—making it look like a poorly made stop-action film. Even so, it was clear enough that I could follow.

time in the corner of the monitor read 22:16. Barely gone quarter past ten. I saw a few people about, although there wasn't the crowd there would be when the pubs closed. The camera was angled to show where Guinea Lane joined the Paragon.

There appeared in the frame a familiar figure in a dark shirt and trousers, walking away from the camera. He had his head bent over his phone. It was Milo. Or John. No, not John.

"That's Milo," I said, pointing to the screen.

Behind him came a cluster of people crowded on the pavement. Then a large man wearing a light-colored suit pushed through. He jostled Milo, who turned to look behind him. The others walked round the two and continued up the road as the large man stepped back, turned toward the camera, and hurried off. Milo paused for a moment, then walked into the park and out of view.

"Recognize anyone else?" Kenny asked as he switched off the monitor.

"Charles Henry," I whispered, staring at the blank screen. I looked from Hopgood to Pye. "Have you arrested him?"

"Not as yet," Hopgood said.

"But he knows you've seen him?"

"Dill admits to this encounter with Overton," Pye said.

"He told you about punching John, and now he's admitted to this encounter with Milo?"

"Oh yes, he's talking all right," Hopgood said. "I could barely get him to stop. Dill told us that just by chance he noticed the man he thought was Aubrey up ahead of him. He came up close behind him because, he said, he wanted to have a few words. When he realized his mistake, he said he apologized."

"From this view, we can't see if he had a knife," Kenny said.

"But," Hopgood added, "Dill is the right height for the angle of the wound."

"That's why you took the suit he was wearing," I said. Even though there was little bleeding, Charles Henry might've ended up with specks on his suit from stabbing Milo. I shuddered.

"Ms. Burke," Hopgood said, his eyebrows dead still, "tell me again, what were Mr. Overton's last words to you?"

I went back to that moment, bending over Milo as he became weaker and weaker. I looked from Hopgood to Kenny. "The last thing I could understand was, 'I said I am not . . .' He didn't finish."

But now I could complete the sentence. *I said I am not John Aubrey.* Mistaken identity.

By the time I left, I had acquired two bits of information: Neither the weapon nor Milo's mobile had been recovered. I'd asked Sergeant Hopgood if this evidence—that Charles Henry had met Milo within minutes of the murder—was classified. No, the DS had replied, but he'd rather I didn't alert the media, because at the moment, he had enough aggro from them about park safety.

Couldn't this point to a random act? The detective sergeant reminded me of murder statistics, which weighed heavily in favor of the victim knowing his assailant. I wasn't clear whether that included mistaken identity.

I left the station and returned to Middlebank, wishing I could head in the opposite direction and sail away on *La Mouette 2.* Do you call it sailing if you are on a narrow boat?

Mrs. Woolgar came out to the entry as soon as I opened the door. I hadn't been able to prepare any reassuring phrases and was relieved to learn that Maureen Frost had gone home the moment Charles Henry texted her to say he'd been released. So, it was left to the secretary to press me for details.

"Is it true the police suspect Charles Henry murdered this Milo Overton by mistake," she asked, "thinking it was John Aubrey? It's what Maureen believes."

Maureen already knew almost as much as I did. "It's one line of enquiry," I said. "Charles Henry told them he'd hit John here in the library, and then he admitted to an encounter with Milo that evening, at first mistaking him for John."

"He told them? He never could keep his mouth shut," Mrs. Woolgar said.

"It's a murder enquiry," I reminded her. "Do you mean he should withhold information?"

"Certainly not, it's only that . . ." Her hands fidgeted at her belt. She appeared unsettled. Flighty.

I had rarely seen Mrs. Woolgar so close to losing her composure. Even that time last year when she'd turned herself in for questioning concerning a previous enquiry, she had remained stoic. Milo's murder, Dill as a suspect compounded with John's story—they were taking their toll.

She put her chin up and took a slow breath. "Later, I will discuss the situation in more detail with Mr. Rennie."

Over dinner? I hoped Duncan knew how to calm her down.

"Good. I'm sure he will know how to proceed. I'm going up to my flat for lunch."

"Of course. And, thank you for going to the police. It was really for Maureen's sake, you know. Although, whatever we may think of Charles Henry, I don't believe he's a murderer."

As far as I was concerned, the jury was out on that subject. Charles Henry had a tenuous hold at best on the prestige of being the only living Fowling relative, and his hope to gain by that was faint, but if he felt that hold loosening further—if pushed hard enough, could he have killed? Might he have seen a man he thought was John, followed him, stabbed him, and only afterward realize the enormity of his deed?

In my flat, I found nothing that could be called lunch, so instead, I finished sorting the Flambeaux stories in sets ready to distribute to interested parties and carried the pile downstairs to my office. On my desk was a letter addressed to me, but with no postage. I turned it over and read the return address, stamped in gold ink: The Larkin, Henrietta Road, Bath.

I opened it and looked at the signature first. It was from Milo.

Dear Hayley,

I give you this important key to John's background with his full knowledge—although he's not a bit happy about it. He's a private person, but this breaks no confidences or professional standards because John did not engage me in a professional capacity. Instead, he hired me to be his ballast. I believe John will be better off if you knew more than he's telling. He won't admit it, but he knows, too. It'll be easier if the story comes from someone else. With more time, I believe

I could persuade John to tell you himself, but I have been called away by another matter. So I leave this in your hands.

Regards,
Milo

My fingers tingled as if the paper I held had been imbued with a magical power—the power to tell me if John's story was truth or lie. At the bottom of the page, Milo had written the name Dolly Beckwith, Turnstone Cottage, Charmouth, Dorset, and a telephone number.

I went to Mrs. Woolgar's office.

"What's this?" I folded the letter closed, but held out the envelope.

"Oh yes," she said, "it came for you after you'd gone up to lunch. Delivered by hand."

"By whom?"

"A young woman from the Larkin—one of the hotels along Henrietta Road."

"Did you get her name? What did she look like?"

"I didn't ask her name. She's Black. She was about my height, but a bit . . . fuller. She had long ringlets, and she wore glasses with red frames. She had a slight gap in her front teeth. Scottish, with a touch of the Glaswegian about her accent."

I wish I had Mrs. Woolgar's keen eye for detail.

"Oh yes, of course, thanks," I said, as if I'd been expecting the letter all along. "Wait now, I have those Flambeaux stories for you." I got them from my office. "I've made copies for the other board members and thought I would deliver them this afternoon."

Mrs. Woolgar had already turned to the first page of "The Pur-

loined Peacock," and said, in an absentminded tone, "Jane Arbuthnot is away in Norfolk until the end of the month."

"I'll hold hers back."

The secretary looked up. "And why don't you leave off Maureen
today?"

Gladly. "Well then, the Moons and Adele."

I packed three sets in my satchel and prepared to lug them round
the city, because my first stop would be the Larkin to ask about
Milo's letter. He'd died nearly a week ago. Where had it been all this
time?

I crossed Pulteney Bridge and turned up Henrietta Road, a long
stretch of Georgian terraced housing lining both sides of the road. I
spotted the Larkin's sign hanging over the entrance and marched up
the walk, between flanking boxwood standards, and in the door.
The entry was about as big as our kitchenette. A small guest lounge
lay to the left and the reception to the right, where I saw that I was
in luck.

"Hello, good afternoon," the young Black woman behind the
desk said with a smile, revealing a small gap in her front teeth. "Welcome to the Larkin. How can I help you?"

My glance darted to the name tag she wore. "Hello, Felicia," I
said. "I'm Hayley Burke from the First Edition Society here in Bath."
I handed over a business card. "Can you tell me, did you or someone
here deliver this letter yesterday?"

She looked at the envelope I held out. "Yes, I did. At the Larkin,
we are always happy to meet our guests' needs. I daresay you don't
find a 'delivered by hand' service often these days."

"Do you know who asked for it to be delivered?"

"Don't you know?" she asked. Her eyes grew wide. "Wasn't it signed?"

"Yes, it was signed, but I wanted to know if it was written by the same person who left it here at reception. And when it was left. It's only that I think it was written a few days ago."

She frowned.

"I'm ever so sorry about that. A terrible oversight on our part." Felicia put her head over the desk and looked round the tiny, empty lobby. She lowered her voice. "Listen"—but she pronounced it *lehs-son*, bringing out the Glasgow in her—"yesterday was my first day, you see. I only just finished the hospitality course at Bath College, and they've taken me on here as an intern. Midseason, too, so I was lucky to get it. There's to be a permanent vacancy in the autumn, so I'm doing my best to be indispensable to them. First thing, I offered to tidy up the office—you should've seen the state of it!"

I looked round the space and couldn't see so much as a paper clip out of place.

"You've done a bang-up job in only a day," I said.

She nodded to six cardboard boxes behind her. "I've crammed everything into those and I'm taking them one at a time. I started here with the desk. There was a stack of papers you could've drowned in—bills, receipts, guest comment forms, leaflets about last year's Jane Austen festival. I found your letter in the middle of it all. I'd no idea how long it might've been lying about, but I thought the least I could do was to drop it round myself."

"That was very good of you," I said.

"I hope the delay hasn't caused any trouble. Listen, could I get you a coffee?"

"No, you're all right. Thanks so much."

Out on the pavement, I considered my next move. Should I ring Dolly now and hear the entire story, or tell John about Milo's letter and give him the chance to explain?

I rang Val.

"I could just do with lunch. And a kiss."

"I'm more than happy to provide both."

Y ou don't know who this Dolly is and she doesn't know you. Why would she talk with you?" Val asked.

We sat inside at the Boater next to an open window. Over his burger, Val had read the letter and then I'd given him a report from the Larkin as I worked my way through an enormous rocket salad. I'd felt virtuous at all the veg, and so had added an egg and ham to it.

"Did Milo warn Dolly some strange woman would be contacting her?" I asked.

"Why is this subterfuge necessary to find out about John's background?"

"I won't use subterfuge," I said. "I'll tell John about Milo's letter and give him the opportunity to explain first. This whole affair is upsetting too many people. We need to know. I think we should go see this Dolly Beckwith."

"Charmouth is near Lyme Regis," Val said.

"It would be worth it if this is John's home," I said. "We'd get a real sense of him."

"It's a long journey."

"It's the seaside."

"Ah." Val's green eyes glinted. "It's the candy floss you're after. Go on, then."

I rang John. He didn't answer, but in a few minutes responded by text.

In Bristol, but back tomorrow for afternoon open.

That confrontation successfully delayed, I rang the Moons to ask if Val and I could stop by. They would be delighted, they said, and so we hiked up to their ground-floor flat near the Crescent, where the four of us settled on two facing sofas. The open French windows led to a tiny garden, where butterflies flitted about and sunshine played hide-and-seek amid the greenery. I stifled a yawn.

The sherry was out. Sylvia Moon poured as she said to Val, "We don't see enough of you." Then she looked at me out of the corner of her eye. "I hope you're seeing enough of each other."

"We do our best," Val said, his face going pink.

"And you, Hayley," Audrey said, "here you are coming up on your one-year work anniversary."

I stopped with my glass on my lips. One-year performance review—that's what she must mean.

"Yes. Hasn't the year flown by?" Would they evaluate me on my use of clichés? I sipped my sherry and cleared my throat. "I was hoping to talk with you both at last week's open, but of course, other things got in the way."

Audrey Moon clicked her tongue. "Charles Henry has always been a bit of a hothead. It dismayed Georgiana so. She said he was much like his father in that regard. But she and her sister had been close, and so she could never completely dissociate herself from her nephew. Family was important to her because hers was so small."

"What about this John Aubrey?" Sylvia leaned forward. "Will we meet him tomorrow afternoon?"

"Possibly," I said. But would Charles Henry Dill be there as well? Would I need to play referee? Or should I ask for a uniform to be on hand? "I'm sure you know what John is claiming—that he's Lady Fowling's grandson." The Moons exchanged glances. "It's not that I believe him, but I did think it wise to learn everything we could about her ladyship's life just after Sir John died."

"We were girls at the time," Audrey said. "I was fifteen, and Syl wasn't quite thirteen. But my parents and Syl's parents were both friends of Sir John. Remember, Syl?"

"Oh yes, we admired Georgiana so," Sylvia said. "Her beauty and her poise. She had a way of making everyone round her happy."

I feared toppling Georgiana Fowling off her pedestal.

"Do you remember that she went away?" I asked.

"Oh yes," Audrey said. "It wasn't a week after Sir John's funeral."

"Mummy and Daddy were shocked," Sylvia said. "They didn't think it proper for a young widow to take herself off at all, much less so soon."

"Do you know where she went?" Val asked.

Audrey shrugged her shoulders. "I'm not sure anyone said. She was gone for more than a year, and then one day, she was here again. And she was like a new woman, wasn't she, Syl? She came back renewed and refreshed."

"And a bit mysterious," Sylvia said.

Nothing like a lack of details to fuel the imagination. "Do you recall anything else?"

"You mean," Audrey said, "did Georgiana have an affair and leave the baby that resulted behind?"

I held my breath, hoping they didn't think I'd overstepped my bounds.

"It seems unlikely," Sylvia said, "but can't grief do strange things to a person? Still, we weren't privy to anything at the time. It wasn't until a few years after Georgiana returned that Aud and I became friends with her. She always treated us as equals, despite us being fifteen years younger. Age never meant a great deal to her—she was always young at heart."

"I wish we could offer more," Audrey said. "We know it's no good asking Glynis if she suspects anything—you know how she is about Georgiana. We tried to talk with Maureen, but she clammed up."

"So," Sylvia said, clapping her hands on her thighs, "we invited Adele and her girlfriend over this evening. We promised them a meal and some French conversation in exchange for a walk down memory lane."

"She's the only other one who knew Georgiana well. It could be," Audrey said, "that the three of us might be able to piece something together."

"Thank you," I said. "I'm sure we can get our Middlebank mystery cleared up. Now, I know you two have your own set of the Flambeaux books"—I could see them in pride of place on the shelves next to the fireplace—"but we've recently come across a collection of short stories Lady Fowling wrote but never published. I've made you photocopies to read."

I handed them over, and you'd think we'd presented them with the Gold Cup at Ascot. The Moons *oohed* and *ahhed* and turned a page to read the beginning of one of the stories and then glanced through at the other titles.

"Aud, look," Sylvia said. "Here's the one about the peacock."

The room went still.

"Do you know that story?" I asked. "Have you read it?"

"Read it?" Audrey said, peering over Sylvia's shoulder. "No, we heard it from Georgiana. She told us lots of François stories, and we loved them so much we would ask for our favorites again and again."

"Oh dear," Sylvia said. She pointed at another title—"François and Evil on a Moonless Night." "It's the one with that awful man. I remember how it frightened me."

11

Val and I left the Moons as Sylvia began reading aloud from "François on the Boards," which they remembered as a story Lady Fowling made up for Maureen Frost—the girl who longed to be on the stage.

We stood out on the pavement as the sun dipped behind the terrace, casting much-needed shade onto the stone walk. From the terrace roofs, the seagulls screeched, and I thought of *La Mouette*.

"These stories have been hidden away for decades—from before Mrs. Woolgar ever arrived—and now we find that both the Moons and John know them," I said. "What does that mean?"

"You've more of a mystery than you thought," Val said.

We walked down past the Jane Austen Centre and farther, parting at the Theatre Royal—Val back to college and I to drop off Adele's copies of the François stories. I texted when I arrived at the street entrance to her flat, which was above a launderette, and when she released the lock, I climbed the stairs. Her door was ajar, and a madhouse lay within.

There were clothes flung over several kitchen chairs and shoes strewn about the floor. A scuffling noise came from the bedroom. Adele, the calm center of the storm, sat on the sofa with her feet on the coffee table.

From the bedroom, Pauline shouted out a hello to me and then said, "Dress or trousers?"

"Both," Adele called out.

"Don't be daft," Pauline said, and then added in a loud, but muffled voice, "I've not met the Moons."

I took that as directed at me.

"They're lovely," I called back.

"This?" she said, thrusting her arm out the bedroom doorway and holding a long, flowing frock made up of a multitude of gauzy layers.

"I like that one," Adele said.

"Gorgeous," I said. "Summery. Very suitable."

"You think?" Pauline appeared and clasped the dress to her chest. "The Moons adore Adele. I want to make a good impression."

"You could wear your cleaning coveralls and still make a good impression," Adele said.

Pauline grinned and returned to the bedroom. I handed over the bundle of copies. "The rest of François for you. I've just learned that the Moons are familiar with these tales. Not from printed versions, but from Lady Fowling's oral storytelling," I said. "And John's made several references to them, too. It's a clear link."

"When am I going to meet him?" Adele asked.

"Come to the afternoon open when school is finished tomorrow. The Moons will be there. We'll stay after when everyone has gone. Now I have more news for you."

I filled her in on the latest about Charles Henry, including the CCTV footage.

"He thought Milo was John," I told her. "He said so himself, but of course, he says it went no further than bumping into him. A case of mistaken identity. Doesn't sound good, does it?"

"I don't know, Hayley," Adele said. "Do you think Charles Henry has it in him?"

"Voilà!" Pauline said, coming out of the bedroom with a flourish.

"Oooh," I said, "you speak French!" I turned to Adele. "I don't know if he has it in him, but remember, he did walk off with those seventeenth-century serving spoons from Middlebank—during the reception after Lady Fowling's funeral."

I spent my Wednesday morning attempting to create a more detailed chart to compare Flambeaux's origin story with *Frenchman's Creek*—which incidents appeared in one or the other or both and if and how they were altered. This worked well until I had a quick read-through of two of the short stories and came across familiar-sounding bits. I realized the short stories could contain du Maurier elements, too. I would need to read them all and rework the chart.

Fascinating, but unfortunately, it didn't help to calm my growing nerves about the afternoon open. At our morning briefing, I had put a cheery spin on it and even tried for a bit of humor.

"You know, at Sutton House in London," I said, "I'm told that the National Trust lets people make their own tea and toast. Perhaps we should turn the kitchenette into a tearoom after all—and Bunter could oversee things for us as long as he promises to keep out of the milk jug."

Mrs. Woolgar shuffled through a stack of papers on her desk and said, "Mr. Rennie will be stopping in this afternoon." Oh well, at least she had gone off the bouncer idea.

The crowd we'd had the previous Wednesday had come without knowing they'd see a boxing match, and so Mrs. Woolgar and I had debated what attendance might look like this next afternoon. She had kept an eye on internet chatter, but had found nothing on the incident and only a single item about Milo—MAN FATALLY STABBED IN PARK. It made no mention of Middlebank. Still, it seemed likely we would continue to build on the previous week, and so I expected an uptick in attendance. Would this include Charles Henry Dill? I hoped not.

I dashed upstairs to my flat for a quick sandwich—having at last done the shopping, I had something to put between two pieces of bread—before the secretary and I hung out our sign and went to our stations.

Three quarters of an hour into the afternoon, I dropped into a wingback chair, surprised that the *plop* didn't echo in the empty library. Was the public so fickle that they'd let a small set-to put them off visiting one of the finest collections of Golden Age mysteries in the country? Hadn't anyone seen the notice in *Bath Live!*?

Had I remembered to send the notice in for this week? I ran downstairs to check, and make myself a cup of tea.

The secretary had gone back to her office. "Mrs. Woolgar," I said, "I might've forgotten to send in the notice for this week."

"No, Ms. Burke, you didn't. I've just come in to check and there it is. I suppose there is no understanding the vagaries of public interest."

When the front door buzzed, I nearly wept with relief.

There began a stream of library patrons for the rest of the afternoon. Not actually a stream, more like a trickle or perhaps a slow drip. At no time were there more than three people in attendance, but as none of them was Charles Henry Dill, I counted myself lucky. Then, about four thirty, things picked up.

I was talking with the only visitor currently in attendance when Mrs. Woolgar and Duncan Rennie escorted John to the library, standing on either side of him rather like jailors. John seemed to take no notice, but walked into the room and put his hands on his hips in true pirate fashion. He lifted his chin in greeting.

I offered a tiny wave as I said to the woman next to me, "If you walk down the hill, you'll see a cake shop at the bottom of Bartlett Street. They do a lovely tea."

She left, and John turned to the secretary and Duncan. "I find the library much like the one in 'François Watches and Waits,' don't you, Mrs. Woolgar? A fine place to curl up for a quiet moment. I wonder who will arrive next, the hatter or the dressmaker?"

Mrs. Woolgar put her hand on the doorpost as if to steady herself. "It will depend on how many pins he finds."

"Yes, of course, you're correct!" John exclaimed with delight. "That's the key, isn't it?"

The exchange left Mrs. Woolgar ashen.

"Come in and sit down," I said, but she declined, murmuring something about finishing for the day. She left for downstairs, accompanied by Duncan.

"Well, John," I said, "where have you found to tie up?"

"Three times I've been back and forth before locating a spot near the same place as usual," he said. "But they keep an eye on how often you return during the busy season."

I thought about his journey back and forth in a narrow boat on a narrow canal. "How do you turn round?"

Val stepped in just in time to hear my question. "Winding holes," he said. "Every so often there's an open spot to make a three-point turn."

"Well, aren't you just the narrow-boat expert," I said.

"A three-point turn is the goal, Val," John said, "but not always attainable."

The front door buzzed.

"I see Duncan's arrived," Val said, "and it looked as if Mrs. Woolgar had packed it in for the afternoon. I can go down."

"No, you two stay." To John, I added, "We're expecting the Moons and Adele."

"Is there a meeting?" John asked. "Will I be in the way?"

"Yes, there is a meeting, and you are the agenda, John," I said. I watched him carefully for a reaction.

"Splendid," he said. "These are the Moons who knew my grandmother? And who is Adele?"

"Adele," I said, "was a dear friend of Lady Fowling's in her later years. They are all quite the Flambeaux fans."

"Who wouldn't be?" John called after me.

Adele arrived first. "Would you get out the sherry and glasses in the kitchenette?" I asked. "I'll be just a moment." I cut my eyes at Mrs. Woolgar's open office door.

Adele nodded. "Righto." First, she looked in on the secretary. "Hello, Glynis. Oh, hello, Duncan. How are you?"

"Fine, thank you," Mrs. Woolgar said. "And you?"

"*Ça va bien.*"

Adele continued to the kitchenette, but I stayed behind. Mrs. Woolgar looked anything but fine. She'd shut down her computer and removed her glasses and stared at the dark screen. Duncan sat across from her. He looked up at me and gave a small shrug.

"Mrs. Woolgar?"

"You have allowed Aubrey to read her ladyship's stories—the ones you've only just found."

"No, I have not. I didn't need to. John already knew those stories."

Her eyes flashed. "How? How could he know stories that have never circulated?"

How, indeed.

"Sylvia and Audrey Moon are familiar with them, too. They say they remember Lady Fowling telling the stories aloud. Do you recall anything like that when you all gathered for tea at the Royal Crescent Hotel?"

Mrs. Woolgar's forehead knitted together slowly as if she might be trying to sneak up on a memory and net it. "There was always a great deal of talk at those afternoons, and until Ms. Babbage arrived, I was the junior attendee. The others had been meeting for years before."

Being the new girl on the block when she arrived—even if it had been more than thirty years ago—meant the secretary knew less about Lady Fowling than the Moons, Maureen Frost, and Jane Arbuthnot. That group had no doubt been hearing the stories for decades. Mrs. Woolgar had been left out.

"Adele is here because she wanted to meet John," I explained. "The Moons are on their way, too. Won't you and Mr. Rennie come up to the library and we can all have a glass of sherry together? We might learn something."

Mrs. Woolgar replaced her glasses, stood up, and brushed imaginary wrinkles from the skirt of her dress. "No, Ms. Burke. Thank you, but we have other plans. I'll see you in the morning."

"Pass along our regrets, won't you?" Duncan said.

They left for Mrs. Woolgar's lower-ground-floor flat, and I waited near the kitchenette until I heard her door close.

"How many of us?" Adele asked, holding the sherry glasses between her fingers.

"Two less than there should be," I said. "Mrs. Woolgar declined the invitation."

"Really? Normally, she likes to stay in the know."

"Normally. It's almost as if all these years later, Lady Fowling has hurt her feelings. So, six of us for sherry. Did you and Pauline have a lovely dinner with the Moons?"

"It was a right old time," Adele said, "although toward the end Pauline's eyes were glazing over. That's because Audrey, Sylvia, and I went over everything we could remember about Georgiana."

"Any clues?" I asked.

"No, sorry," Adele said. Rummaging in the biscuit tin, she came up with a custard cream and ate it in two bites. "They remembered her stories—not 'How It All Began,' because that was new to all of us, but the others. But I've managed a quick read-through, and I do recall the occasional mention of a story element. This was at—"

"Tea at the Royal Crescent, yes." I was feeling a tinge of jealousy myself for missing out.

"Georgiana would say something about an adder or pins in the library, and the others would chuckle or smile."

"Even Mrs. Woolgar?" I asked.

Adele thought. "No, I don't recall Glynis chuckling. I didn't know what Georgiana was talking about, so one day over lunch at the Gainsborough, I asked her what those comments meant, and she said they were stories she hadn't told anyone for yonks. Glynis could've asked her, too. No one was stopping her."

"You and Lady Fowling had lunch at the Gainsborough? All right for some."

Adele grinned. "That was when I still shaved my head."

I remembered Adele's scalp tattoo in a blue Celtic design—quite impressive, although now covered by a mass of long, red curls.

"I'm surprised Lady Fowling didn't follow suit and get a tattoo," I said.

"She got a temporary one—a dragon that reached from her wrist to her elbow. I thought Glynis would faint dead away when she saw it."

Handing me the sherry decanter, Adele picked up the tray of glasses, and we headed for the library. "At the end of that lunch, the head teacher from a local girls' school arrived. Georgiana had set it up, of course, because she knew they had a post opening up. And hey, presto, here I am all these years later, a teacher at said school. That's Georgiana for you, always doing something for someone."

We paused on the library landing for a glance up at Lady Fowling. "But about the origin story," I said. "Apart from the *Frenchman's Creek* elements, did you recognize anything?"

Adele shook her head. "It looks like John was the only one who had read that."

In the library, Val and John were in a deep discussion about narrow-boat batteries and solar power, but broke it off when the door buzzed, and Val went to answer.

"Adele Babbage, John Aubrey," I said.

"It speaks to my grandmother's love of life that she called you a friend, Adele," John said, "even with so many years' difference in your ages. She knew no barriers, did she?"

"Good to meet you, John," Adele said.

When Val escorted the Moons in, John went to them at once, and I followed with introductions.

"My dear ladies," he said, smiling as he gently shook each hand in turn, "I am so very happy to meet you."

"Well, we've been quite looking forward to this moment ourselves," Audrey said. "We are, so to speak, your litmus test, Mr. Aubrey."

"As you may have heard," Sylvia added, "we knew Georgiana for seventy years."

Good on you, Moons. I was afraid they'd be swept up in the romance of the moment—and the dimple—and was delighted to know they would start off with a skeptical eye.

"This is an honor for me," John said. "To know that I am in such a presence. And please, will you call me John?"

Sylvia blushed.

From one aspect, the gathering was a great success. Val and I played audience members as the Moons charmed John, and he returned the favor. Adele joked with him and he joked back. But as usual, he brushed off any question that had an iota of reality attached to it.

When Sylvia asked, "Can you do your job from the narrow boat? What do they call it, work . . ." She looked to Adele, who filled in with "remotely."

"No one bothers with my coming and going," John replied.

"It sounds as if your grandfather was a great influence on you," Adele said. "When did he die?"

"I like to think he lives still, because of Flambeaux," John replied.

Once or twice, I suspected a grain of truth had dropped in—to be quickly worked into the story, like rubbing butter into flour, so that a new thing was made of two different ingredients, truth and fiction.

"Not everyone can see that life is an adventure," John had said, briefly losing the animation in his face and immediately gaining ten years. "Some would mock a boy who talked of a grandfather who had been first a pirate and then a detective."

Sylvia reached over and patted his hand. "Some people have no imagination."

At the end of our sherry hour, what had been gained? John had won support of all three board members. I knew the moment it happened. It was when he brought up a scene from "How It All Began."

"Do you remember when he asked her to open a tin of soup? Such a simple request, and yet when he turns, it is to find her weeping." A look of pain crossed his face. "What a poignant way to show her heartbreak and healing, all at the same time."

Yes, it wasn't all *Frenchman's Creek* fan fiction in Flambeaux's origin story. Lady Fowling had managed to work in threads of her own life. Sir John's fortune had come from tins—that is, the sort of tins that hold peaches in syrup, baked beans, and tomato soup. Could the mere sight of a tin carry such emotional weight, reminding her of her late husband? Had this been the truth of Lady Fowling?

Sylvia murmured, "She was so young to feel such pain." We all grew quiet.

Adele was first to mark the conclusion to the gathering.

"You'll have to excuse me," she said. "I have a class this evening." Rustling began as everyone rose to leave, and, as we made our way to the entry, invitations were extended. The Moons asked John to dinner and hoped he would bring a friend. John suggested a drinks party on his narrow boat for board members and their partners.

At that reminder—partners—good humor in the air evaporated.

Audrey leaned toward me. "Hayley, have you spoken to the police again since—"

"Not yet," I said.

"The police? This is about Milo?" John asked.

Glances darted right and left, and the silence became painful.

"It's only that the police wanted to talk with Charles Henry," I said.

"Why?" John asked. "It was not what happened here in the library last week? Because I told them nothing."

"Charles Henry told them about it himself. No, not that. It's because, as it turns out, he saw Milo the evening of the murder. He told police about that, too. One line of enquiry the police are following"—*don't I just sound the junior detective?*—"is that Milo's death could have something to do with how the two of you looked a bit alike. From a distance, you know, and from the back."

"Did we?" John asked. "Are you saying police suspect Charles Henry of murder? No. Even if my cousin mistook Milo for me, I don't believe he could do such a thing."

"It's kind of you to see the good in people," Audrey said.

"I admit that, at times, there is no good to see," John replied. "Some person killed Milo. Was it because the killer thought he was killing me? Selfishly, I hope not, but regardless of the reason, it was evil." He clicked his tongue. "Was it also a moonless night?"

There was a brief moment of heavy silence, and then Adele said, "I didn't know she could write about such darkness."

Sylvia shuddered. "Just the thought of it."

"François and Evil on a Moonless Night." Must get to that one.

John looked round at the faces cast in shadow and said, "But brighter days ahead, yes? I am on the adder's holiday and so now must be away!"

The Moons laughed. Val and Adele snickered.

Val gave the sisters-in-law a lift home and John strode off down the hill. Adele and I went to the kitchenette and washed sherry glasses.

"So, do you believe him?" I asked.

"That he's Georgiana's grandson?" Adele replied. "I'm not sure any of us believe that."

"But he knows so much. Don't you want to find out how?"

"Of course I do. Do you have a plan?"

"Yes."

Adele laughed. "No, really? I thought I was joking."

"Well, I'm not. Milo told me about someone who knows John's story. I'm going to visit her."

"Does this have something to do with the murder? And if it does, shouldn't you tell the police first?"

"It has everything to do with the mystery at Middlebank. If there's a shred of information that concerns Milo's murder, I will immediately give it over to the enquiry. Satisfied?"

12

Mrs. Woolgar looked her usual self at our briefing Thursday morning. As her fingers were busy on the keyboard, she asked, "Have you settled on what software you want to use to track the patrons from Wednesday afternoons?"

"No, I was hoping you might be able to take care of that," I said. Choosing the software, setting up parameters, filling in the data every week. Better her than me.

"Have you read through the stories?" I asked bravely.

Her fingers paused, and she dropped her hands in her lap. "These stories and the Flambeaux books were before my time, but even so, I thought I knew about her ladyship's life. She never seemed to be hiding anything from me. Apparently, I was wrong."

"Time passes and we forget how important things were, and even who knows what. I can't imagine she kept anything back on purpose. Not from you, of all people."

Mrs. Woolgar's face twitched, as if she were fighting with herself whether or not she would accept this wee bit of sympathy. We were saved by the ring of my phone. I ran back to my office for it.

"Hayley, Maureen Frost here. I wonder if you might have time this morning to stop in for a coffee."

No, please, no. "Yes, I'd love to."

"Good, I'll see you at eleven."

The call ended, and I whispered, "Yes, ma'am."

I wouldn't say Maureen was a dislikable person. I couldn't say it, because I barely knew her. She had loyal friends, was admired in the city, and had been a name on the stage, but to me she was inscrutable.

"Maureen Frost has asked me over for coffee," I reported to Mrs. Woolgar.

"She isn't an ogre, Ms. Burke," the secretary replied, reading my mind.

"No, of course she isn't. I wonder, will Charles Henry be there, too," I said.

I changed clothes before leaving, not wanting to show up in my curator's dark trousers and white blouse as if I were about to guide someone through an exhibit at the Victoria Gallery. I set off too early, walked down and across the Pulteney Bridge, and turned up Grove Street and stood in front of the block of flats with fifteen minutes to spare. I continued up the road until I reached St. John's at the end and loitered at the bus stop, hoping one wouldn't come along thinking I wanted to board.

I thought about Maureen Frost—daughter of one of Lady Fowling's friends and then, once her mother had died and Maureen had moved back to Bath, a friend herself. She continued her acting career, and I recalled that ten or twelve years ago, I'd accompanied Dinah and a group of girls from her school to a performance of *A Flea in Her Ear* at the Theatre Royal. I believe it had been a class assignment and the girls were to write a review of the production. Good fun, those French farces, full of slapstick and innuendos. Even the most blasé of the school group had sniggered at a joke or two. Maureen Frost had been in that production, but of course at the time, that meant nothing to me.

Five minutes before eleven, I hurried back up Grove Street, rang Maureen's flat on the entry phone, and was let in. I took the lift to the next floor and walked almost to the end of the corridor.

"Come through, Hayley," Maureen said when she opened the door. "It's good of you to take the time."

"It's very nice of you to ask me." I walked in and glanced about. Would Charles Henry leap from a hidden doorway at any moment?

"It's only the two of us," she said. "I hope that's all right."

"Fine," I said, losing only half of my apprehension.

I followed her down a long hall past framed theatrical posters. I caught Maureen's name on one for *The Merry Wives of Windsor.*

She gestured into an open doorway on the right. "I'll bring our coffee in."

I stepped into the sitting room, done in white with white accents; black-framed artwork hung on the walls. Tall windows looked out over the river and I crossed to admire the view, avoiding the white rug in the middle of the room.

When Maureen returned with the tray, I said, "What a lovely spot."

"I grew up out in Bathford, but the family home was sold after my mother died and I moved into town. Please, sit."

I resisted brushing off my bum before sitting on the white sofa. We were quiet as Maureen slowly pushed the plunger down into the cafetière and then poured out two cups. I added milk, and she offered a plate of purple, red, and blue macarons.

"You always have such wonderful pastries for our board meetings at Middlebank," she said.

I reached for the purple—black currant—and then recalled Charles Henry doing the same at his hiring meeting. At the last second, I chose the raspberry. I leaned over my coffee and took a careful bite. Bloodred flakes scattered like confetti.

"You probably know why I asked you here," Maureen said. "It's about Charles Henry."

I'd been about to take the rest of the macaron in one bite to get it over with, but held off long enough to say, "Yes, of course. How is he? Are the police still . . . talking with him?"

"He's offered the police all the assistance they should need from him," she said. "I believe they'll come to the conclusion that he had nothing whatsoever to do with that man's unfortunate death."

Mouthful of macaron, I made no reply.

"Hayley, you may wonder why I am willing to come to Charles Henry's support on the odd occasion. It's sometimes difficult to see what lies beneath a relationship, don't you think?"

The moment of silence told me this was not a rhetorical question.

"Yes," I said.

"Charles Henry was kind to me at a difficult time in my life, and when that happens, a bond is formed. You remember the core of the connection, and it's easier to brush away the occasional anomaly."

Occasional anomaly? She made him sound like a lab experiment.

Maureen had taken a macaron, but it lay in her saucer untouched. "I married late, you see. I'd been far too busy with my career, but the time comes when one should 'settle down,' as they say. At least, that's what we're led to believe, isn't it?"

"Yes."

"The man I married was a theatrical producer in London—a big name. He said he loved me and that we were a melding of artistic talent and financial savvy and destined to be one of the great couples of the theater. I believed him." She took a sip of coffee. "Five years later, I stumbled upon the fact that he'd been near destitute when we married and had subsequently spent vast amounts of money. My money. He'd signed my name to a mortage on our Mayfair flat and to several loans. He'd made poor investment choices and, oh yes, he'd bought a boat."

"But did you fight it? Recover your losses?"

A slight shrug. "He got one thing right—he'd hired the smartest solicitors, who wove such a tangled web that I couldn't see my way out. I looked like a silly fool. We separated—quite a show of its own—and I came back to Bath, beaten, lost, betrayed. I felt worthless. That's when I met Charles Henry. Met him again, I should say, because we'd been acquainted from the summers he visited Georgiana when he was a boy. By this time, his mother had died and he was often here in the city. In him, I found protection and strength, and my soul healed. Can you believe that?"

Could I? Fortunately, no answer appeared to be needed.

"My husband and I never divorced—that was the best advice I got. He died a few years after, but by then Charles Henry was off on a few adventures of his own. It was only at Georgiana's death that we saw each other again."

I had to admit this was a good story, if only I could cast someone else in Charles Henry's role.

"It must've been a great help to you to have someone by your side."

Maureen smiled. It transformed her face, and I saw in her what the theater crowd had seen—a soft yet steely beauty.

"And now," she said. But before she went on, she ate her macaron and sipped her coffee and looked out the window at the river. "About Charles Henry's rather possessive view of Middlebank. In his defense—and I would never say anything against Georgiana, of course . . ."

But let me now say something against Georgiana.

"Charles Henry's mother, Georgiana's younger sister, was not the most loving person, and he looked on his youthful summers here in Bath as a respite from a dull, cold existence. When Georgiana died, it's true that he hoped to make Middlebank his home, so it's understandable that he was disappointed when he received only a bequest."

After a gripping story, Maureen was about to lose me, because I knew how much money Lady Fowling had left her nephew, and it was a pile.

"A part of him realizes that his resentment is baseless, but some of us still have that small child within who wants more. He means no harm, but he's been shocked at this John Aubrey's declaration of being Georgiana's grandson. You can't believe that's true, can you?"

"John is a storyteller," I said. "He's asking for nothing except to meet people who knew Lady Fowling or know of her. He does seem to be familiar with her writing—her Flambeaux stories—even those that no one else has seen before."

"Yes, Glynis told me you'd come across more of Georgiana's writings."

My cue. Out of my satchel, I took Maureen's copies of the short stories, including "How It All Began."

"These are for you—and Charles Henry, of course. Well," I said. Unconsciously, I brushed off my trousers and then flinched at the tiny red flakes that fell. "I had better be on my way. Thank you for asking me over and explaining ... things."

We parted if not warmly, at least on friendly terms. I had a bit more understanding of Maureen, although nothing she had said could entirely wipe away the idea that Charles Henry was a suspect in Milo's murder.

On my way to Middlebank, I went up the Paragon to Guinea Lane and alongside Hedgemead Park—the same way Milo had walked that evening when Charles Henry Dill overtook him. A hot, sunny afternoon with plenty of people about, but still I glanced over my shoulder, feeling as if someone's eyes were on me. Of course, no one was paying me any heed. I paused at the park gate and then went in.

The temperature dropped dramatically when I walked into the shade. It had been dusky at ten thirty when Val and I were returning from our dinner. On the pavement outside this lower entrance, Charles Henry had encountered Milo. And stabbed him? Or had Milo been attacked in here under the trees? The light here would've been dim. If Charles Henry hadn't done it, had someone lain in wait here in the park?

The path took a long zigzag up to reach the other gate, where we had found Milo. I stopped halfway up to let a mother pushing a pram with one hand and holding the hand of a toddler with the other pass me. Farther along, I saw a figure standing in the dappled shade. A shiver went through me, but then he stepped out and it was Kenny Pye.

"You gave me a turn," I said, walking up closer. "Don't you have your coaching session with Val later this afternoon?"

"I do, and I'm just about on my way," Kenny said.

"Are you here about Milo's enquiry? Are you still searching for evidence?"

"Refreshing my memory of the scene," Kenny said.

I glanced round as if perhaps the murderer might give himself up.

"You see Milo come into the park on CCTV," I said. "And do you see him at the gate where Val and I found him?"

"We do," Kenny said. "It takes him about fifteen minutes."

"It isn't that long a journey—three or four minutes. Did he meet someone in here? Could Charles Henry have circled round and come in another way, unseen?"

Kenny's eyes darted to me and away. I took that as a possibility.

"You must have Milo on other CCTV," I said, "before he got to this point. So that you can see where he came from and if he spoke to anyone else."

"Chance would be a fine thing. Cameras aren't always turned at the angle we'd like."

"It could've been a robbery," I offered.

"He still had his wallet—credit cards and sixty pounds. Only his mobile was missing."

I liked it when Kenny was in a talkative mood.

"But can't you locate his mobile?"

"We could do," Kenny said, "but it's either not in working order or switched off."

"What about Charles Henry?" I asked.

"Would it be easier on you if he wasn't a suspect?"

"Probably," I admitted, "not that I would stand in the way of the enquiry."

"We're tracing Overton's route up to where Dill overtook him, looking for any other encounters, but it means combing through a wider and wider CCTV landscape. We're also tracking the movements of anyone else through the park—although someone could've slipped out over the railing unseen by the cameras. It'll take time."

"So, no other leads yet. That must be frustrating. How is Sergeant Hopgood taking it?"

"Why do you think I'm up here?" Kenny asked. "Doesn't help no one has come forward as a witness."

"But you know the attacker is tall, like Charles Henry? Didn't you say something about the angle of the wound revealing that?"

Kenny stepped off the path, which was cut through a steep slope, and although the DC and I were about the same height, he now stood a head above me.

"So," I said, "whoever did it would have needed only to stand off the path in the right place."

Kenny smiled. "That's me away. See ya, Hayley."

Detective Constable Pye had told me once before that he liked talking with witnesses or anyone involved in a case because you never knew what another person might remember later. A bit different from Detective Sergeant Hopgood, whose push-broom mustache bristled at the thought of too much fraternizing with the public and who preferred to ask a question and get an answer.

I went back down the path and out the way I'd come. Back to Middlebank for lunch or out to John's narrow boat? I headed for the canal—Mrs. Woolgar would never miss me. I was eager to give John the opportunity to tell me his story. It's possible I wouldn't even need to talk with this Dolly Beckwith. I'd nearly reached the Pulteney Bridge when I spotted a Panama hat atop a mint-green linen suit coming straight toward me in the crowd.

I scooted into the nearest shop and backed in far enough to be unseen by a passerby. Just because Maureen Frost and I had reached some sort of an understanding didn't mean Charles Henry and I were about to become all hail-fellow-well-met. When he came into view, I instinctively ducked behind a rack of summer frocks and then waited a minute before stepping out onto the pavement. He was nowhere in sight. I crept to the corner, looked up Grove Street, and saw his Panama hat.

After that narrow escape, I continued on my way across the bridge, but when I'd reached Laura Circle, a familiar form caught my eye. Celia, her streaky blond hair drooping, sat on the pavement with her back up against the iron railing, her legs stretched out in front of her, and straw bag in a heap in her lap.

"Hello, Celia."

When she looked up, I took a step back. Her eye makeup had run and made her look like a harlequin clown. The only shade came from a nearby light pole—the sun was beating down on us, and the pavement must be boiling.

"Hiya, Hayley," she said, and it seemed to take great effort.

"What's wrong?" I asked. "Are you not well?"

"No, yeah, I'm fine." She sniveled and wiped her nose on the back of her hand. "It's only that I went to see him"—she waved her arm in a direction vaguely behind her—"and he's gone."

"He . . . your boyfriend? You mean he arrived and already left? You didn't have much time together, did you?"

"It wasn't my fault," she squeezed out through a sob.

Holidays don't suit every couple, do they? This was easy to read—Celia and her boyfriend had had a spat, and he'd legged it, leaving her alone, away from home, and feeling rotten.

"Of course it wasn't your fault." I looked down at her pathetic figure and wondered if I was losing my grip as curator of the First Edition Society and its library and instead becoming an agony aunt, commiserating on the failed relationships of others. I sighed. "I tell you what, come with me. We'll get lunch and go sit down by the river and cool off."

I gave her a hand to help her off the pavement and propped her up outside the newsagent while I nipped in for sandwiches, drinks, and as many paper napkins as I could grab, and then we went down and settled in the grassy shade by the weir. Celia used up most of the napkins blowing her nose and wiping her eyes, and then I gave her a choice of sandwiches. She took the chicken and stuffing, so I had the ham and cheese. I handed her a bottle of fizzy elderflower water. We didn't talk until she had wolfed down her sandwich.

"Did you have an argument?" I asked.

Celia shrugged.

"Perhaps you'll smooth it over when you get back to Plymouth." Her eyes filled with tears. "Everything I touch goes bad."

This was no time for a "stiff upper lip" comment, so I stayed quiet, and eventually, Celia heaved a great sigh and began to notice her surroundings. "Nice, here." Something across the weir in the Parade Gardens caught her eye. She squinted and then muttered, "Bloody hell."

I followed her gaze over. "What's that?"

Celia clambered up and began collecting our rubbish. "Best be on my way."

"Is it your boyfriend—has he come back?"

Her gaze darted to me and away.

"Look, if you're in trouble or feeling unsafe," I said, "you should go directly to the police. I'll go along, if you like. I know someone you can talk with."

She brushed grass off her dress. "You know the local police? How's that?"

"Oh, well"—better to stick with the most recent events—"a man died near Middlebank last week, and my boyfriend and I came across him. He'd been stabbed in the park. Dreadful, really."

Celia clutched our sandwich cartons to her chest. "That's awful. Do they know who did it?"

Nothing like a murder mystery to distract a woman from her own troubles. Celia seemed to have perked up a bit, and so I continued. "No, they don't. That is, it's an ongoing enquiry. One possibility is that it was a case of mistaken identity. You see, he looked a bit like this other fellow that . . . oh, wait, you saw him. Remember at the library, the fellow who got punched?"

Celia squinted at me. "Yeah."

"He and the victim were similar at first glance."

"Says who?"

"Well . . ." I caught myself before I threw Charles Henry under the bus. "Of course, police look at all evidence. It might not be mistaken identity. Perhaps this fellow had enemies or it was a random attack."

"You know a lot about it," Celia said.

I screwed the cap back on my bottle. "Not really. It's nothing to do with me."

13

We parted on Pulteney Bridge. Celia stopped in the news-agent for cigarettes, and I checked the time. Gone three o'clock. I sent John a text to say I'd like to have a chat, and he'd answered that he was aboard *La Mouette 2* and would look forward to my arrival. I rang Mrs. Woolgar.

"I'll be away a little longer than I expected," I told her.

"I'll leave the correspondence for you to deal with upon your return," the secretary answered. "There was an email about a dead-line tomorrow for an article you offered to write. The Society of Curatorial Professionals? Something about ideas for cataloging a historical genre collection?"

"Excellent," I said with a sinking feeling. "I'll be back before the end of the day to do a final edit on the article so that it's ready to send off tomorrow morning."

But first I'd have to write it.

More than a month ago, I'd suggested the article to the SCP on a whim, inspired by Lady Fowling's musings in one of her notebooks. I intended the article to be tongue in cheek, throwing out the idea that books could be cataloged by setting—a country house with hidden passages, a country house built over a medieval crypt, a country house that had been used as a hideout by Charles I. I had thought it would be a breeze to come up with a thousand words on the subject, and one more way to get the word out about the First Edition Society. The SCP had accepted the idea, and the next moment, the assignment had flown clean out of my head.

Surely I could dash this thing out after seeing John. On the walk out to *La Mouette 2*, instead of practicing what I would say to him, I concentrated on the article, trying out several leads, each one sounding weaker than the one before. That's how I came upon the narrow boat unprepared to tell John about Milo's letter.

"Hello, Hayley," John said, coming out of the cabin. "Tea?"

"Yes, please."

John put the kettle on and then straightened a handful of loose papers on the table as I sat down. I glimpsed a pencil drawing and asked, "Do you sketch?"

"These?" he asked. "These are only the beginnings of ideas. But not all; here is one." He shuffled through the papers and handed one over. It was of a narrow boat—in fact, the *La Mouette 2*. I knew that because of the name on the side of the boat. And in the sky were marks similar to those I'd seen on the sticky note John had signed.

"Birds?" I asked.

"Gulls, Hayley," John replied with an exaggerated eye roll. "Obviously, I am no artist."

When tea and a plate of jammy dodgers had been served, I looked for a way to begin.

"Have you heard anything about the enquiry?" John asked.

"No, not really."

"Sergeant Hopgood shouldn't waste his time on Charles Henry. I am looking into Milo's past to find a clue."

"Investigating is the job of the police," I said, "and we should let them do it." And this time I really meant it, because didn't we have our own mystery at Middlebank to solve?

I tapped the edge of my biscuit on the plate. "John, before Milo died, he said he wanted to give me some information about your background, and you objected."

A curtain descended behind John's eyes, just as a curtain drops on a stage.

"I told him there was no reason to do that," John said.

"He said he felt it would be better if you were honest with us, and I agree."

John set his mug down hard. "I have not lied to you."

"Have you been entirely truthful?" I asked. He didn't answer. "There you are, then."

"These details," he said, "they make no difference."

"Why don't you let us decide that? Don't we deserve to know your whole story in exchange for welcoming you into Middlebank?" He looked at me out of the corner of his eye. "All right, not everyone has welcomed you," I corrected. "But why wouldn't there be suspicion when you won't explain. You aren't being fair to us, John, surely you can see that."

He didn't answer and didn't look at me. In the quiet, I heard the voices of people from the towpath, and out the window, I could see a continuous stream of foot traffic.

"You know things that no one else did," I said. "About Lady Fowling's writings. How?"

"You know how I know," John said, his voice rising. "I know because it's my history."

"Is it?" I asked. "Is that the truth?"

He jumped up from the table and in three strides made it to the back of the boat.

"You cannot tell me what is true about my life!" he shouted, pointing a finger at me. He backed farther until he bumped into the wall. "Only I can say that!"

I stood and kept my voice level, but firm. "If it's the truth, why does it upset you? Aren't we entitled to proof?"

"I am the proof!" he shouted back. "I won't let you do this!"

For all of being an adult male, he suddenly reminded me of a thirteen-year-old Dinah protesting when I'd said I wanted to meet her new friend's parents. I put my hands on my hips and said, "How will you stop me, John? More importantly, *why* will you stop me?"

"I warned Milo not to do this." His voice, still loud, shook. "What did he tell you?"

"He told me I should talk with Dolly Beckwith in Charmouth. Who is Dolly?"

John crossed his arms, clutching them tightly to his body. His eyes were bright, but his face a blotchy red. His voice dropped to almost nothing. "Dolly is . . . Dolly."

"If you don't want me to see her, then tell me what she would say."

I waited for what seemed like forever. Gradually, I saw the tension leave John's shoulders. "No," he said quietly. "It's better you hear it from Dolly."

I had my permission.

I hadn't thought it possible, but I arrived back at Middlebank before the end of the workday—all of two minutes before—and I caught Mrs. Woolgar coming out of her office.

Inhaling through my nose to control my breathing and hoping she wouldn't notice the sweat streaking down my face, I said, "Well, I'll just take another look at that article before I send it off."

"Yes, Ms. Burke," she said, walking back to her stairs. "Have a lovely evening."

I would have no evening at all, and I suspected that she suspected as much.

"You, too. Frances will be here in the morning," I reminded her. "Perhaps we could ask her to give us an update on her project. What do you think?"

Mrs. Woolgar paused, hand resting on the newel. "I'd quite like that."

Good to end the day with that crumb of approval. I waited until I heard her door close, and then I dragged myself up to my flat.

But only for a shower. In no time, I was back in my office, laptop open, cup of tea at my elbow, and texting Val to tell him what I was about. Then I settled down to work. Bunter, unaccustomed to my spending the evening on the ground floor, prowled around, hopping up on surfaces and slinking under furniture, sniffing candlesticks, lamp switches, and the coal bucket as if he'd never seen these items before in his life. Finally, he wrapped himself in a ball in the wingback chair and fell asleep. I got up to make another cup of tea—I'd yet to finish the first paragraph.

But by ten o'clock, I had really got into my stride. I could see where I wanted the article to go and aimed myself in that direction with newfound zeal, having consumed four cups of tea and an entire package of custard cream biscuits.

My fingers flew over the keyboard, and I had just come up with a humorous but important key point about cataloging when my phone went off. I couldn't take any disruption at this crucial stage, but when I glanced at the screen, I answered.

"Dinah sweetie, how are you?"

"Hiya, Mum."

I put her on speaker and we chatted while I kept going on the article, afraid if I paused for any length of time I'd lose my focus.

"Look, Mum, when you're at Gran's on Saturday, why don't I drive over and we can go out. A drive in the country. What do you think?"

"What a lovely idea," I said, thinking that for the Golden Age of Mystery, books could be organized by the number of murders within one book. "But sweetie I won't be able to go to Liverpool this weekend because I've a . . . work thing to do." Driving to Charmouth in Dorset to see Dolly Beckwith. It may not have been on my job description, but it most certainly had to do with Middlebank and the Society. "I gave your gran a quick text about it already."

"That's all right," Dinah said, sounding not a bit put out. "We'll go just the two of us this time. It'll be a trial run for our Burke women on the road, won't it?"

"Yes, that'll be lovely."

How many different cataloging systems existed in the world? Did everyone use the Dewey classification? I proceeded with a quick internet search while Dinah said something else about her driving.

"Yes, sweetie, it is wonderful that you're able to share the car with Ginny," I said. "And I'm sure you're being careful."

What system did they use in the States?

". . . and you know how difficult it is to get onto Gran's schedule," Dinah said.

"Your gran likes to stay busy, doesn't she? Isn't she heading up the summer fete for Cats Rescue People?"

What I needed in the article was a description of how the First Edition library would look using my imaginary system. I typed away as Dinah said something else, ending with, "Do you think?"

"Lovely."

"Ace, Mum. See you then."

"Bye, sweetie."

A t two thirty Friday morning, I read through the article aloud, which must've annoyed Bunter, because he woke up, jumped down, and stalked out of my office. I didn't blame him. I was a fair bit annoyed myself, but mostly I was exhausted. My head hit the pillow at five past three.

The alarm on my phone went off at seven. I'd set it across the room to make sure I got to my feet. I cooked an egg for my breakfast, and, guilty for having nothing for my dinner the night before apart from biscuits, I didn't even put marmalade on my toast. Then I walked down to the Bertinet and brought back a box of pastries for later.

Frances arrived promptly at nine and I walked her up to the library.

"Mrs. Woolgar and I would love to hear how you're doing," I said. "Would you have a few minutes later?"

"Certainly, anytime," Frances said. She arranged her laptop, notebook, pencils, and two stacks of paperbacks before putting her hands in her lap. Then she moved the pencils, shifted her laptop, and picked up one of the paperbacks.

"Well, Hayley, Friday already. Do you have plans for your weekend?"

"Usually I go visit my mum in Liverpool," I said. "It makes a nice break, you know."

"Yes, I'm sure it does." Frances opened the book and then closed it again. "But not this weekend?"

"No, this weekend Val and I are off to Dorset."

"Dorset," she replied, and looked up at me. "That's a change, isn't it?"

I held her gaze for a moment and saw her cheeks bloom a rosy pink.

"I love the seaside," I said.

I waited until after ten to phone Dolly Beckwith. As I listened to the rings, my heart raced *thumpity thump*. What was I to say to this person, and why would she agree to talk with a stranger about things that John obviously wanted kept secret? Was this a fool's errand?

"Double-oh-seven-double-four-six-eight-six-three-six."

I grinned. It had been ages since I'd heard someone answer a phone with the phone number.

"Hello, is this Dolly Beckwith? My name is Hayley Burke."

My name would mean nothing to her, but at least it showed good faith.

"Hello, Hayley, yes, this is Dolly."

She sounded elderly, and her voice was a bit loud, but I reined myself in from shouting back at her—she probably had the volume on her phone set quite high.

"I'm ringing to ask if . . ." Again, what was I supposed to say?

"You'd like to have a talk, wouldn't you?"

"Yes," I said, "I would like to talk with you. It's about—"

"Oh, I know what it's about. John told me. But," she added, "we won't do this on the telephone, will we?"

14

❧

I wonder what she'll say," I said to Val on Saturday morning as we headed south. "What if she's just as vague as John? What if we go all the way to Dorset and learn nothing?"

"What if it's all her plot to make you spend the rest of the afternoon looking in the tide pools at Lyme Regis?" Val asked, cutting his eyes at me. "Oh, wait, that would be your plot, wouldn't it?"

"Doesn't hurt that we get a night away, does it?" I asked. "I'm glad Dinah's going to see Mum in my place, although I'm a bit worried about her driving them round."

"Didn't she receive top safety marks on her driving course?"

"She did. A few more months of short journeys, and perhaps she'll bring Mum down to see us."

Over lunch at a roadside service, I said, "John wasn't best pleased about this, but I gave him his chance, and he wouldn't tell me anything. Instead, he rang Dolly and told her she'd be hearing from me. What a muddle."

"Are you sure you don't want to talk with her alone?" Val asked.

"No, I want you there," I said. "It's better the two of us."

Val squeezed my hand. "What if he is Lady Fowling's grandson, then what?"

"That's not for us to decide—fortunately. Not even Mrs. Woolgar will be able to control it. That's for science. Someone will have to ask Charles Henry for a DNA sample."

Turnstone Cottage lay up a winding lane in the village of Charmouth. It stood out amid a cluster of other cottages, its clean white stucco and the door and window trim painted sea blue. Honeysuckle had gone wild over the front gate, but everywhere else the garden looked tidy. We arrived after two o'clock and walked up the path lined with heartsease to the front door. I raised the brass knocker and let it drop.

A thin woman with white hair in a pixie cut answered. She wore dark blue trousers and a pale yellow cardigan—an echo of the flowers along the path. She smiled, accentuating the fine lines that burst from the corners of her eyes. No dimple to be seen.

"Hello, I'm Dolly. Welcome to my house," she said, pronouncing it *owse* in good Dorset fashion.

We introduced ourselves, and she opened the door wide to let us in.

"I hope you didn't mind coming all this way from Bath," she said as we followed her down a short corridor.

"Not at all," I said. "We had a lovely drive, didn't we?"

Val agreed and asked, "Have you lived here long, Mrs. Beckwith?"

"Oh, now, it's just Dolly. This has been my home for fifty-odd years, if you can believe it."

In that case, she'd certainly kept up with the times, I thought. The sitting room she led us to wasn't large, but felt light and fresh with muted floral prints. A few watercolors hung round the room, and a large mirror over the fireplace.

"Now then," she said, "are you ready for your tea, or would you like to wait a bit?"

She may not want to give us tea when we'd finished. Still, I'd rather get right to it.

"Perhaps later?"

Val and I sat on the sofa, and Dolly faced us across a low table. The sun streamed in at our side, and a breeze drifted through the open window. I could almost smell the sea.

"Well, Dolly," I said, "I realize this is a strange thing that Val and I should come down here to ask about John when he's in Bath. Why couldn't we just hear it from him?"

I was half hoping she might answer that question, but instead, she smiled and made a little indulgent noise like a hen clucking at its chick.

"I've known John his whole life," she said, "and so it doesn't seem a bit strange to me. I'm happy to tell you what you want to know." She sat up straight with hands on her thighs. "Fire away."

She was the opposite of John in that case—offering the truth instead of . . . whatever it was that we'd had thus far.

"We've heard a great deal about John's grandfather. Did you know him?"

"No, I didn't. And neither did anyone else. I doubt even Margaret, John's grandmother, knew him more than was necessary. If you take my meaning."

"Margaret?" I whispered.

"Margaret Aubrey," Dolly said.

I looked at Val, and he took the next question.

"John told us his parents died in a road traffic accident when he was quite young. Is that true?"

Dolly shook her head. "No, his parents . . . I see that I'd better take it from the top, as they say."

"Please do." The first two answers had so flummoxed me, I wouldn't't've known what to ask next.

"John's grandfather, that is, the man he talks about," Dolly said, "is taken from stories he was told all his life, stories he embraced when he couldn't face the real world. He changed them a bit to make them his own. He made them real."

"Do any of his stories take place in Brittany?" I asked.

"Oh, indeed they do," Dolly said. "That's where it all began."

With François Flambeaux?

"Well, here's what John's told us," I said. "That his grandmother went to Brittany and met a man. They had a child. And then she went away, leaving the baby behind."

"Margaret would no more have abandoned her baby than she would fly to the moon," Dolly said.

The scaffolding of John's life began to crumble, and Dolly must've seen the realization on my face. Had I wanted Lady Fowling to be his grandmother?

"It was never John's intent to deceive you," Dolly said. "Not on purpose. You keep that in mind, all right?"

She popped up, went to the sideboard, brought back a photo album, and sat again, holding it in her lap.

"Now, Margaret was what you'd call a 'free spirit.' A year or two after the war, barely eighteen, she followed some fellow to France."

"Did you know Margaret?" I asked.

"I was a little girl when she left and only got to know her after she returned," Dolly replied. "I married in 1964, and, as Margaret was a niece of my husband's uncle's wife, she became a relation of sorts. They both did."

"Both?"

"Yes. She'd come back from Brittany in 1951 pregnant. By her own account, she barely made it to land before giving birth."

"She had a son?" Val asked.

"No," Dolly said, "she had a daughter. Georgie, she was called, short for Georgiana."

"Georgiana!"

Dolly acknowledged this with a nod. "After that first fellow had legged it, Margaret had stayed on in Brittany, getting work as a cleaner in some village, eking out a living I don't know how. That lasted a couple of years, but when she fell pregnant, she began to see the predicament she was in—away from home, alone, and with a baby on the way. She felt a bit desperate. Then she met a widowed English lady staying in the small hotel where she worked, and this woman befriended her."

"Lady Fowling," I whispered.

"From all we heard," Dolly said, "your Lady Fowling was the loveliest person—and a bit lonely herself. To take Margaret's mind off her troubles, she told her stories. Oh, those stories! It's just the sort of thing that would suit Margaret, taking her away from the real world. So, this English lady went home, and finally Margaret came back, too. She and Georgie set up in a tiny cottage in the village and kept themselves to themselves."

"Did Margaret work?"

"Nothing steady," Dolly said. "The two of them spent their days walking the cliffs and living on their own terms. And she kept those stories alive by telling them over and over to her Georgie. The girl was much like her mother—head in the clouds most of the time. And so, somewhere along the way, the stories became more than tales to Georgie."

"Do you know the stories?" I asked.

Dolly laughed. "Oh, pirates and such. I never paid much attention. I had more practical things to tend to. My husband fell ill, you see, right about the time Margaret died. I had to keep working while I was his carer, and we were occupied with our own lives. I was aware that Georgie was living the way she had been reared—another one of those free spirits."

"A few years passed. My husband had died, and I kept working. Then one day, I saw Georgie down at the shops with John, who was barely a year old. I knew about the baby—didn't everybody?—and just as her mother before her, there was no father to be found. We got to talking, and Georgie told me she and John were leaving, going off on an adventure to spend their fortune. Dear girl had no more common sense than her mother—anyone could see they didn't have two tuppence to rub together. I said no, don't go, come move into the cottage with me, the two of you."

"That was kind of you," I said.

"Oh well," Dolly said, "I needed someone to do for me, and besides, I wanted the company." She opened the album to the middle and handed it to us. "Here now, you take a look through there while I put the kettle on."

She had opened the album to a snapshot taken in front of her own cottage. It was of a smiling woman looking down at a boy of four or five. He had blond curls, stood with his hands on his hips, and wore a loose, white shirt tucked into black trousers. There was that dimple—it matched the one on his mother's cheek. A miniature John with his mum.

"Ah, look at him," I said, my voice thick. "He's the boy who wouldn't grow up."

"Mixing your genres there, my love," Val said, resting his arm round my shoulders and kissing my temple. "Although you're right—there is a bit of Peter Pan about him."

"Margaret lived off the money Lady Fowling had given her, didn't she? There was truth in that."

"Lady Fowling must've had an account set up," Val said. "Has Duncan found anything?"

"No," I said, "but then he wasn't quite sure what to look for. Now we can give him a name: Margaret Aubrey."

We turned to the front of the album and looked through pages of snapshots showing Dolly and her husband through the years. The middle section included more shots of John and his mother. At the very back was a page with three old black-and-white photos— the kind with scalloped edges—and one empty space.

The photos were of a young woman. They couldn't be Georgie, and so must be Margaret—there was that dimple. In one, she sat at a table with a glass in front of her, posing for the camera. In another, she wore a loose-fitting dress and leaned against a rocky outcrop on a sandy beach. In the third, she stood in front of a hotel with another woman—a young Georgiana Fowling.

I ran my finger over the space where the fourth photo had been. I thought of the one in John's wallet.

Dolly came back with the tea tray, and Val jumped up to carry it for her.

"Thank you, dear. The teapot seems to grow heavier the older I get. You won't tell John I said that, though, will you?"

The tray held enough food to feed a crowd—home-baked shortbread, seedcake, a bowl of raspberries, cheese, brown bread, and butter.

"He hasn't had it easy, our John," Dolly said as she poured the tea and gestured for us to tuck in. "Father unknown and a mother that lived in the stories her mum had told to her, and that she now told to her son."

"And what about Georgie?"

Dolly paused with the milk jug in her hand. "John was nine years old when she died. He'd been kept after school that day, not an uncommon occurrence, and she had gone walking along the cliffs, just as she had done with Margaret. She went out so often it was well after tea before John and I began to feel . . . I don't know, edgy, like. I rang the constable and they put up a search. John wanted to go with them, but I kept him indoors, and so we sat in here and waited, and he talked about pirates and detectives and I don't know what all. They found her the next morning—the cliff had collapsed, and she had been buried at the bottom."

"How awful," I said.

"We had a rough few years after that, John and I did," Dolly said.

"It seemed the only way he could manage was to disappear into all those stories of Georgie's and Margaret's before her. I thought, if it makes him happy to think his grandfather had been a pirate, who's to say that's a bad thing. We don't all fit into this life the same way."

"And, how did you and John manage?" I asked. "Did you continue to work?"

"I did, until I didn't need to any longer, because of John. You see, he's different from Margaret and Georgie in this—John has a practical, down-to-earth side of him, and he's smart as a whip. He didn't bother with school after he turned sixteen. He'd settled down by then, and he'd sold a few of his ideas."

I have ideas, he had said.

"Inventions?" Val asked.

"Of a sort," Dolly said. "They were little things to begin with. When he was twelve, he said to the fellow who ran the village shop, I can show you how to sell more packets of crisps, and the fellow said, you go on then. John built some contraption to show them off, the shop sold more crisps, and he got five pounds for it. You'd think he'd won the lottery. After he left school, he got on at the local garage and showed the man who owned the place a better way to store used oil. Fifty pounds for that one! You see, he's always coming up with something—better window latches on trains, chairs that turn into tables, I don't know what all. For years, he would take a job here and there, all the while selling his ideas and making a bit of extra. He finally made enough that I could quit my job."

"Does he have a workshop?" Val asked.

"No, these days John isn't interested in building, only in coming up with the ideas. Not that he isn't a handy fellow when he needs to be. He had an idea for cupboards that don't waste space in the kitchen. First, he built them here for me, and then he sold the idea to a cabinetmaker in Exeter. They call it 'More Room Than Narnia.'"

"What?" I was gobsmacked. "I've seen their adverts in magazines. That was John's idea?"

Val snapped his fingers. "He's used that in his narrow boat—he reconfigured the layout."

"That one paid for the refurb on my cottage. You see how practical he can be," Dolly said. "Now, two years ago, he got on with a company in Plymouth. They make scooters—the sort that pensioners take to the shops and all. John had an idea that would make them drive better, but don't ask me how. They paid him quite handsomely for that, and he bought his narrow boat. But then, last year, I had a scare with my health."

"Oh dear," I said.

"Not to worry, I'm fine now. But at the time, it sent John into a tailspin, because it had been the two of us for so long. It's as if it all came back to him about his mum. He feared that if he lost me, he would lose his hold on the real world. Ballast, John calls it. He needs something—that is, someone, to keep him stable. That's what I'd been for him. About the same time, he came across notices about your Society."

I thought back to almost a year ago, when I'd been hired, and remembered that it had been announced and a press release sent out.

"Lady Georgiana Fowling was mentioned, and there were even a few old pictures of her. You see, he'd never known Margaret, but he knew the pirate-detective Flambeaux. He began telling the stories again. I was that worried about him, but this time, a part of him understood that he needed to keep one foot on the ground, and so he hired Milo. Milo worked for John, but he also kept an eye on him." She smiled. "John said Flambeaux could've used someone like Milo."

But Flambeaux did have someone like Milo. That is, in *Frenchman's Creek*, the pirate Jean Benoit-Aubéry had William, his valet or butler or whatever. But then, John hadn't read the du Maurier book, I reminded myself. His life was based on Lady Fowling's writings.

"John told me what happened to Milo," Dolly said, "and I'm so sorry about it. He was a good man, and I'm sure he helped many people." Her hands worried the edge of her cardigan. "You don't think his death had anything to do with John, do you?"

She'd probably held that question in as long as she could. A web of worry lines broke out on her face, and her hands couldn't stay still.

Val and I looked at each other and back at her, both of us shaking our heads. "No, it's nothing to do with John," I said.

Not unless it was a case of mistaken identity. Did the police have anything else, or was Charles Henry Dill the prime suspect?

W e helped Dolly clean up the tea things, and it gave me a chance to see John's idea for better cupboards at work. I probably had loads of unused space in my own kitchen, and I wondered if the Society would let me get these installed in my flat.

After such an afternoon, Val and I barely talked as we drove over to our B&B on the Cobb, the harbor in Lyme Regis. We checked in and then took a long walk along the seafront, dodging old-age pensioners in their scooters along the way. We stopped, leaned on the railing, and looked out, the wind whipping my hair round. I fancied I could see all the way to Brittany from there.

The tide was coming in. A wave hit the seawall, sending a fine, cold spray into our faces.

"John told me that his narrow boat gave him freedom without entirely losing sight of land," Val said. "Now I understand what he meant."

I slipped an arm through his. "You're quite taken with the narrow-boat experience, aren't you?"

He shrugged in a casual way. "Might be fun to try it out."

"For our next holiday?" I asked. I had two more weeks to take in August and Val had the entire month off. "Seems like a great deal of work, though, doesn't it? All that business with opening and closing the locks. I rather like a holiday where I can lie back and enjoy things."

Val turned and pulled me close, his hands sliding down to my bottom. "Oh, I think that could be arranged."

His lips were warm and a bit salty from the spray. We kissed until a passing knot of children shrieked, and he loosened his grip.

"No," Val said, "I think we should stay the course with our survey of every seaside resort in Britain. What's next?"

I studied his face for a moment. "Well, we're spoilt for choice, aren't we? I tell you what, as you planned our last week at the seaside, why don't you let me plan this one? I'll make certain there's a good pub nearby."

"You're on," Val said, taking my hand. "And speaking of which, I could just do with a pint."

15

We looked in on Dolly before we left the next day, and she sent us off with sandwiches, the remainder of the seedcake, and fresh raspberries. We took the long way home on small roads and stopped to have our lunch. I rang Mum, and we told her what we'd learned about John, and she told us about her outing with Dinah as driver.

"She's careful and sure, and you don't need to worry about longer journeys. We'll be just fine. Look now, I'll send you a snap of the two of us."

A text came in—a photo of Dinah in the driver's seat and Mum leaning over toward the window.

"That was a good day out," I said.

"It was. See you soon, love."

We rang off. Not exactly "soon"—my usual visit was a week away. By the time Val left me at the door of Middlebank and went home to get ready for his Monday classes, it was early evening. I was greeted by Bunter, who peered out cautiously from Mrs. Woolgar's office. When he saw it was me, he raced across the entry, jumped on the hallstand, down again, and began weaving a figure eight round my legs. Good thing I always kept a spare catnip mouse in my bag.

As the cat scrambled round the entry chasing his fresh prey, I went up to the first-floor landing, dropped my bag down, pulled out a Chippendale chair, and sat across from Lady Fowling.

"That was a kind thing to do," I said, "put aside your own grief to help a young woman in trouble."

I saw a gleam in her eye.

"John's an odd mix, isn't he—fantasy and practicality. Do you mind what he's told people?"

The enigmatic smile softened.

"He seems to have a great memory for stories he was told as a boy. The details, you know."

I studied Lady Fowling's face and imagined I caught a glimpse of the young woman at the seaside in Brittany.

"I'll talk with him tomorrow, and after that I'll explain to Mrs. Woolgar, and after that I'll let the board know. I wonder what John will do now. Will he hire another William? And, what about Milo? We may have settled our mystery at Middlebank, but his murderer is still on the loose. What about . . . what about Charles Henry?"

But at that, Lady Fowling turned back into a painting.

I hadn't said a word to Mrs. Woolgar about my weekend plans or Milo's letter or Dolly Beckwith. Now that I knew a great deal more, I was unsure if she would be relieved or incensed that John had put the wind up her. I would tread carefully.

Sitting on this information made our morning briefing uncomfortable—at least for me. I let Mrs. Woolgar direct the agenda, and she gave me a report on her research into software that would help us track patrons, asked if I would republish my article in the Society's newsletter after the curatorial group had done so, and mentioned the silver plate needed polishing. I attempted to be the very model of composure throughout.

Finally, she asked, "Ms. Burke, anything on John Aubrey?"

My face felt as if it were on fire.

"Regarding?"

"Well, Audrey and Sylvia Moon seem quite taken with him, and that's all well and good, but it's no proof to his wild claims about family. We need to settle this business immediately, make it clear that there is no connection between him and her ladyship. It's for the safety of the Society and Middlebank. He needs to take a DNA test."

"And compare it to . . ."

Mrs. Woolgar frowned. "Yes, I realize that means Charles Henry must take one, too. It's best to approach that subject through Maureen, but they may be preoccupied with the matter from last week." *Charles Henry Dill, prime suspect.* "It's only that John Aubrey hasn't been here since Wednesday. I don't want to be taken by surprise. Again. Has he gone?"

"Things do seem to have calmed down a bit, haven't they?" I asked. The secretary waited for more. I could tell her now. It would be a relief to get it over with, and look how reasonable she seemed this morning. Still, if Duncan Rennie were here, too, I'd have a cushion, so to speak.

I was saved from a decision by the buzzer at the front door. "That'll be Charles Henry," I said, exasperation covering my relief. "He's a bit early. I'd better get him started."

But it wasn't Charles Henry at the front door—it was Sergeant Hopgood.

"Sergeant Hopgood, good morning." I stepped aside.

"Good morning, Ms. Burke. Good morning, Mrs. Woolgar," he said as he came in, aiming the greeting at her open office door.

"Good morning, Sergeant," she replied, but made no move.

"What can I do for you?" I asked, leading him to my office. "Have you found something? More CCTV that shows Milo and his attacker? Evidence? The weapon?"

The door buzzed again.

"Sorry, let me just—"

I left the sergeant in my office and retraced my steps to the front door. As soon as it was opened, Charles Henry strode in, his satchel under one arm and a takeaway coffee in the other. "You know, Ms. Burke, it would save you a great deal of trouble if I had a key to Middlebank. As I am an employee, it doesn't seem an unreasonable..."

He looked across the entry at Hopgood and stopped dead.

"Mr. Dill." The DS gave a nod.

Charles Henry seemed to kick-start himself, sputtering for a moment before saying, "'Morning. Yes, I'll just get to my work, shall I?" and before I could reply, he hurried up the stairs faster than I'd ever seen him move.

"Did you want to talk with Charles Henry?" I asked the sergeant.

"No, Ms. Burke, I am trying to locate Mr. Aubrey."

"Why?" Not expecting an answer, I followed up with, "Have you tried his mobile?"

"Switched off, apparently."

"He's probably moored somewhere along the towpath."

"We've been up and down the towpath from Bathampton through the city, and he isn't there."

"Is it urgent?"

"It's a matter of police business."

"About the murder? Didn't John give you the information you needed? And after all, you're the police. Why don't you send a helicopter along the entire Kennet and Avon Canal from Bristol to Reading?"

"Police time and police budgets, Ms. Burke, that's why."

I didn't like this, not at all. Milo had his mobile taken from him, and now John couldn't be found.

"He may have had to move his narrow boat farther out," I suggested. "He could be at Devizes—I've heard they have a great many locks to get through there, it takes time."

"Has Mr. Aubrey said anything to you about having an argument with Milo Overton?"

"An argument? No."

"Did Mr. Aubrey tell you that he objected to Overton revealing to you details about Aubrey's past?" Hopgood asked.

"Milo said . . . wait. Did John tell you this? Because, I know they had a disagreement, but that's all it was."

"Would you say Mr. Aubrey has an explosive temper?"

"A temper . . . I've never . . . he didn't . . ." I seemed incapable of finishing a sentence or deciding which direction to take, because what the DS was asking me was based on the previous Thursday afternoon, a conversation I'd had on John's narrow boat when I went out to tell him about Milo's letter.

I took a sharp breath. "Where has all this come from? Because it's obvious that whatever you've heard has been blown out of all proportion. Who told you?"

"Ms. Burke, this is a murder enquiry, and you of all people should realize we must follow every lead and from any source. It just so happens that this bit of information came to us on Friday morning." I noticed the end of one eyebrow lift slightly, and I could've sworn it pointed toward the library.

I looked up to see a vanishing figure on the landing. "Excuse me for a moment, Sergeant."

When I walked into the library, Charles Henry sat at the far end of the table, puffing slightly. He ignored me, tapping away into his laptop, but just before I came near enough to see the screen, he snapped it closed.

"Yes, Ms. Burke?" he asked, and then he saw Sergeant Hopgood at the library door. His eyes widened.

"Mr. Dill, were you following me last Thursday afternoon?"

His jaw dropped. "What? Follow you? I am shocked at this unfounded accusation. Follow you where? Why? I don't understand."

I let him bluster until he ran out of steam, and then I shook my head and clicked my tongue. "You've been caught by CCTV once," I said. "You'd think you would've remembered that the city is well covered with cameras along its streets and—correct me if I'm wrong, Sergeant—along the canal towpath, too. Should I ask for proof? Is this harassment?"

I prayed Hopgood wouldn't disagree. When I cut my eyes at him and saw his brows in neutral, I realized this was just what he'd wanted, for me to know Charles Henry had been the source and to watch us bang heads and see what came out of it. *Well played, Detective Sergeant.*

Dill had lost his voice for a moment, but after a small gurgling sound, he said, "It so happens that I wanted to speak with you about a . . . work-related matter, and I saw you walking past and followed only meaning to catch you up."

"Where? Where did you see me?"

Dill's face squeezed up in concentration. "I believe it must've been on the bridge?"

"That's a long way to follow. You didn't try very hard to catch me up, did you?" I asked.

"You set yourself quite a pace, I must say, and by the time I neared, you were already otherwise engaged with Aubrey. I lingered briefly in the hope that you would finish whatever business you had with this con man, but then I heard raised voices." He leaned back in the chair, as if settling in. "It was quite a heated argument and the tone of Aubrey's voice disconcerted me, I can tell you that. I was concerned for your safety, Ms. Burke. I feared you were in danger. You don't know what that man is capable of."

"Concerned for my safety?" I asked in a low voice. "Concerned for my safety?" I shouted at him. "You were so concerned that you turned right round, went back to Maureen's flat, had a peaceful afternoon and evening, a lovely dinner, went to bed, and got up the next morning, had breakfast, and *then* went to the police?"

"Mr. Dill," Hopgood said, and although his voice was quiet, we both paid attention. "You told us nothing about Ms. Burke being in danger."

"What?" Charles Henry paled. "Of course I did. I'm certain I did. It may've momentarily been overshadowed by the . . . you know . . . rest of the story."

"Which was?" I asked.

"The exchange as you reported it to police," Hopgood said, "concerned Aubrey's statements about Overton. 'I warned him,' you told us Aubrey said. 'I had to stop him.' Those were his exact words, you told us."

"Exact?" Dill whispered. "Did I say that?"

"Sergeant Hopgood," I said, "I will swear to you right now that John never said, 'I had to stop him.' "

"Didn't he?" Dill said, putting on a perplexed look. "Well, it must've been something very like it." He threw back his shoulders. "I'm terribly sorry if I've misconstrued the exchange, which I only quite by chance overheard. Perhaps the two of you were having a lovely chat about pirates."

"What we had a chat about is none of your business, Mr. Dill," I said, sticking my finger in his face. "And here's a piece of advice for you—don't be a fool. Don't be Godolphin." Charles Henry pulled his head back and frowned. I straightened and sniffed. "And now I suggest you get back to your work while you still have a job."

I stalked out, and the DS followed me downstairs. In the entry, I kept my voice down. "Last Thursday when I went out to the narrow boat, John and I were talking about his family," I said. "It's an emotional subject for him, and for only a moment, the discussion became heated. I was never in any danger."

"A person can be provoked, Ms. Burke," Hopgood said. "He or she can be under such strain that the mind snaps. Perfectly reasonable people have been known to do so."

"Yes, I'm sure that's true, but not John."

"It remains that I want to speak to Aubrey," Hopgood said.

"You can't possibly suspect him of murdering Milo."

"I suspect anyone I can't find, Ms. Burke."

"John worked for a company in Plymouth that manufactures scooters," I said, hoping that a solid piece of information would help.

"Marshall's Ability Transport," Hopgood answered. "We've been in touch with them. Overton worked in HR, but part-time only."

"Well then, you know more than I do."

"Yes, Mr. Aubrey has phoned several times to tell me this or that. He's given me Mr. Overton's ex-wife's name, told me the make of car he drove—although the car was left in Plymouth. It's only when I instigate contact that we run into a snag."

"He's probably busy looking for moorage," I said with more conviction than I felt.

A fter the detective sergeant left, I sent John a text, asking if he was in Bath. A tiny red warning appeared beside the message, telling me it hadn't gone out. I put my phone down and sat at my desk, forcing myself to focus on the Society's fall membership drive—an idea I'd yet to float with Mrs. Woolgar, who preferred for people to find the Society of their own accord rather than the Society chase them down.

Just before eleven, afraid Charles Henry would come downstairs in search of tea, I started up to the library with his cup and a plate of Maries. As I got to the landing, I heard him talking. I paused.

"Yes, Mr. Yoxford, this is Charles Henry Dill . . . no, please don't apologize for taking so long to return my phone call. After all, as the premier solicitor in the country when it comes to estate law, you must be terribly busy."

The door was half closed and he spoke quietly, but still I could hear that oleaginous tone ooze into his voice. I crept forward.

His volume dropped. "Well, you see, sir . . . oh, you can't hear me? I'm awfully sorry. It's only that I wanted to clarify a point or two of law when it comes to inheritance. Particularly"—he dropped his voice again, and I took another step closer—". . . say perhaps a previously unknown direct descendant . . ." I lost a few words. ". . . if the will . . ." I leaned in. ". . . would it then be easier for another blood relative to . . ."

I trembled, and the cup and saucer rattled on the tray. There was an immediate silence in the library. I held my breath. Then Charles Henry spoke, loud and clear.

"Thank you so much for that information. It will help immensely in my job."

I waited another moment before pushing the door open and taking in his tray.

"Ah, Ms. Burke," Charles Henry said. "I'm afraid I've been taking a short break from my work to phone a fellow about my pension and how my pay from the Society may affect it. I hope you don't mind."

His face looked like a beetroot, round and deep crimson. Mine felt as if it might look the same.

"No, it's fine." I set down his tray and turned to go.

"I do have a question about the newsletters," he said.

I came back to the table, and he held an issue from 1977 in which Bunter had written a piece about the history of the monocle. "The cat was always a favorite, I see," he said. Then he shuffled through his untidy stack and picked up another, this from June 1973. "Here's an item about one of the members. It reads, 'With good wishes on your wedding and in hope you will not have a *Busman's Honeymoon*.' That's one of the mysteries, isn't it, Ms. Burke? Who wrote that one?"

"Dorothy L. Sayers," I said. Although I recognized this as his attempt to distract me from what I might've overheard, still I took the bait. "Are there other notices like that?"

"Occasionally," Dill said, sliding papers round. "Here's one on the birth of a baby to a member in New Zealand. Aunt Georgiana seemed to feel as if she knew each member personally."

"Are they in every issue?"

Charles Henry huffed. "I didn't think these small items were worthy of the index, Ms. Burke. I do wish you had told me to begin with. Will I need to go back now and record every single one?"

"No, leave it. Just carry on as you were."

I sat at my desk letting my own tea go cold as I thought about the incomplete, one-sided phone conversation. Charles Henry talking with a solicitor about estate law. He'd tried before to break Lady Fowling's will, and now he seemed to be asking about it again. Mrs. Woolgar looked in on me just before one o'clock.

"Was there a problem this morning?"

"No, not really. Sergeant Hopgood stopped by only to . . . check in." I had no desire to save Dill from looking like Godolphin, but that could wait. "There is something I want to talk with you about. You see, I know more about John now, and I think I can explain what's happened. Would you have time later today? And Mr. Rennie, too—I believe he should hear this." Perhaps I could ask Duncan about what I'd overheard—before I took it to the police.

The secretary fingered the rhinestone brooch on her wide lapel, staring off into the middle distance for a moment. "Yes, all right. I'll check with him and let you know."

"Good, thank you." She left, and I took a deep breath to clear my head of murder. I needed to organize my thoughts in order to tell John's story properly to Mrs. Woolgar. Perhaps I should write it out in Lady Fowling style.

> *She had arrived on the shores of what had been an ancient Celtic civilization, but now bore signs of the tourist industry with a creperie on every corner. The water lapped gently on the side of the boat in which she sat like a thirsty Irish wolfhound, and a rustling in the undergrowth told of secret creatures in the night going about their business of . . . whatever business they had. What adventure awaited her in this new country? Suddenly a nightingale sang. Was she in Berkeley Square? Only time would tell.*

On second thought, I'd better not. No one's prose could hold a candle to Lady Fowling's.

Charles Henry and I left Middlebank at the same moment—not the timing I would've chosen, but I wanted to dash down to the newsagent's for a sandwich and work through lunch, so I steeled myself for an uncomfortable walk.

We hadn't gone far—only to the entrance to Hedgemead Park—when he slowed to a stop, as if the location had given him the cue.

"Ms. Burke, I feel I must address the heart of this matter, speak to the unspoken, so to . . . speak. I hope you don't believe I had anything to do with the murder of this Milo Overton. It's true, I did see him that evening and mistook him for Aubrey, whom I wanted to have a word with to . . . to apologize for my behavior that afternoon. But I realized it wasn't Aubrey, and I left the man alone."

"Thank you for explaining," I said, aiming for an even, non-committal tone. I would not mention I'd overheard his phone conversation. Or that I'd seen the CCTV.

"However, I remain steadfast in my belief that this Aubrey is a menace."

But useful if his death helps you get your hands on the Fowling fortune? He should've quit while he was ahead.

"Mr. Dill, did Lady Fowling give your mother a set of the Flambeaux books?"

"Books? Flambeaux? Like the set in the library? She may have done. Yes, perhaps I do recall she did."

"And so, you must have the books now." It was a statement, not a question. A challenge.

"Do I?" he said quietly, as if asking himself.

"Have you read the François Flambeaux stories I left with Maureen?"

"No, I can't say I have had that pleasure yet."

"They've never been published—not like the full-length novels—but John knows them well. He grew up with them. Did Lady Fowling ever tell you stories during those summer holidays you spent at Middlebank?"

Charles Henry stretched his neck, as if the collar of his shirt were too tight. "She may have, but really, Ms. Burke, what young boy wants to listen to a load of stories about pirates and detectives, eh?"

What young boy wouldn't?

We parted ways at the newsagent, and I returned to Middlebank to eat my ham-and-cheese sandwich while reading Lady Fowling's earliest newsletters, this time carefully combing through member news for a familiar name. I finished lunch with nothing to show for my effort and checked the time. Val and I were meeting at the Minerva for a drink before his evening class. I had just enough time to dash upstairs and change into summer togs.

When I left, I pulled the front door closed and turned to be faced with Jelley, the little owl. It looked as if he'd slept on his feathers wrong. His hair, that is. Bits of it were sticking up here and there, and he had the decided look of yesterday's clothes about him.

"Milo here?" he asked.

"Don't you know?" That was a silly question, because obviously he didn't, but why was it up to me to be the bearer of sad tidings to people I barely knew? "I mean, Milo said he caught you up."

"Yeah, well, that was the other week. I want to know where he is now. He said he'd be round here a fair while."

Just tell him, Hayley. "Don't you know where he was staying?"

Jelley stared at me, blinking slowly behind his glasses. "What's the problem? If he's here, say so. If he's not, tell me where I can find him."

John should be doing this. No, Sergeant Hopgood should. Anyone but me.

"Do you live in Bath?" I asked.

"Why aren't you answering my question?" Jelley said, frowning.

"Do you work with Milo?"

"My business with Milo is my own," he snapped. "He's got something of mine, and I want it back."

At that moment, the Minerva seemed far away, and I wished Val were here. I decided I didn't like Jelley.

"Look, I'm sorry you haven't heard this already"—*and mostly sorry I have to be the one to tell you*—"but Milo is dead."

Jelley blinked. "Dead what? Dead keen on hiding from me?"

"Dead. Actually dead." A thought occurred to me. "The police will want to talk with you."

His head swiveled left and right. "The police?" he repeated. "What for?"

"Milo was murdered, that's why."

"And what's that got to do with me?" Jelley asked.

"You knew him. When did you see him last? You might have some vital piece of information that could help them with their enquiry."

"Bollocks." Jelley turned and walked off.

I followed. "No, really, it's true. Look, ring them, will you? Are you local? Where are you staying?" I trotted after Jelley as he swept down the hill and took a sharp right, crossing the road against traffic. I kept on his heels and heard a car horn. "What's your first name? Do you want to give me your phone number and I'll tell the police?"

He stopped and whirled round so abruptly I knocked into him. We almost toppled over and he grabbed both my arms, squeezing hard. That close, I detected an unwashed odor. Fishy.

"Out of my face!" he shouted.

Two passing women stopped and one of them called, "Oi! Get your hands off her."

Jelley let go and brushed himself off. "Look, this has nothing to do with me, so leave me alone or . . . or I'll phone the police."

He stalked off, and I stayed put, but shouted after him, "Yes, that's the point. Phone the police!"

Tosser.

16

I had a delayed reaction to my encounter with Jelley. After first walking away in indignation, I made it halfway down Milsom Street before I came all over funny. I started to shake. Determined not to swoon in the middle of Bath's crowded shopping district, I edged along to the Minerva and sank into a chair at the end of a table with my back to the wall. I stared out the window, watching every passerby walking up and down Northumberland Place.

When Val entered, I popped up, smiled brightly, and took my bag off the chair I'd been saving. "Hiya," I said. "Lovely day, but did you see those clouds off to the west? It's quite close out there, isn't it? A bit of a change in the weather, don't you think?"

Even I could hear the shrill tone to my voice.

He took my hands and said, "What is it?"

"I'm fine, just a bit"—I patted my chest. "Sorry, I should've ordered for us."

"I'll go," Val said. "You're all right here." He looked round at the pub and back at me. "Aren't you?"

"Oh yes," I said, and requested a half pint of bitter.

When he returned with our drinks and packets of crisps, I told him what had happened, making it to the end of the crisps and my story at the same time.

"Did he threaten you?"

"No, not as such. But he was a bit . . . intimidating."

When I reached for my glass, Val's face darkened. He took hold of my hand and gently pushed up my short sleeve. Bruises had already bloomed where Jelley had caught me.

"You have no idea who this fellow really is and what he might do," Val said, running a finger lightly over the purple marks. "Drink up, we're going to the police."

At the station, the desk sergeant smiled and said, "Detective Sergeant Hopgood is out, but Detective Constable Pye is available. Shall I give him a bell?"

I'm not sure how I got on her good side, but was grateful. Kenny came out, and after I told him what had happened and Val suggested I show my bruises, we were taken back into the inner workings of the station. I described what Jelley looked like to a man at a computer, and the result was an E-FIT graphic of a face.

"They never look much like people," the DC said as he studied the printout, "but this bloke looks like an owl."

"Yes, that's him," I said, adding that he was no taller than I was and rather wiry.

"He's violent," Val said.

"And he knew Milo," I said.

"No first name, no known address, and no idea of his connection to the victim," Kenny said.

"Jelley said Milo had something that belonged to him and he wanted it back," I said. "Maybe finding out Milo's dead set him off."

"Perhaps John knows Jelley," Val said.

"And speaking of Mr. Aubrey," Kenny said. "We've not seen him again, and we do have further questions."

"If it's about Charles Henry's wild tales," I said, "I hope you'll keep in mind the source. I gave Sergeant Hopgood a more accurate account of the conversation John and I had Thursday afternoon. I'm sure you'll hear from John soon." Unless now that Val and I knew the truth about his past, he'd done a bunk

"Right," the DC said. "We'll put the word out about this Jelley. If you see him again, let us know immediately."

"Did you get all Milo's effects from his hotel room?" I asked.

"We did, but there wasn't much. He didn't even have a laptop with him—Aubrey said he used his phone."

As Val and I left the station, he asked, "Look, why don't I walk you back to Middlebank?"

"You have class," I said, "and I'm in no danger. Jelley was upset, but I don't think it had anything to do with me. I thought I might take a stroll along the towpath, just in case John has returned. I've told Mrs. Woolgar that I have news for her, and she's setting something up with Duncan. It's time they knew. But should I ask John before I say anything to them? I wish he'd turn his phone on." I'd tried another text, and now two were sitting there, unsent.

"No more secrets, I'd say. And, if you don't hear from him by tomorrow, phone Dolly."

"And worry her," I said.

V al left, and I started up Manvers to North Parade, where I could walk out and catch the towpath. A text came in, and I almost dropped my phone in the hurry to read it. It was from Mrs. Woolgar— a rare occurrence—telling me that Mr. Rennie wouldn't be free until the evening and would seven o'clock suit me or would this best be done during the business day.

I replied that I would see them both at seven, then checked my stalled messages to John and saw that at last, they'd gone out. While I was looking at the screen, a reply came in.

Bath Marina, Brassmill Lane, slot 37

On my way.

I located Bath Marina on my phone. It lay west of the city center along the river. A long walk or . . . lucky I was so near the coach station. I caught the number 39 bus, got off at the nearest stop, and then became lost in a caravan park, amid swarms of children at play. I couldn't quite get my bearings—where had the river gone?

I spotted the caravan park office and went in. It doubled as the local shop, and a handful of people stood in a queue to buy milk, bread, float toys, and sun hats while the man behind the counter growled into his mobile, "It's clearly posted no tent camping. No, it'll have to wait. Not unless you want to run him off." He tossed his phone down, looked up, and shouted, "Next!" into the face of the man at the head of the queue.

I stood at the back, asking the woman in front of me about narrow boats, but she'd just arrived and had no idea where they were. I waited, and at last my turn came.

"Aren't there narrow boats here?" I asked when I reached the counter.

"Not moored on dry land, there aren't. They're over at the marina." The man directed me farther along the road, where I came upon both the river and the marina, which was like a large, square pond, surrounded by tall trees and shrubby undergrowth. Two rows of boats occupied the center—pulled in at an angle as if they were in a car park. Others lined the edges, and that's where I found *La Mouette 2*, in the dappled shade. John sat in a deck chair at the front of the boat, shoulders sagging. He looked old and sad and, at the same time, young and afraid. When he saw me, he rose and helped me aboard.

"I'm sorry I took so long," I said. "The bus let me off up by the caravan park."

"I thought you and Val might drive out."

"He's in class." It was an awkward moment, and I wasn't quite sure how to get to the point. "You've a nice spot here."

John shrugged. "They let moorage slips by the fortnight, but someone left on Friday before their time was up, and so I've taken the last few days. I must move again on Wednesday. Sit down, please."

We settled in deck chairs and were silent, until John started off.

"Well, Hayley, now you know," he said, looking at his feet. "I am a fraud. Not only a fraud, but a coward, afraid to tell you and Val the truth."

"Nonsense," I said. "On both accounts. First, you aren't a coward. It's only that you were too close to the story to tell it. You were right that it was better to have Dolly explain. She's wonderful, by the way."

There was the dimple. "Dolly is an amazing person. How do you think she looked? Well?"

"Oh yes, quite well. How old is she?"

"Eighty-four," John said. "She enjoyed meeting you and Val. She has many friends to look in on her, but she's always happy to meet new people. Still, I shouldn't've forced her to tell you of my folly. It's only that when I'm living in the stories, I have a job of it to find my way out again."

"And second, I don't believe you're a fraud, either," I said. "It's quite evident that you love and appreciate Lady Fowling as few others can. You've shown us a side of her that no one else has seen—and it only deepens what we know of her generosity of spirit and her sense of adventure. Even though you never met her in person, you are the conduit of those traits. And there's this, John—you knew about Flambeaux's origin before anyone else."

His face lightened. "Did I?"

"Yes. Although the books were published, those stories had lain hidden for decades, and the others—Audrey and Sylvia, Maureen, I daresay Jane Arbuthnot, and Adele—only remembered snatches from when Lady Fowling would regale them over tea."

"And Mrs. Woolgar remembered, too?" John asked.

"Well, apart from Adele, Mrs. Woolgar hasn't known her ladyship as long as the others. The stories have come as a surprise to her, and that's been difficult, because she thought she knew Lady Fowling better than anyone. I believe she felt left out. That's part of the reason she's been a bit . . . standoffish with you."

"Yes, thank you for putting it in such a delicate way."

"To think it all started with Margaret, your grandmother. Lady Fowling must've invented the stories to help her cope with her situation."

"They were both remarkable women in their own way," John said, his eyes shining. "I never met my grandmother, but, growing up, as my mother and I shared the stories, Margaret and Georgiana Fowling seemed to become one person to me. And when my mother died, those thoughts were a great comfort."

"I'm amazed at what a good memory you have for all the details. You were just a boy the last time you heard them."

"I remember my mother telling me, yes," he said, "but I didn't need to have a perfect memory."

At that moment, the sky darkened and a gust of wind whipped through. The flags on the boats snapped, and branches on trees were tossed about. I looked up to see only a patch of blue left.

"Come in," John said. "I will show you how Lady Fowling's stories stayed alive."

We went into the cabin and John raised the seat of the settee and took out a leather satchel so worn it looked like soft suede. "My old school bag," he explained. He unbuckled it and drew out a thick stack of paper—crisp, crackly onionskin. I caught sight of the top page—the print was easy to read, yet a bit fuzzy around each letter.

"François Flambeaux:

How It All Began"

by

Georgiana Fowling

Below her name she had written with a blue fountain pen: *To Margaret with fond memories of Brittany and best wishes to you and little Georgiana*, and under that, an illustration. From a thrifty number of lines sprang the suggestion of a ship half hidden by foliage, and in the sky, simple marks that gave the impression of birds in flight. Gulls.

"Oh my God," I said. "She made carbon copies."

"My mother told me Margaret had cherished them, and so, when my mother died, I made sure to keep them safe."

A different kind of "safe" from the tea chest in the cellar. After the typewritten stories had made it through the rest of Margaret's life and then all of Georgie's abbreviated existence, it had been up to a young boy to keep them from harm. No wonder they looked as if they'd been through the wars—corners curled with age, small tears here and there, and flecks of dirt and tea and who knows what else spattered across the pages. John rubbed his hands on his thighs as he leaned over and watched me sort through. It looked as if every François story was accounted for.

"These were all I had," John said. "And the photographs. I gave those to Dolly."

I thought of the snapshot in John's pocketbook. "The photo you have of Lady Fowling is signed 'Georgiana.' Did that confuse you, because it's your mother's name, too?"

John shook his head. "Not until she died and was buried next to Margaret and I saw her headstone. I had only ever heard her called Georgie. Of course, I grew to know the difference between the two women, but knowing a fact and believing a memory are two different things."

"What about the money, the living Lady Fowling left?"

"Another part of the Aubrey family lore," John said. "Mum thought it had been a vast fortune. I have no idea how much it really was, but enough for my grandmother to live on modestly. There was little left for my mother. That's when Dolly came to our rescue. The story of the money has always been in the back of my mind, and last year, when I became . . . interested in Georgiana Fowling again, I made some enquiries. It took months, but at last I tracked down the account and what was left. But I don't know how or when it began. Has Mr. Rennie picked up the trail?"

"I don't believe so, but now we can tell him what to look for, and that will help. How did you know Duncan's grandfather's name?"

"The firm's website has a fine history of the Rennie family. Tea?" John asked.

Over our mugs and jammy dodgers, I asked, "You know that Sergeant Hopgood has been trying to reach you?"

"Yes, messages received—all of them. Now that I am settled here for the next few days, I will see him first thing in the morning. I've told him Milo had some business that evening, but I don't know what it was. Is there a breakthrough in the enquiry?"

"No, not really." I broke my biscuit in half and didn't look at him. "You told the police where you were the evening Milo was killed."

"Yes, I did."

I continued to break up my biscuit, getting jam on my fingers, not meeting John's eye.

"Are you asking me where I was, Hayley?" John asked.

I looked up. "Yes."

He gave a humorless laugh. "It's no surprise that you would—not after the way I've treated you. I was here on *La Mouette 2* all that evening until quite late. Well, not here, but over along the towpath near the Sydney Wharf Bridge."

"Was someone with you?"

"I didn't kill Milo."

"I know that, but now there's been more annoyance. Last Thursday, when I told you about getting Milo's letter, Charles Henry was lurking on the towpath. The next day he went to the police saying you had admitted to threatening Milo."

"He what?"

"Don't try to understand it," I said. "Today, he added onto his tale by saying he heard you threaten me as well. That seemed to have slipped his mind on Friday."

"Ah," John said, sounding exasperated, "doesn't he know he's making himself out a fool?"

"He is, isn't he?" I replied. "If he wore a wig, I would tell him he'd better watch out."

John burst out laughing. "Good thing he doesn't wear one, or I would be sorely tempted to take it from him."

I saw Charles Henry's actions in their proper light now—even the sketchy details from the phone conversation. "He's oblivious to what he's doing, but I believe Sergeant Hopgood and Kenny both have the measure of the man. Still, they do want to talk with you again."

"And I with them," John said, "because I have something that may be of interest."

"What is it?"

"Milo kept his schedule on his phone, but his phone is gone."

"Yes."

"I didn't know all of his business. When we met, he was a consul-
tant in human resources at the Plymouth factory where I brought
my idea for the scooters. He gave that up when I hired him."

"To be your ballast," I said.

John nodded. "As well as doing a bit of business for me."

"Yes, your ballast and your William."

John smiled. "You must explain to me who this William is. You've
mentioned him before."

"He's a character in . . . oh, another time."

"Right, well, you see, when I decided to come to Bath, it was to
see Middlebank and be near the people who knew my . . . Lady
Fowling, but also because I have an idea about washing-powder dis-
pensers at launderettes, and there is a local company I wanted to
talk with."

There it was again, fantasy and reality—if John could keep the
right mix, it wouldn't be a bad way to live. But who would be his
ballast now that Milo was gone?

"Milo continued to see many of his clients privately," John said.
"In case we needed to coordinate our time, he texted me a link to
his calendar. I never looked at it—I hadn't needed to—and only just
remembered." John picked up his phone. "Would you like to see?"

"Oh yes. Have you already found something?"

"Unfortunately, nothing I can interpret. Look here, you see Milo
indicated appointments by using his clients' initials, not full names.
Even when you tap through to the contact, there is limited personal
information. Therapists must be careful about that."

"Therapists?" I asked.

"His profession. He was a mental health therapist. He talked
about the delicate balance—to be on an intimate level with your

client and yet not personally involved." John held out the phone. "Here."

We scanned through the calendar. The week before John had arrived at Middlebank, Milo's days were sprinkled with initials: MT, AR, TWS, GA.

"Do you recognize any?" I asked.

"No, but certainly the police can go further with this. It could lead to a break in the enquiry."

It seemed a faint hope.

"What business did he have that evening?" I asked.

"Ah, you see, there is an asterisk on that day." John tapped the symbol, and it led to a screen that read *Delusion and Transference*. But it was a link that wouldn't go anywhere. "That one isn't my file," John said with chagrin. "Milo was writing a paper about me he titled 'Trauma and Recovery in the Young Mind.'"

"You do have an unusual history," I said, "and you have coped remarkably well. In your own way."

John laughed. "I admit your caveat is necessary."

"You never know—the police may find something of interest from the calendar, so well done, you. Now, I must be off, because . . . because I'm going to talk with Mrs. Woolgar and Mr. Rennie. I said I would tell them what Dolly told us about you. Is that all right? Would you rather I say nothing? It's only that she—"

"Please," John broke in. "Please, tell her. Tell them both. Tell everyone. I will apologize to Mrs. Woolgar in person, although I don't know how she could ever forgive me for such deception. I'm sorry to you, too, Hayley. Last year when Dolly fell ill, my mind became a jumble. I was with her every day through her treatment, and it was a success, but I couldn't get myself back on track after that. And then those thoughts of Georgiana returned. I imagined that I would find a sort of family here—that Dolly and I would have more than just the two of us."

"Whatever Mrs. Woolgar's reaction, I believe you can count on support from Adele, Val, and me. Certainly the Moons."

I rose to leave, but when John opened the cabin door, a gust of wind slapped us in the face.

"I'll phone for a taxi," John said.

"No, I'll be fine. It isn't raining yet, and the same bus I came out on will take me almost directly to Middlebank." I checked my phone. "And the next one is in ten minutes."

John walked me up to the bus stop. The ponderous, slate-gray clouds had turned the late afternoon to evening, and the wind whipped flags and caught my shirt, making it billow out like a sail. When we passed by the river, I could see across to the other bank, where the trees danced and a blue tarpaulin flapped.

The number 39 came into view just as something occurred to me.

"John, do you know a man named Jelley? He wears glasses and looks like an owl."

He frowned. "A man who looks like an owl?"

That did sound a bit daft. "It's his eyes. And he blinks slowly."

"No."

"He stopped by Middlebank asking for Milo before I knew who Milo was. They had some sort of business to settle, I think. He turned up again today looking for Milo."

"He didn't know?"

"Apparently not. He became upset—angry, really—when I told him Milo was dead. I've let the police know about him. Which reminds me," I said, boarding the bus and turning back. "First thing tomorrow, what are you doing?"

He stared up the road and didn't answer.

"John?"

"Yes, tomorrow I will ring Sergeant Hopgood."

As the doors closed, there was a flash in the sky followed close on by a sharp *crack* of thunder. The clouds ripped open, and the rain came bucketing down. I waved at John as he dashed off, then I found a seat, and spent the return journey gazing out the window, seeing nothing as the rain continued to come down in sheets. When I got off at the stop nearest Middlebank, I fought my way against a head wind, and although it took me less than a minute to reach the door, I was soaked through. Inside, I stood for a moment, dripping on the entry flagstone.

Quarter to seven. I ran up to my flat, changed, towel-dried my hair, and made it back as I heard voices coming up from the lower ground floor.

"Ah, Ms. Burke."

Mr. Rennie still wore his three-piece pin-striped gray suit, and Mrs. Woolgar, the same dress she'd had on during the day—a peach-colored frock with a narrow skirt and a pleated bodice in contrasting thread. This marked the occasion as still work related. I had changed into denims and a long-sleeved loose shirt and left my hair down.

"Good evening," I said. "Shall we go in my office?"

Mr. Rennie stepped back to allow Mrs. Woolgar in before him and then held up a bottle of wine.

"I thought, as it was evening, we might want a glass of something."

I caught sight of the label—a very good bottle of claret, which I recognized only because I'd seen it on the eye-level shelf at Wait-rose. That is, the higher-priced bottles. Who did Duncan think needed it more, me or Mrs. Woolgar? Regardless, it would make a nice change from my usual plonk.

"Lovely, thank you."

Duncan went into the kitchenette to open the bottle, and I shifted the third wingback chair over to the fireplace while Mrs. Woolgar held Bunter, who had been disturbed from his early-evening nap in the move. When she put him on the floor, he promptly jumped up on my desk and sat on my closed laptop.

We settled with glasses in hand and began with a minor exchange about the weather—"summer rain," "fresher air," "short sharp showers," and the like. If I hadn't had a story to tell—a case to present—then I would've quite enjoyed it. I wasn't often in a social situation with Mrs. Woolgar, and perhaps with a glass of wine in her, she might've let her guard down and told me about her childhood or her family or . . . but it was not to be. Not this evening.

"Before you begin, Ms. Burke," Duncan said, "There is something you should know. I had a talk this afternoon with a solicitor friend who specializes in estate law. He'd had a phone call from—"

"Charles Henry," I said.

"Yes, that's right."

"I happened to overhear him this morning talking with a Mr. Yoxford. It was when I took his tea up to the library. I didn't hear any details."

"The details are sordid," Duncan replied. "At least on first hearing. Mr. Dill wanted to consult Yoxford on what he called a 'hypothetical situation.' He wanted to know that if a direct descendant were found—one unnamed and unknown when the will was read—would he be considered a beneficiary. If so, and in the event of his death, could another relative inherit."

When Duncan laid it out, it sent a shudder down my spine. "He wants to know that if it turns out John is Lady Fowling's grandson, can he benefit from the Fowling estate, and could Charles Henry then benefit if John dies. That's despicable," I said.

"It is. And poorly thought out. Yoxford recognized it for what it was—fishing. He wasn't breaking client confidentiality by telling me. Dill didn't want to pay for legal services, he only wanted free advice."

"Despicable and so like him," I said. "Should we tell the police? Does it sound like evidence?"

"I'd say we have no choice."

"Good, then, yes, we will. Thank you, Mr. Rennie."

Mrs. Woolgar had remained quiet during this exchange, but now spoke up.

"Ms. Burke—about Mr. Aubrey?"

I took a sip of my wine. "Over the weekend, Val and I went to visit the woman who had brought John up. She lives in Charmouth, not far from Lyme Regis."

"A relative?"

"A distant relation through her late husband," I replied. "John would've told us this himself eventually, but he felt it would be better coming from Dolly. That's her name, Dolly Beckwith. She's a lovely woman and thinks the world of John."

The secretary's face remained in neutral. Duncan smiled encouragingly.

"Of course you were right, Mrs. Woolgar, about John's

grandmother—she wasn't Lady Fowling. But her ladyship had a great influence on his real grandmother's life and, naturally, his. I believe that what happened is another example of what a kind and generous woman she was."

Never hurts to butter up the listener first. Noting the approving but wary look on the secretary's face, I then proceeded to tell the story in as simple and clear a way as I could. I began with Margaret Aubrey living in Brittany, and her friendship with a kind English-woman at a difficult time in both their lives. I went through Margaret's return to Dorset and leapt over the years to the moment Georgie and John—not even out of nappies—moved in with Dolly. Then I rushed forward to the day Georgie died, still a young woman, leaving behind a little boy with nothing but stories and dreams and a fictional world that he was all too eager to live within.

"Through all these years, the François stories have been precious to him, and so, how could he not carry a deep love and admiration for Lady Fowling even though, of course, he may not have shown that in an appropriate manner. But it's as Dolly said, we don't all fit into this life the same way. And so, I realize he's wasted a great deal of our time, and has caused unnecessary upheaval in everyone's life . . ."

Mrs. Woolgar said nothing and Duncan looked down into his glass.

This would not do.

"No," I said, "that isn't right. John hasn't wasted anyone's time."

Both heads snapped to attention.

"And just how terrible was this upheaval?" I asked. "Because of him, we've discovered Lady Fowling's early writings, the origins of

Flambeaux. We now have a collection of short stories that could be published. Audrey and Sylvia Moon, as well as Adele, Maureen Frost, and, you, too, Mrs. Woolgar, have spent time recalling your friendship with Lady Fowling and how much she meant to you. We've learned more about her ladyship's generous spirit, and I don't see why we shouldn't be thanking John for what he's done. Even if it did start out in an . . . unusual manner."

The silence reverberated in my ears. I took a gulp of wine, holding the glass in both hands. Mrs. Woolgar stared into the cold fireplace, her face revealing nothing. At last, she cleared her throat and looked to Duncan. I gripped the arms of the chair.

"Well, Ms. Burke," the secretary said. She took off her glasses and pinched the bridge of her nose. She reached for her wine and, holding it by the stem, took a sip. If she didn't continue, I would go mad. After what seemed like forever, she sighed.

"Even before your explanation, I had given the situation a great deal of thought. I saw that others, although skeptical of John Aubrey's tale, were not nearly as incensed as I. Why was that? I asked myself. At last, I came to realize that it was my own bias that kept me from looking beyond his eccentricities to see the situation for what it was."

She took another sip and I a gulp.

"But my mind was closed," she said. "That's because, when he arrived at Middlebank"—she frowned slightly—"I seemed to recognize something in him. Something of her. And it frightened me. I thought, what if what he was saying were true. I felt if that were so, then our memories would be tainted. I should've realized that even if his story had been based in fact, it wouldn't change the person Lady Fowling had been. Not at her core. But instead, I disregarded his guileless demeanor and thought only of myself. You are correct—we owe John Aubrey our gratitude, but I owe him an apology."

This is what I wanted from Mrs. Woolgar—to get to know and understand her better. Still, I found myself at sea for a response.

Duncan came to our rescue. He put a hand over Mrs. Woolgar's and said to me, "Well, then, the 'living' wasn't John's imagining. I'll have someone pull out the Fowling ledgers from the fifties and search for Margaret Aubrey's name. I'm sure we'll find the original arrangements. Another story for the Fowling legacy, isn't it? More wine?"

With our glasses refilled, I felt at ease. Warm and cozy. And hungry. Had I eaten lunch? Val would arrive in an hour or so, and I had a Waitrose ready meal for us—chicken tikka masala.

In the meantime, we continued with small talk. That is, Mrs. Woolgar talked. She asked about Dolly and about John's ideas. She spoke of the dangers of Dorset cliffs. She recalled a fancy dress party for which her ladyship dressed as a pirate.

"It seemed an odd decision at the time, but now, of course, I see she was demonstrating her ties to Flambeaux's past."

The fictional pirate, Lady Fowling's second love. That thought sparked another: Had there been a living inspiration for François Flambeaux? It didn't seem an unreasonable idea. Who's to say Georgiana Fowling hadn't fallen in love during that short time in Brittany all those years ago? There could've been a man and a brief but intense relationship. Her offspring from it might not have been a child, but it could've been the pirate turned detective of her dreams. My thoughts drifted across the Channel to a hidden creek, a ship, and the moaning of—

My phone rang and I jumped, splashing precious drops of claret

onto my denims. Bunter sprang off my desk and took shelter behind
the coal bucket, shaking himself in indignation. I didn't recognize
the number.

"Hello?"

"Hayley, it's John. You arrived at Middlebank safely?"

"I did, yes." I could hear odd noises in the background—a beep-
ing and the tinny announcement over a speaker system. "John,
where are you?"

"Nothing to worry about, Hayley, but I am in hospital."

17

Hospital?" I exclaimed, and both Mrs. Woolgar and Duncan looked up. "What's happened?"

"After you left, I was returning to my boat in the rain and wind. Someone came from behind with a knife."

"You were stabbed?"

I heard a gasp from Mrs. Woolgar.

"The wound is not bad, although I suffered a hairline fracture of my collarbone in the fall. Still, I believe they will let me go before long." I heard a woman's voice, but couldn't distinguish the words. "Or perhaps," John said, "in the morning."

"Did you ring the police?"

"Yes. Sergeant Hopgood is on his way."

"So am I."

I ended the call and described the situation as I put my phone down, picked it up, looked for my bag, and remembered it was upstairs in my flat. "I'll ring for a taxi and then let Val know—he can meet me there."

"I'll give you a lift," Duncan said.

"Thank you, but I wouldn't want to disrupt your evening."

"Let Duncan do this," Mrs. Woolgar said, standing. "Is it serious?"

"No, he said not."

Not one of us spoke the obvious—a knife in the dark sounded too familiar.

I ran up to get my bag, and when I arrived back in the entry, Duncan and Mrs. Woolgar were waiting. The secretary opened the front door and said, "Please tell John that . . . tell him I'd like to talk with him. As soon as he feels able."

At the hospital, I tried A&E and was told John had been moved into a ward. I found the floor, and as the doors of my lift opened, I caught sight of a familiar figure stepping into the next one. I jumped out, but the doors had glided closed and a nurse came up and said, "It's a bit late for a visit."

"Hasn't Detective Sergeant Hopgood arrived?" I asked in an officious tone. "I thought he'd make it here before me."

"Oh yes, it's about Mr. Aubrey. He's in the ward just there," she said, nodding to a door past the nurses' station.

"Yes, thanks," I said, "I'd better let the DS know I'm here."

I confess to a tiny thrill at my ability to talk my way in after visiting hours as if I were a police officer myself. But as I marched off, the nurse said, "You are Hayley Burke, is that right?"

"Oh, yes"—I began fumbling in my bag—"do you need to see . . ."

"No, that's all right. Go along. They're expecting you."

John was in a ward with six beds, all occupied. The other men looked up at me when I entered, but then returned to their magazines. Sergeant Hopgood stood at John's bedside. The patient looked wan and had his left arm in a sling secured to his chest. But he smiled.

"Hayley, you see I am fine. You didn't need to come, I only wanted to make certain you were all right."

"And I you," I said.

"Ms. Burke," the DS said, "you save me from calling on you tomorrow. Mr. Aubrey tells me he walked you to the bus stop just before his attack. Did you notice anything or anyone along the way that gave you pause?"

I frowned in thought. I recalled the wind through the trees sounding as loud as surf and the flags dancing. People had dashed out of boats to retrieve washing hung out to dry or to secure chairs and tables. The ripples on the river. The snap of the blue tarpaulin.

I shrugged. "Nothing of note. Sorry. John, are you in pain?"

John shook his head. "No, the doctor has seen to that."

"Where were you stabbed?"

"In the back of my shoulder on the right," John said, cocking his head to one side to indicate. "Not deep."

"Someone came from behind?" I asked.

"Yes. I saw nothing," John said. "He knifed me. When I threw him off, he pushed me hard, and I put my left arm out to stop my fall, resulting in the collarbone injury. There were many people nearby who came to my assistance, but it was darker than it should've been at that time of day, and with the heavy rain, my assailant disappeared into the undergrowth."

"Pye is at the scene taking statements," Hopgood said.

"Do you have a description?" I asked.

John sighed, but Hopgood answered. "A large person. Round."

We were quiet for a moment. "There'll be CCTV, won't there?" I asked.

"Being gathered. Well, Mr. Aubrey, stop in tomorrow and we'll take a look at your phone and see if there's anything from Mr. Overton's calendar that might be of use."

As Hopgood left, I saw Val coming. The two men stood in the corridor talking for a moment.

"I'll be right back," I said to John and went out. "Sergeant Hopgood, may I ask you something?"

"I'll go check on the patient," Val said and went into the ward.

Hopgood waited, his eyebrows migrating upward slightly.

"Is John in danger?" I asked.

"Well, Ms. Burke, a murder followed by the same sort of attack would seem to confirm that John Aubrey was the intended victim all along. Milo Overton was mistaken for him, and now the killer has tried for Aubrey again."

"'Would seem to confirm'? That doesn't sound like you're entirely sold on the idea."

"We keep our options open," the DS said.

"Sergeant, I have other news for you."

The caterpillars rose to attention. I gave a brief account of Charles Henry's renewed interest in estate law.

"He was asking about inheritence by a direct descendant," Hopgood repeated. "And if another relative could then inherit in the case of . . ."

He left that sentence dangling long enough for me to pick it up.

"You want to know whether I heard Charles Henry ask about the death of the direct descendant. If he died, would the next blood relative inherit. No, I didn't hear that." And at that moment I couldn't decide if I was relieved or disappointed. "Mr. Rennie can tell you more."

"I'll be happy to listen," Hopgood said. "Have a good evening, Ms. Burke."

I returned to the ward to find John and Val deep in discussion about narrow boats.

"You see, Val," John was saying, "I'm on the river at the marina, but I prefer the canal. Easier boating without strong currents or such fluctuating water levels."

"Ahoy, there," I said. "Do you need us to fetch anything for you? Fresh clothes in the morning?"

"Thank you, but no, I have made arrangements."

"Have you now?" I asked in an offhanded manner. "Is Frances bringing them by?"

Val did a double take, and John cut his eyes at me as the dimple surfaced. "Ah, Hayley, you are the true detective here."

"No, I'm a woman. Plus, I saw her getting on a lift when I arrived. How long has this been going on?"

"For me, since the morning I first met her at Middlebank," John said, resting his head back on his pillows. "From that moment, I could sense in Frances a depth, a capacity for emotion as well as a desire to—" He stopped. "Then came the afternoon Charles Henry punched me. She came to my aid, a kind and immediate action of help. I was sorry she left before I did, but when I walked out, I saw her at the corner. We said hello. We went for coffee. We had dinner. We sat on the deck of *La Mouette 2* and talked for hours."

"That's quick work," Val said.

John held up a forefinger. "Only talked."

But I added what he hadn't said. *Only talked—that first evening.*

"In the days since then, I have found strength in Frances. I had the courage to tell her what you have learned from Dolly. It was a risky endeavor, but she listened and has not run away. As you might both imagine"—his face, at first pale, now warmed—"I've not been lucky in love. Most women find me too much work. But Dolly has always believed that one would come along and that we would be the right fit. Like a puzzle. I have hopes."

"Frances has kept this quiet," Val said. "She stopped in to see me earlier today to talk about her project on the paperback-book covers and never said a word about you."

"Frances is a private person," John said. "I accept this."

"But she could confirm your alibi for the night of the murder," Val said.

"I don't need an alibi, Val. I didn't kill Milo."

"Here, now," a sharp but quiet voice said. We all three looked to see a nurse standing in the doorway with hands on her hips. "That detective sergeant left. You two need to be on your way. It's late, and my patient needs his rest."

"One more thing, John," I said as Val and I made the motions of leaving, "Mrs. Woolgar would like to talk with you."

John looked wary. "Am I banished from Middlebank?"

"Not a bit of it. In fact, if you're feeling up to it, perhaps you'll stop by tomorrow." The nurse had remained in the doorway. "That's us away."

Val and I paused in the car park. The rain and the clouds had cleared, and the air smelled fresh. I took a deep breath. It would be a lovely cool night.

"So," Val said, "are police now certain that Milo's murder was a case of mistaken identity? That John was the target?"

"Seems so, doesn't it, although Sergeant Hopgood wouldn't say for certain. I forgot to ask if John was attacked with the same sort of knife that killed Milo. He's got off lucky, didn't he? Considering." Under my breath, I added, "Attacked by a large round person."

"It all keeps coming back to Charles Henry."

I filled him in on the latest. "It's looking bad, isn't it? But he probably has Maureen as an alibi."

Val paused with his hand on the car door. "But how would Charles Henry have known where John had moored?"

Tuesday morning, Val and I sat in my flat over tea and toast and did not talk of murder. Instead, we focused on our upcoming holiday.

"Have you decided which seaside it'll be?" he asked.

"Mmm," I replied. "The possibilites are nearly endless. But re-member, I'm planning this one. You'll need only to be packed and ready to leave on—my God, that's next week. I can't believe it's al-most August."

"I wonder, will they find Milo's murderer before the end of the summer?" Val asked.

I reached for the marmalade. "They've got no weapon, no finger-prints, no blood on Charles Henry's suit—which actually doesn't prove anything one way or another, because there was barely any blood from the wound."

"They know little else after the attack on John last night," Val said.

"This is where I am happy to leave it to the police."

We went downstairs just before nine and I kissed Val good-bye.

"How many coaching sessions do you have today?" I asked.

"Six writers—two noir, three traditional, one police procedural. And your day?"

"It might very well come down to it that I do my proper job today. I need to finish the newsletter, and we've received a proposal from a women's fiction society in Canada to collaborate on a paper about the influence of gender on genre. But first"—I heard footsteps on the stairs coming from the lower ground floor—"the morning briefing."

Val and the secretary exchanged "good mornings" and he went on his way. I followed Mrs. Woolgar into her office. Before she even switched on her computer, she asked, "How is John?"

It wasn't the sort of start to our meeting that I could've predicted three days ago.

"A small wound in his right shoulder, but he has a hairline fracture in his collarbone on the left side, so his arm's taped up to keep him immobile."

"Dreadful. How did it happen?"

"The storm had just whipped up and with the wind and rain, visibility was poor. Someone came at John from behind. Witnesses reported seeing someone large . . . and round."

Without the glare from the computer screen on her glasses, I could see the secretary's eyes widen.

"Charles Henry can be an unpleasant sort," she said, "and I would never defend him . . ." The pause told me she recalled doing just that and quite recently. She had the good grace to blush.

"I'm sure he can account for himself," I said. "Maureen will corroborate his alibi. If they even ask."

"Maureen." Mrs. Woolgar put a hand on her phone and then took it away. "Maureen is in London. She left yesterday morning and won't return until tomorrow."

The silence that ensued spoke more than words could say.

"Mrs. Woolgar, about the board members."

"Yes, we should explain to them about John and find a way to welcome him. Jane is still away, but I'll ring her."

"I'm happy to talk with the Moons and Adele."

"And so that leaves Maureen to me," Mrs. Woolgar said.

"Well, only if you think that would be . . ." *Yes, please.*

"How was your coffee with her last week?"

I remembered a dusting of red macaron on a white sofa and Maureen's story of her unhappy marriage. "It was good of her to explain to me about how she and Charles Henry had met and how he had helped her. I don't think he's evil, Mrs. Woolgar, I've never said that." I might've, but I'd meant it in an offhanded way. "But he tries my patience, that's for certain, and the way he talks about Lady Fowling is so mercenary."

"Too right," Mrs. Woolgar said with heat. "His own mother brought him up to equate love with things, possessions, money. Her ladyship tried to counteract that on his summer holidays here, but I believe it was an uphill battle. Still, I do try to remind myself not to blame him. Entirely."

A giggle escaped before I could stop it, and Mrs. Woolgar smiled. She smiled!

"I'll ring the Moons and ask if I can stop by later." I had phoned

Adele and brought her up-to-date after Val and I returned from the hospital. "Oh, and I told John you would like to talk with him. He's with the police this morning—he may have information on Milo they can use—but after that, I daresay we'll see him. And so, before I get to work, why don't I nip down to the bakery."

T o the Bertinet and back took no time. Bunter greeted me upon my return, giving the pink bakery box a careful sniff, before trotting halfway up the stairs. There he paused with one paw in the air. Voices drifted down from the library—not raised voices, but in conversation.

As I went up, I heard Mrs. Woolgar say, "She was a bit of a rebel, no one can deny it. She and your grandmother must've recognized that in each other."

I stood for a moment in the doorway to take in the cozy scene—the secretary and John in wingback chairs near the fireplace, both leaning forward slightly, tête-à-tête. When he noticed me, John stood. He still had his left arm strapped to his chest, but he'd regained color in his face and the dimple was in fine form.

"Sorry to disturb the two of you," I said.

"Hello, Hayley," he said. "Mrs. Woolgar has been kind enough to share her memories of Lady Fowling with me this morning."

"Won't you join us, Ms. Burke?"

"I will, thank you. First, I'll go make us coffee. You two carry on."

When I returned with the tray, Mrs. Woolgar said, "Shall we sit at the table? Won't it be easier with your arm, John?"

I served as the two of them continued their discussion.

"How kind of Margaret to have named her daughter after her

ladyship," Mrs. Woolgar said. "We must find a way to honor their lives."

As they chatted, Mrs. Woolgar came up with anecdotes about Lady Fowling, and John compared François short stories, recounting a few of his favorite parts. They both commented on the ingenious clue of how many pins François found in "Watches and Waits" and chuckled about what the adder packed to go on holiday. I was more than happy to be the fifth wheel. I topped up coffee, offered a second pass at the pastries, and only when it seemed things were winding down did I ask John if he had seen the leather-bound Flambeaux books before now.

"No, we had no books," he said sadly. "But to see them here on the shelf was a thrill. That first afternoon, I looked at *Flambeaux and the Painted Night,* and it was familiar to me because of the story 'François Paints the Night.'" He turned to Mrs. Woolgar. "But the stories have never been published? That's a shame."

Now that I thought about it, it made sense he'd never seen the books. By the time Lady Fowling had them published, Margaret had died and Georgie, although cherishing the stories of the past, had no contact with her namesake. That other set of books must've gone to Charles Henry's mother after all. Even if he didn't remember.

John insisted on helping to carry the coffee things down to the kitchenette, so I gave him the cafetière, empty apart from the layer of sludge at the bottom.

In the front entry, he said, "I thank you both—Hayley, for not turfing me out that first day, and you, Mrs. Woolgar, for such compassionate understanding."

The secretary seemed to quiver, and I wasn't entirely sure she could answer, so I jumped in.

"You're-very welcome, John. We're happy you found us. I'm sure you'll stop in for tomorrow's afternoon open."

I closed the door and turned back to Mrs. Woolgar. I could see the color in her cheeks.

"What a remarkable young man," she said.

"Did he tell you about his ideas?" I asked.

"The kitchen cupboards," she said. "And he said he has an idea about the conveyor belt at the grocery till—how to keep the eggs from tumbling along and the apples from bruising. Imagine coming up with such useful inspiration."

"Well." I sighed. "Here's to a quiet rest of the day."

"Gracious," Mrs. Woolgar said, "with all that's gone on, Ms. Burke, I've forgotten about your visitor yesterday."

Not Jelley, I hoped. "Who was it?"

"She wouldn't give her name, but I recognized her because she's come to two of the afternoon opens. Thin woman, with streaks of blond in her hair and such heavy mascara and black kohl round her eyes I wonder how she can see."

"Celia," I said. "She's quite a fan of the Golden Age of Mystery writers, and she's here in Bath for a while. I saw her last week. Monday, I believe. She seems a bit lonely at the moment—quite friendly, but at the same time . . ."

"On edge?" Mrs. Woolgar offered.

What a relief to spend the rest of the morning at my desk. I read a few recent blog posts from a book conservator at the British Library and then picked up "François and the Purloined Peacock." I hadn't finished that one and so began where I'd stopped and made it to the end, laughing aloud at the last line. A peacock and a vicar, indeed.

I thought I might as well continue. Next in the stack was "François and Evil on a Moonless Night." I remembered Sylvia and Audrey shuddering over the title, as they recalled Lady Fowling telling the story at afternoon tea in the Royal Crescent. I passed it over and picked up "François and the Adder's Holiday."

At the end, when the adder's shed skin had been retrieved and presented to Flambeaux as a token of appreciation, I heard a sound behind me. Bunter. By chance or by design, a catnip mouse had worked its way behind a stack of cartons that contained . . . really, I needed to clean out my office.

"You, cat," I said. "Lunch."

I gave Bunter some tuna concoction and he tucked in, and I retreated from the fishy kitchenette to my flat.

Later, I carried the last of my grapes downstairs and set them on my desk. Mrs. Woolgar was back in her office, and we both settled into our usual routine of working separately. I shifted the rest of the François stories to the wingback chair by the door and reread the proposal from the Canadian writers organization. I had started to formulate a reply when the front-door buzzer went off.

I went out to the entry, saying, "I'll get this," as I passed Mrs. Woolgar's office.

Charles Henry Dill waited on the doorstep. He had gone back to baby-blue linen, had his leather satchel slung across his body, and held his Panama hat in front of him, fingering the brim.

"Good afternoon, Ms. Burke."

How was I to treat this? Had the police questioned him about his phone call to the estate law solicitor? Or the attack on John yesterday? If he had attacked John, why was he free? Specifically, why was he free and here at Middlebank?

"Good afternoon, Mr. Dill. Do come in."

He took two steps in and stopped, as if playing chess on the flagstones, and began what sounded like a rehearsed speech. "You are no doubt wondering why I have appeared at your door on a Tuesday afternoon. It's because I'm eager to continue with my indexing project, and I feel that too many distractions yesterday morning kept me from my work. So if you'll allow me my little corner of the table in the library, you won't hear a peep out of me for the next couple of hours."

Coming from anyone else, I would accept this statement at face value and be glad for the person's work ethic. Why was I so suspicious of Charles Henry? Had my bias at how he thought of the Fowling estate as rightfully his colored my entire view of the man? I should give him his chance to shine, even if it was only in working up an index for the newsletters.

"What a fine idea," I said. "Yes, go right up and get to work. I'll be in my office if you have any questions."

As he marched up the stairs, I looked in on Mrs. Woolgar and shrugged.

I wasn't in my office long. About twenty minutes later, the front door buzzed. I went out again and noticed Mrs. Woolgar's door closed. Perhaps she was making her calls to Jane Arbuthnot and Maureen Frost.

Detective Sergeant Hopgood and Detective Constable Pye stood waiting on the doorstep and, behind them parked at the curb, a police car with two uniforms inside. My stomach clenched, forming a solid mass of excitement, panic, and fear. Something had broken—the enquiry into Milo's murder or John's attack? Or both?

"What's happened?" I asked as I opened the door wide, and they stepped in. "I mean, hello, good afternoon."

"Good afternoon, Ms. Burke," Hopgood said, keeping his voice low. He looked round and glanced at the secretary's door. "As you know, we didn't find Mr. Overton's mobile at the murder scene, and our attempts at tracking it down have failed, whether because it had been destroyed or switched off, we weren't sure. But we have continued to try the number, and, an hour ago, it was switched back on."

"You've found it?"

"Not quite," Kenny said. "The locator doesn't pinpoint the phone exactly, but it gives us a reasonably sized area to search. It showed this terrace and the other side of the road. Middlebank seemed the likeliest place to start."

"Pye," Hopgood said, "give it a go."

Kenny pulled his mobile out and tapped in a number. From upstairs in the library, I heard a phone ring.

18

❧❀❧

DC Pye and DS Hopgood turned to me as the phone in the library—Milo's phone—continued to ring.

"Is someone up there?" the sergeant asked quietly.

"Charles Henry," I mouthed.

DC Pye ran up the stairs without a sound. Sergeant Hopgood turned to me before following and said, "Stay here."

Stay here? Not likely. I went after them and made it to the landing as the detectives stopped in the doorway to the library. I peered over their shoulders at Charles Henry, sitting at the end of the table in front of his laptop. He had a puzzled expression on his face as he looked from the silent mobile in his hand to his satchel—still ringing—and then to us.

Pye walked in slowly. "Mr. Dill, is that your mobile ringing?"

"No," Charles Henry said, frowning. He held up his hand. "This is mine."

Sergeant Hopgood went up to the table. "Would you turn out your bag for us, sir?" he asked.

The phone ceased, but the ringing seemed to echo round the library. Without asking why, Charles Henry picked up his satchel by the bottom. Out tumbled its contents—a folded newspaper, wallet, various papers including a playbill, several pens, a packet of chewing gum, and crumbs. Then, out of a side pocket, slid a mobile phone, its screen illuminated with a notification: Missed Call.

Charles Henry leapt up and sprang away, knocking into a shelf. "Where did that come from?" he asked, pointing at the phone.

"Indeed, Mr. Dill, I was about to ask you the same thing," Hopgood said.

"It isn't mine."

"No, it isn't—this mobile belonged to Milo Overton."

"Who?" Charles Henry asked indignantly. Then he twigged it. "What? No! That can't be."

He reached forward as if to take it, but the DC put a hand out. "Leave it!" From the pocket of his jacket, Pye brought out thin latex gloves. He pulled them on and took a plastic bag, picked up Milo's phone, and dropped it in. Charles Henry watched in horror.

"This is impossible," he said. "Why would it be in my bag?"

"You've never seen this phone before?" Hopgood asked.

"I have not."

"Where have you been this morning, Mr. Dill? What time did you leave your flat?"

"I . . . well, er . . ." Charles Henry screwed up his face, looked at his watch, and glanced at the floor, then the ceiling. "I left just after one, I suppose, and went for lunch at that Italian place near the theater."

"Did you talk with anyone while you were at lunch?" Pye asked.

"No. That is, I spoke to the server."

"Was the place crowded?"

"It was lunch," Charles Henry said. "There was a queue to be seated."

"How many people in the queue?" Hopgood asked.

"I didn't count!" The police said nothing, and Charles Henry took a sharp breath. "There were several groups ahead of me when I arrived, and a few people came up behind me. It got quite crowded then, or must've, because the fellow behind stood too close and I bumped into him when I turned."

"What did he look like, the man who stood close?" Hopgood asked.

"Yes, that's it!" Charles Henry said, hope in his voice. "He could've planted this on me."

"What did he look like, Mr. Dill?"

Charles Henry waved his arms in the air as if trying to re-create the fellow, but then gave up and shrugged.

"Do you recall his face?"

"I don't think I looked at his face."

"One more thing, Mr. Dill," Kenny said. "Where were you late yesterday afternoon?"

"Yesterday? But the murder was . . ." Charles Henry scowled. "Hang on, what am I being shopped for?"

"Who would want to fit you up for murder, Mr. Dill? Or for assault with a deadly weapon?"

He paled at the accusation. "Assault? What's happened?"

"There's been another knife attack, sir," Pye said. "Again, where were you yesterday late afternoon?"

"I daresay you'll be asking Mr. John Aubrey this same question?"

"Oh, we know where he was," Hopgood replied, "because he was the victim."

Charles Henry sank into the chair and held on to the table with both hands.

"He isn't . . . is he all right?"

"Yes. Once again, Mr. Dill, where were you?"

"Yesterday? Late afternoon? I went out for a walk to clear my head."

"There was a storm."

"Don't I know it," Charles Henry said. "I was trapped under a beech along Royal Avenue. It provided little protection from the rain and there were no taxis in sight. Rain running down my back, my suit nearly ruined. Took me ages to get home."

"Is there anyone who can confirm this? Ms. Frost, perhaps."

I held my breath—Mrs. Woolgar had said Maureen was away. Would Charles Henry lie about that?

He paled. "No, she is in London. She had a meeting yesterday with the director of a show at Wyndham's for next spring. But you can ask my dry cleaners—I had to take that suit in and hope for the best. Michael's—that's the place. On Quiet Street. You talk with him, he'll remember me."

It had rained all over the city, and Charles Henry easily could have been soaked dashing round the Bath Marina as he could in Victoria Park—but neither detective seemed moved to mention this.

"Well, Mr. Dill," Hopgood said, "we have no further questions at the moment, but we do ask you to remain available during the rest of the enquiry."

We left Charles Henry slumped at the table, and I saw Hopgood and Pye out.

"How can you let him go if the descriptions from witnesses to John's attack match Charles Henry?"

Kenny shook his head. "As it happens, we have contradicting accounts from yesterday. Several witnesses said the attacker was large and round, but another was certain it was a thin or moderately built person wearing a rain poncho. It could have been a trick of the wind."

I recalled my top being caught by a gust and billowing out like a sail.

"What about the weapon that was used on John—was it the same as used on Milo?"

"If we had said weapon in hand, we would be able to tell for certain. We're looking for a filleting knife, it seems—long, thin, narrow."

"You don't think it was Charles Henry—either time?"

"Overton still had his phone when Dill walked away," Kenny said.

"Then why was it in his satchel just now?"

"And only recently turned on?" Hopgood said. "In an outside pocket, too—easily slipped in without him knowing. Convenient, isn't it? I'm not hopeful, but we'll see if there are any prints on it."

The detectives left, and the Battenberg police car followed. I went to the kitchenette and made tea. Mrs. Woolgar's office door remained shut. I took a tray to the last place I wanted to be at that moment—the library. Charles Henry hadn't moved, and the contents of his satchel were still strewn across the table. He stared at them, morose and deflated.

"Tea?"

He mumbled something that might've been "Yes, thank you," and swept his detritus to the side to make room.

I poured out two cups and set a plate of custard creams on the table. Charles Henry eyed them as he added milk and sugar to his tea.

"Is Aubrey all right?" he asked, a strain in his voice that suggested that he knew it a proper question to ask, although he wished he didn't need to.

"He was stabbed from behind, Mr. Dill, and the knife went into his shoulder. Lucky that—Milo was stabbed a bit lower and it went straight through, causing internal bleeding. That's how he died."

Charles Henry squirmed. "But Aubrey . . . escaped?"

"The attacker escaped. John has a stab wound and a hairline fracture in his collarbone. He spent the night in hospital all the while thinking about how Milo died and how close he came to it happening to him." *Snap* went the custard cream as I bit it in half.

"Ms. Burke, do you think I'm guilty of these violent actions? Murder? A knife attack?"

I chewed my biscuit and watched Charles Henry as I thought about what he had asked. I didn't know if he remained on Hopgood's suspect list—or if he did, how high up. Was he being set up, or was it all a ruse on Dill's part to make it look as if he were being set up? Did I truly believe him to be a murderer or to be innocent? Either way, I could be wrong.

"No, Mr. Dill," I said with great effort and fifty percent conviction, "I do not believe you murdered Milo Overton or attacked John yesterday."

He straightened. He put his shoulders back and his chin in the air. It was as if I could see him begin to reinflate.

"But," I said, "you must get this idea out of your head that you're in competition with John—that if one of you is good, the other is automatically bad."

Charles Henry jabbed his finger on the table. "He is not my aunt's grandson."

"You're right, he isn't."

He sat back at this stunning pronouncement.

"You know that for certain?" he asked, his voice full of excitement. "Can we bring charges against him? Duncan will know, won't he? This'll put a cork in Aubrey's attempt to talk his way into a fortune."

"*You* put a cork in it!" I said, my finger in his face. "Would you listen to yourself? All you can think about is what you can get out of this. Here are the facts: After Sir John died, Lady Fowling met John's grandmother, who was going through a difficult time. They became friends. Through the years, stories survived in John's family—not only about Flambeaux, but also about what a kind and generous spirit your aunt had. John may not be her blood relative, but he is imbued with the same qualities. Go on, talk with Duncan. While you're at it, talk with Audrey and Sylvia Moon, and Mrs. Woolgar. Ask them what they think about John, and you'll hear the same. When Maureen learns the truth, I wonder what she will say."

Charles Henry looked away, a frown growing on his brow. It occurred to me that it didn't need to be a literal wig snatched off Godolphin's head to make a man look a fool.

"Well," I said, "I'll leave you to your work."

He stayed in the library another hour—doing what, I didn't know—and then left without a word.

THE LIBRARIAN ALWAYS RINGS TWICE   257

I soldiered on at my desk until Val rang.

"Come to mine this evening?" he asked. "I'll cook. We'll watch an old movie."

I felt as if I'd been rescued. "I'm all yours. Seven o'clock? I'll be stopping to tell Audrey and Sylvia the latest."

Looking forward to the evening kicked me into gear. When Mrs. Woolgar emerged from her office, I offered tea and made hers—Fortnum & Mason Assam Superb—separately. It was second nature to me now, and I didn't mind.

We sat across the desk from each other in her office with a plate of shortbread fingers between us, and I related the afternoon.

"And so," I said, wrapping up, "it looks as if the police don't believe it was Dill."

"But how did Milo's phone get in his satchel?"

"They suspect it was planted," I said, "by a man who was in the queue behind Charles Henry at that Italian restaurant near the theater."

Mrs. Woolgar tsked. "I'd say he'd better tell Maureen about it straightaway. Of course, we know where her loyalties lie, but she sounded quite sympathetic to John's story when I told her." The secretary reached for a shortbread finger. "I'm sorry I missed all this, but it took a while to catch Jane up on all that's gone on. She remembered a character in one of the Flambeaux books named Margaret, who is instrumental in catching the thief. I believe she said it was in *Flambeaux and Gall of the Oak*. We should locate it and tell John."

"Adele knows, and I'm seeing the Moons after work."

"I will talk with Maureen tomorrow."

I checked the time. "I'd better change my clothes. I'll just clear up—"

"No, Ms. Burke, I'll take care of the tea things. You go on."

It was actually a bit early to leave for the Moons', but that was on purpose, because I had another stop in mind first. I walked over to Abbey Green, and looked in at the Crystal Palace, the pub that had become Celia's local. There were two bars, but she wasn't in either of them. I went out the back to the garden. All the tables were occupied, including the one up against the wall of fake ivy on lattice, where Celia and I had sat that evening. I checked the table on the other side of the ivy wall, too. No Celia.

She had probably made a fair few friends since she'd been in Bath, and so I didn't know why I thought her well-being my responsibility. Still, I went out and over to her flat and rang the bell. Checking up on library patrons—add another task to my curator duties. At least I could remind her of the afternoon open tomorrow.

A sea of people flowed past me as I waited. I shaded my eyes and looked up to the first-floor window that I thought was hers. I rang again.

After a minute, the door opened a crack, and I saw one heavily kohled eye squinting at me.

"Celia?"

"Oh yeah, Hayley, hi." The door opened wider. "Come in, why don't you?"

I stepped past her. Before she closed the door, Celia scanned the crowd of day-trippers outside the Abbey.

When my eyes adjusted to the change in light levels, I saw we stood in a small entry, bare apart from the recycling bins and a few adverts strewn about the floor below the letter box.

"Mrs. Woolgar told me you stopped by yesterday. I was sorry to have missed you. I wanted to say that I hope we'll see you tomorrow at the afternoon open. How's your holiday?"

"Good, yeah, well, you know. Want to come up? I've only just got my face on."

A bit late in the day for it, I thought as I followed her up to her flat. It was a bedsit. Isn't it amazing what can be fit into one room? The bed occupied one corner and a sink, fridge, microwave, and toaster the other. I could see into the bathroom, which looked just about big enough to turn round in. A wire bistro table and two chairs sat under the front window that looked out and across to the Abbey, eye level with the stone angels that climbed up and down Jacob's ladder.

"Lovely view," I said.

Celia lit a cigarette, opened the window next to which a "No Smoking" sign was posted, and then walked back to fill the kettle and switch it on.

"I've only got until the end of the week," she said.

"And then you'll go back to Plymouth?"

She had her back to me as she took two mugs down from a shelf. "I'm not going back to Slough, I can tell you that. I'm sick and tired of . . ." Celia turned and pointed her cigarette at me. "You remember Rockingham, don't you, Hayley? He was a bad one. You remember how she took care of him?"

A shiver shot through my body. In *Frenchman's Creek*, Rockingham had started out unpleasant, but ended up evil.

"Are you in trouble, Celia? Is this about the boyfriend?"

Celia looked stricken. "It wasn't my fault."

We'd been here before. "No, of course it wasn't. Look, if someone is bothering you, you should go to the police."

Celia bit her lip. "I'm rubbish with men."

I didn't recall enough of her story to know where to go from this point. The kettle boiled and switched off. Celia dropped tea bags into the mugs and poured in the water.

"I'm out of milk," she said.

The room was quiet except for the muted sound of the crowd below drifting into the open window and the metallic *clink clink* as Celia stirred two spoonfuls of sugar into each mug. It came to me that no one knew where I was.

Tucking the cigarette between her lips, she picked up both mugs and walked over. "Here, sit down."

I lowered myself onto a wire chair. I felt the legs splay out slightly, and I took hold of the table to steady myself. "What sort of place is it where you work?"

Celia squinted at me. "We make scooters," she said. "Not scooters like Vespas—these are the ones for old-age pensioners to get round on. Yeah?"

Yeah. This information settled over me. Scooters. Plymouth. A boyfriend who had been her therapist. She'd followed him to Bath, and now he was "gone."

The tea was scalding and sugary, but I took a sip regardless, to cover the fact that I couldn't speak. I held the mug as the steam swirled up in front of my face like a scrim. I wondered how much I would have to drink before I could leave.

Say something, Hayley, so she doesn't think you suspect her of murder.

"What's his name, Celia? Your boyfriend?"

"Doesn't matter now, does it?"

"Do you know for certain he's left Bath?"

"Oh yeah, he's gone." In an instant, her eyes filled with tears.

"Are you in some sort of trouble?"

She squinted out the window to the pavement below, a few tears dribbling down her cheeks. "Ears like a . . ." She took a sharp breath. "We should stay away from the Rockinghams, shouldn't we, Hayley? But easier said than done."

I needed air and I needed to get to the Moons'. I reached in my bag and handed her one of my business cards. "We'll see you tomorrow at the afternoon open, won't we? You let me know if you need anything, all right?"

"I can take care of myself. Bloody nerve." She reached out and touched my arm. "Sorry, Hayley. Not you."

On the way to Sylvia and Audrey Moon's, I went over what had just happened at Celia's holiday flat.

Had I been a coward for not confronting her, asking her point-blank if Milo had been her therapist "boyfriend"? At times, it could be difficult to follow her line of thought, but that's what it seemed to add up to. Were her cryptic remarks about Rockingham meant to be about Milo? Had she killed him to save her own life? Was her mind unbalanced?

Tomorrow, I would go to the police with these coincidences and assumptions. They could check her out, couldn't they, because Celia must have worked at the same company as Milo, a factory that made scooters? Companies have employee records—she'd be listed. Let

Sergeant Hopgood find out if the disparate, odd remarks I'd collected would hold together.

After a visit with the Moons and at last relieved of my obligations for the day, I took a taxi to Val's house. He had been keeping an eye out and opened the door as I came up the walk. He drew me in as the aroma of chicken roasted with lemon and olives and thyme enveloped us.

I threw my arms round his neck. "It smells like heaven."

Val kissed me and then gave the corner of my mouth a nibble. "Mmm," he said. "A visit to the Moons is never complete without sherry. How many glasses?"

"Two," I said, standing nose to nose with him. "And a boatload of tales from the past."

Two glasses of sherry were enough to cast my encounter with Celia in a different light. She seemed a troubled woman with a nervous nature who hadn't had an easy time of it. I didn't intend to keep my visit to her a secret, but first things first. Dinner.

In the kitchen, Val took the chicken out of the oven to rest, and I started on a salad. I was quite at home here, even though the house held memories for him that I was no part of. It's where he and his wife, Jill, had lived and where he brought up their twins, Bess and Becky, who were just a year or so older than my Dinah. Jill had died when the girls were quite young. This was a second life for both Val and me.

As we worked, I first told him about how the police found Milo's mobile in Charles Henry's satchel.

"It's getting a bit ridiculous, isn't it?" Val asked. "He can't be that dim."

"True. Although, a part of me would like to see him get into trouble just to put him in his place."

I sliced the bread, Val opened the wine, and we sat down to our meal.

"Now for the romantic portion of my day," I said.

"And where was I for this?" Val asked in mock indignation.

"In my heart, of course," I said, and his eyes crinkled at the corners.

"Good save."

"Audrey and Sylvia had me go through everything we learned about John twice over, and the second time they started fitting in little bits from the François stories. They've known them all these years from Lady Fowling's oral storytelling, but now that they have the printed documents, they can check details. When I told them how Margaret and Georgie walked along the cliffs on the Dorset coast, they said there was a reference in 'François Stops Time' to the detective walking the cliffs and looking across the Channel and remembering his past."

Val raised his glass. "She was a clever one, that Georgiana Fowling. Did you notice in 'The Purloined Peacock,' he receives a letter from 'the city where the Royal Mail was reborn'? That's here, of course—Bath, where Ralph Allen reformed the postal system. You know, it's as if we could write her biography from her stories."

After dinner we moved out to the living room and scrolled through a myriad of movie choices on the television screen until I said, "That one!"

"*My Cousin Rachel*?" Val asked. "I see a du Maurier theme here."

We'd both seen it before, and I knew the film wasn't everyone's favorite, but I loved the tension that built scene by scene, and Richard Burton's descent into such a state that he didn't know what sort of woman Olivia de Havilland was. I should read the book.

"Wait now." We'd made it only two minutes into the movie, when I remembered I had more news. "Before I saw the Moons, I saw Celia." Val paused the film, and I related my visit.

"So, she's either a delusional client from his therapy practice or Milo was Rockingham from *Frenchman's Creek*?"

"You see why I didn't ring up Kenny Pye immediately," I said. "I think I'll run it past John first—find out what sort of a temperament Milo had."

"You'd think he'd need to be fairly levelheaded to work with John."

We went back to the film, but a few moments later, Val paused it again. There was a phone ringing. Mine.

I tracked it down in my bag in the kitchen, saw the caller, and answered immediately.

"Ms. Burke," Sergeant Hopgood said. "The ME has gone over Overton's phone and come up with something."

"Fingerprints? Whose were they?"

"No dabs, it was wiped clean. Or, almost. At the side of the screen, rather tucked under the edge of the cover, as if pushed there when the thing was wiped, she found several fish scales."

19

⟨꧁⟩

F ish scales?" I repeated. "Are you saying that Milo was a fisher-
   man?"

"That's what we want to find out." That was Kenny's voice—
Hopgood must have me on speaker.

"I don't know, so you'll need to ask John. You could ring him."

"But is he in the mood to answer his phone?" Hopgood said.

"There's that."

Hopgood and Kenny had an exchange about something I couldn't
quite make out as I thought about fish scales smeared on a mobile
phone.

"Hayley, is John's narrow boat still at the marina?" Kenny asked.

"Yes, he got the last few days of someone else's booking."

"I'll see if I can catch him up there," the DC said. "I've got to go
back out myself in the morning. The manager of the caravan park
gave me an earful yesterday when we were there, complaining about

a tent camper. I had a couple of uniforms go over, but the site had been abandoned, and I didn't have time to deal with it."

"Celia," Val whispered to remind me.

I nodded. "Sergeant, I have something for you about Milo," I said.

"Information?" Hopgood asked.

No need to get their hopes up. "Nothing solid. And possibly not even about Milo. There's a woman who has come to two of our afternoon opens. She's visiting Bath from Plymouth and works in a factory that makes scooters." I paused.

"Go on," Hopgood said.

"She told me she'd been in a bad marriage and that when it had broken up, she'd seen a therapist and that they had started a relationship. She and her therapist. At first, she said they were meeting here in Bath, but I don't think they ever did. She's never actually said his name, and she's been quite nervous and vague about things the last couple of times I've seen her. Not unhinged or anything, but emotional and teary. Angry, too."

"What is her name?" Hopgood asked.

"Celia. Celia . . . I don't know her surname." And then I remembered our guest book. "But I might have it at Middlebank. I'm not there this evening. I'll check first thing tomorrow and give you a ring."

Over cornflakes quite early the next morning, Val said, "I've a class followed by a meeting followed by two coaching sessions. I'll drop you at Middlebank, and I'll be there for the open, but not until toward the end."

"Afternoon open," I said. "I should've put up different displays for

this week. Maybe I still have time to change them out. Mrs. Woolgar sent the notices to the online calendars, so that's sorted. Our
attendance has been up and down—the first week, we had a few
people, the second week a mob—"

"And a boxing match," Val added.

"And practically no one at the third. What will today look like?
We need a hook to lure people in. A proper hook, one that doesn't
include Charles Henry attacking anyone. If these afternoons aren't
a success, the board may think they are a waste. Mrs. Woolgar has
gone along with it, but I wouldn't say she's been the biggest supporter."

"What are you wasting?" Val asked. "Any contact with the public
is a benefit. This is different from the salons and the exhibition—a
scheduled public open time is for the long term. I think you'll need
to look at attendance over at least six months, probably a year before
you can tell if it's a success."

I scraped the last few soggy flakes round my bowl. "My one-year
performance review is coming up."

"Think you'll be sacked?" Val asked, hanging his head to catch
my eye.

It made me laugh, but only for a moment. "Will they think I've
been skiving off work lately? I had the mystery at Middlebank to
solve, didn't I? But I don't want them to keep me on just because
they don't want to look for another curator. I want to be worth my
salt."

The next morning, I said to Mrs. Woolgar, "I thought a display
theme of foreign settings might be of interest, as it's the sum-

mer holiday season and all. It'll be easy to pull together before this afternoon. What do you think?"

"Well . . ." the secretary said.

Try again. "Or murder methods?"

"We would need to stay away from knives, don't you think?"

"Yes, I suppose so. We could begin with poison."

"We don't have enough table space for all the books that use poison as the method," Mrs. Woolgar said. "No, your idea about foreign settings is interesting. What were you thinking it might include?"

And here we were back at my lack of knowledge about the books in our library.

"Miss Marple went to the Caribbean, didn't she?" It was the one book I was certain of.

"Christie can account for quite a few—the Nile, Mesopotamia, the Caribbean," Mrs. Woolgar said. "Marsh sent her British detective off to New Zealand, didn't she?"

"Yes, of course, Inspector . . . Alleyn." His name came to me at the last second. "Sort of an interesting turnabout," I added with more confidence, "as she herself was from New Zealand."

"So, foreign settings it is." Mrs. Woolgar jotted something down. "And were you able to find that woman who stopped to see you—Celia, was it?"

"Celia!" I set my mug down hard. "It had gone clean out of my head. I told the police I would look in our guest book for her surname."

"What would the police want with her surname?" Mrs. Woolgar asked.

I explained my tenuous supposition and ended with "And so, there's a slim possibility that she was a client of Milo's—his therapy practice. You know how the police want to look into every tiny thing in an enquiry. I'm sure it'll amount to nothing."

The secretary was already up and pulling the guest book off the shelf. She opened it to the first day and set it on her desk so that we could both see the list of eleven names. We'd had twelve people that day, actually, but John hadn't signed.

Mrs. Woolgar pointed halfway down the list. "Oh yes, she's the one."

Celia had written her first name in a loopy script, but where her surname might have been was a scratching of black ink. She'd obliterated whatever had been there and used such a heavy hand it caused the paper to pooch out on the back side. The pen had practically gone through.

I took the guest book to the window and held the page against the light, but couldn't read anything.

"She didn't leave her email address, either," I said.

"Some people prefer their privacy," Mrs. Woolgar replied.

"Yes, but she was so excited to find us, and she knows so much about the authors and their books," I complained. "You'd think she'd at least want to sign up for our newsletter. Wait—she was here the second week, too."

"Skip forward," Mrs. Woolgar said. "I had to find an undamaged page."

"No, she didn't sign the second week. I'd better take the entire book to the police," I said. "I may have to leave it with them."

"That's fine. This afternoon, we'll use the guest book from the exhibition. There are a few pages left at the back."

"Well, that's me away. I'll arrange the displays when I get back."

* * *

Will you be able to tell what she crossed out?" I asked Kenny Pye as we stood in the lobby of the station. "Because then you could match her up with Milo's client list."

"I don't remember a 'Celia' on it," Kenny said, holding the page up to the light.

"But she said she saw a therapist and found him through work at the scooter factory. She followed him to Bath. If it wasn't Milo, who was it?" Expecting no answer to that question, I added, "Will this be any help at all?"

Kenny ran his finger lightly over the blank page that held an impression of Celia's firm hand. "You never know. Where is it she's staying?"

Something I actually knew. I gave him directions to Celia's holiday flat. "She does seem a bit . . . she isn't unhinged, only confused. I don't think she could . . . I hope she didn't kill Milo."

"Someone did. Aubrey's had a look at Overton's client list, but he says he doesn't recognize any names. Still, we're in the process of contacting each one."

"I wouldn't have the nerve to question people the way you and Sergeant Hopgood do," I said.

"It's not bad when you remember there's a truth there, somewhere, and the goal is to find it."

"Did you ask John about fish scales on Milo's phone?"

"No joy there—Overton didn't fish. All I returned from the marina with was that abandoned tent and tarpaulin from the camper. Bit of a tip the place was, disposable barbecue pans left in a heap."

"Didn't think rubbish collection was part of your remit as a detective constable," I said.

Kenny grinned. "Our talents are endless."

Back at Middlebank, I ran what seemed like an endless circuit up and down the stairs. First to my flat, to splash cool water on my face and change my blouse, then down to my office for a quick internet search on Golden Age of Mystery books with international settings. Back up to the library, where I pulled the books, and at last to my flat to eat a sandwich while standing at the kitchen sink. Finally, to the ground floor, where I collected brochures and moved the small table out to the entry.

Now for the table displays—and look, it was only half past twelve. But the front door buzzed. Mrs. Woolgar wasn't up from her flat yet and so I answered, hoping it wasn't an early patron or, worse, Charles Henry. Or the police.

It was Frances.

"Hello. How lovely to see you," I said. I made a show of looking past her and down the pavement. "On your own?"

She drew in her chin and smiled. "John told me we've been sussed. I wanted to stop by and offer an explanation."

"You are under no obligation to explain anything," I said, opening the door wide. "But, of course, I'm all ears."

I led her to my office, but the floor, my desk, and the seats of the chairs were covered in old newsletters. We turned in to the kitchenette instead, and without thinking, I put the kettle on. We sat at the table, and I smiled at her, but said nothing.

Frances took on her usual serious, businesslike manner with her chin tucked in. "You may think this is all quite sudden, especially as I had told you that I was . . . reluctant to enter into another relationship."

"You made yourself abundantly clear that you had sworn off men."

"I had and I meant it. When my marriage broke up, I was hurt, and rather than strike back, I retreated. I hid from life. It can take it out of you, can't it? Make you feel worthless."

A wave of emotion came over me as I recalled the months and months after I'd caught Roger cheating and we'd gone through the soul-numbing process of divorce. I had been suffocated by the thought that if my husband had turned to others, it must have been my fault. My brain knew that was wrong, but it took a long time for my heart to catch up.

The kettle began to whistle, and I threw tea bags in the pot, pulled the milk out of the fridge, and retrieved two mugs from the shelf behind Frances. "But John changed your mind?"

There it was, that smile creeping in, this time accompanied by a rosy glow. "I'm not much given to flights of fancy. You might've been able to tell that about me."

I grinned. "I might've."

"The first time John and I met, here in the entry, I was shaken. It's because I sensed something in him—a need for a real connection." Frances poured milk into the mugs. "I never had that in my marriage. I never felt as if I truly mattered, and I had grown weary of being a convenience, an accessory, a legally sanctioned 'plus one' for important events. Once, at a party, my husband started to introduce me to a coworker, and I swear to you that for a moment, he couldn't remember my name. Shows you how much of an impression I made. Since then, I've learned a great deal about myself, and I know this, Hayley—I need someone who needs me. Is that too much to ask?"

Not as far as I was concerned, but I didn't answer, because I heard Mrs. Woolgar's steps coming up from her flat.

"I was just about to put the sign out," I said when she appeared at the kitchenette door.

"Lovely. Hello, Frances, how are you?"

"Fine, Mrs. Woolgar. And you?"

"Very well, thank you. Will John stop in this afternoon, do you think?"

So I wasn't the only one who knew. As I went out to the entry, Frances replied, "Yes, he will."

With Frances's help, we had plenty of time to set up the table displays, particularly as no one appeared until half past one, when a man and woman arrived and got in a discussion about *4.50 from Paddington* by Christie and the importance of a reliable railroad timetable. They drifted off, and after a few quiet minutes, Frances picked up an anthology of short stories from 1964. I selected *Flambeaux and the Fragrance of Freesias*, and we settled in the wingback chairs to read.

In a while, a handful of girls about thirteen years old came skipping up the stairs chattering in French. They stopped just inside the library.

I stood and ventured, "Bonjour." This prompted them to rush toward me as one, all talking at the same time. Where was Adele when I needed her? Fortunately, a woman came in after them, said something, and the girls fell quiet.

"Hello," the woman said. "Do you have books in French for the girls to see? I want to show them how popular the mystery is."

This led to a busy half hour and ended with the table strewn with foreign editions. The group left, and Frances and I began to reshelve when a single visitor arrived, someone I knew.

"Hello, Felicia. Nice of you to stop in."

I introduced her to Frances, who said, "Lovely to meet you. I'll carry on with shelving, Hayley, so you two can chat."

"Thanks. So, Felicia, how are things at the Larkin?"

"The hotel business is smashing, thanks." Felicia gazed at the shelves. "I took a look at your website and thought I needed to see the place for real. Oh, look." She went straight to the display table and picked up a book. "I just watched *Murder on the Orient Express* last night. Loved it. I must read the book now."

Before I could ask her which version of the film, she continued. "I noticed you have a winter salon series. You must bring in special lecturers for that."

"Yes—London, Edinburgh. There was an American here, too." Fortunately, we hadn't had to pay for travel.

"Do you put them up in a hotel?" Felicia asked. "Because if you do, I'd love to talk with you about what the Larkin can offer. Top-notch rooms, cozy atmosphere, excellent service. A really personal touch. As your salon season is winter, I'm sure we could come to an agreement on a good rate. We could even extend the offer to any of your out-of-town attendees." She lowered her voice. "I haven't actually said anything to the owner about my idea, thought I'd get a feel for your reaction first."

"It's brilliant—tell your boss I said that. Why don't you work up a proposal and we'll talk about it come September?"

Felicia's smile, showing off the slight gap in her front teeth, was infectious. "Grand," she said. "Now, how did you get on with your mystery letter?"

Milo's letter to me about John. Milo. Milo and Celia. An image flashed in my mind of finding Celia sitting on the pavement at Laura Circle, only a few doors away from the Larkin.

"The letter? Fine. Felicia, I wonder if you might recall a friend of mine going into the hotel recently. She wasn't staying there, but she might've been looking for one of your guests. She's thin with streaky hair, and she wears a great deal of eye makeup."

"Lord, yes, I remember her," Felicia said. "It was early last week I saw her. She was nice, and I was so sorry I couldn't help. I thought it better to let the manager take care of it."

"Do you remember who it was she asked about?"

Felicia squirmed, pressed her lips together, and exhaled in a huff.

"He had died," she said. "The man she was looking for. Oh, not in the hotel, nothing like that. Outdoors one evening just before the pubs closed. He was *murdered*." The last word came out as barely a whisper, and she glanced round the room as if the books on the shelves might be leaning in to hear of a new plot.

"Milo Overton?" I asked. "Is that who it was?"

"Yes, he's the one," Felicia said. "It happened the week before I started working, you see. One of the cleaners told me that the police came and took all his belongings. The owner has made it quite clear she would prefer to keep the whole thing quiet. It wouldn't make a terribly good impression on the sort of guest we're after. Did you know him?"

"That's who wrote the letter," I said.

Felicia's mouth dropped open. "Cor, you really are in the mystery business, aren't you?"

"Only in books," I said. I'm not sure I believed it any more than she did.

"I hope you didn't mind," Frances said when we were alone again. "I couldn't help overhearing. Was someone asking about Milo at his hotel?"

"Yes. Celia. She's been here for two of the afternoon opens, and I've run into her round the city. She doesn't live in Bath and told me she was here to meet her boyfriend-therapist. She's never said his name, but there are a few coincidences that can't be overlooked. First"—I stuck out my thumb and began counting off—"he was a therapist. Second, he was from Plymouth. And third, he worked at a scooter factory."

"Would John know her?"

"If he did, I'm sure he would've recognized her—she was here that afternoon when Charles Henry . . . you know. John said that Milo would never date a client, that it was unprofessional, but there must've been something going on. Or Celia thought there was. What Felicia said just now is concrete proof of their connection. I'll need to ring the police."

A man about my age walked in, and I remembered what I was supposed to be about.

"Hello," I said, "welcome to the First Edition Society library. Our books are from the Golden Age of Mystery, and we have an extensive collection of interesting reprints and foreign editions, too."

"Don't like mysteries, actually," he said, hands in the pockets of his denims, looking along one shelf at a time. "Don't see the point, actually."

I bit back my response—*And so, why are you here, actually?*—and instead replied, "Isn't it good that we don't all like the same thing? It would be a boring world otherwise, wouldn't it?"

"I like American westerns," he said. "Do you have any of those?"

Behind me, I heard Frances give a muffled snort.

"As it happens, we don't."

Perhaps he didn't believe me, because he spent the next fifteen minutes reading the spines on the shelves before he finally gave up and left.

"I'll just nip down to get my phone," I said to Frances. But I heard the front door open and close, followed by voices, and so waited another minute. Soon Mrs. Woolgar appeared with John, back in his pirate togs and arm still secured against his chest. His face lit up when he saw Frances.

"Oh, hello there," he said. "Here's a happy surprise."

Happy, yes. Surprise? I doubt it.

Frances beamed in return.

I slipped out, saying, "Just after my phone. And look, it's nearly four o'clock. A slow day, wasn't it? Shall I put the kettle on?"

In the kitchenette while I waited for the water to boil, I rang Kenny, but got his voice mail, so I tried Sergeant Hopgood, who did answer. I explained, after which he had the nerve to act like a police officer.

"You had a letter from the victim?" he asked. "You've not mentioned this."

"That's because it was about our mystery—the mystery at

Middlebank." Bunter sauntered in and began performing figure eights round my ankles. I reached over for his treats, scattered a few in his dish, and continued. "About Lady Fowling and John's grandmother. But, sorry, I should've at least told you I had it. About midday on that Wednesday, Milo told me he had something that would explain John's . . . great affection for Lady Fowling, so he must've written the letter that afternoon or evening before he died and left it at the hotel desk to be posted. It was overlooked and then hand-delivered last week."

"We'll want to take a look."

"Yes, of course you will. But Celia. This is actual proof, right—not just me doing my sums wrong."

"It's interesting, I'll say that."

But there was a snag with this—something apart from thinking that Celia might be a murderer. "The thing is, Sergeant, if Celia killed Milo, why would she go back to his hotel and ask to see him?"

"Why indeed?"

"Have you talked with her yet?" I asked.

"Pye called on her, but she wasn't in her flat. He'll make another stop again later. You don't have her mobile number?"

"No. She has mine, though."

"That only helps if she uses it."

I lugged the tray with the teapot, plate of custard creams, cups, saucers, milk, and sugar as far as the entry when the front-door buzzer sounded. I hoped it wasn't a library patron wanting to view the collection. I nudged the guest book off the entry table with the back of my hand. It tumbled to the flagstone floor, and I set the tray down.

Val waited on the doorstep.

"Well timed," I said, giving him a kiss. As the door closed, I heard a call.

"Hang on a tick!"

Adele came panting up. "Thanks." She noticed the tray. "You aren't opening your own tearoom after all, are you?"

"Certainly not—this is for friends. We're in the library. You two go on up, and I'll follow."

Val took the tray, and I went back to the kitchenette, put the kettle on again, and gathered more cups and saucers. By the time I made it back to the library, the five of them were settled round one end of the long table. Bunter had joined the group at a safe distance from atop the mantel—and the conversation was in full swing. The topic: narrow boats.

"It isn't really a concern how far you can go in one day," John said. "It's the journey that matters. That being said, a moderate pace is about three miles an hour, but that doesn't account for locks. It's a relaxing way to travel."

When Mrs. Woolgar asked if John had painted *La Mouette 2* on the boat himself, conversation turned like a meandering river and wound its way through boats, seasides, the best fish-and-chips, the enduring popularity of the little Belgian, and finally to books.

This led us to the subject of Flambeaux, both the books and the unpublished stories. John asked Mrs. Woolgar if she thought Lady Fowling had meant for "The Purloined Peacock" to be the lighter side of Flambeaux.

"She had a sharp wit," Mrs. Woolgar said, and she and Adele started in on a few funny Georgiana anecdotes. I nibbled on a biscuit, all the while keeping one eye on John and Frances.

They were a case study in the attraction of opposites. Quiet Frances and gregarious John. But like those opposing magnets, an unseen force drew them close to each other. I saw John reach over and touch Frances's hand, and she leaned into him to say something. The dimple surfaced.

The door buzzed again. Val went to answer and brought up two more—Sylvia and Audrey Moon.

"Oh, look, Aud—the party has already started."

"John," Audrey said, "how are you feeling? We were shocked to hear what had happened."

Everyone shifted to add two more places at the table—John dragging a chair with one arm as he told the Moons his injury was nothing compared with the broken leg Flambeaux had suffered in "François on the Boards." Sylvia commented that the detective had learned the hard way that tap dancing wasn't his forte, and everyone laughed.

I went downstairs and returned with two bottles of sherry—one was half gone—and a tray of glasses just in time to hear Audrey Moon tell about the time Georgiana tried to do her own translation of *Flambeaux and the Lost Cravat* into German, leaving us in tears of laughter. We barely heard the front door buzz. It went off again, and Val rose, but I waved him back down. "I'll go. It's nearly five. It can't be anyone for the library."

Another anecdote had caused the group to burst out in laughter, which died an instant death when I returned with Maureen Frost and Charles Henry Dill.

20

ohn leapt up, and everyone else froze.

"Well," I said, "you see we're a merry group"—*at least, we were*—"and you're very welcome. Tea? Sherry?"

"No, thank you, Hayley," Maureen replied. Behind her, Charles Henry shuffled from foot to foot, but Maureen smiled at the gathering. "It's fortunate you're here, John, because we've stopped to ask how you're doing."

John nodded to his arm strapped to his chest. He cleared his throat and swallowed. "I am on the mend, thank you. I had planned to call on the two of you tomorrow morning in order to offer my apologies, but I will give them now so that others can hear, too. I'm truly sorry for any pain I've caused you—especially you, Mr. Dill—in my claim to be a relation of Lady Fowling's. These claims are false, as you well know. I can offer no reasonable excuse but my own failings. If there is some way I can make amends, I hope you will let me know."

Maureen's head inclined ever so slightly, perhaps to acknowledge what John had said or perhaps as a signal, because at her nod, Charles Henry began to speak.

The words came out in a halting fashion, as if some inner prodding mechanism had to be employed to produce each one. "Mr. Aubrey. I accept your apology . . . and I . . . would . . . like to . . . offer . . . my own . . . in return." He breathed in and out and continued as everyone round the table kept silent, their eyes moving back and forth between the two men. "Now that Maureen has explained to me the circumstances of your visit to Middlebank, I can see that I reacted without thinking and without taking into consideration my aunt's long life and how she had such a great influence on so many people. I'm sorry for dismissing you out of hand."

John offered an abbreviated bow. "Thank you for those words. Yes, of course I accept your apology."

Lovely speeches on both sides. Now what?

"Are you sure you wouldn't like a sherry?" I asked.

Charles Henry certainly looked as if he could use a stiff one—likewise John, who rested his free hand on the table for support.

"Another time," Maureen said. "We'll need a bottle for the next board meeting, I'm sure, because we will have a great deal to discuss, won't we? Aren't we coming up to your one-year anniversary as curator, Hayley?"

"Why, so we are," I said. "I'm looking forward to reviewing events of the past year with the board." Most of the events. I hurried on. "I'll make sure to have an overview of the salon season and the exhibition—including the press coverage, the increase in membership, and the feedback from attendees."

"We won't forget these last few weeks, either," Maureen said, "and your part in it."

A veiled reference to the trouble Charles Henry got into? Got *himself* into, that is.

"You've reminded us, Hayley," Maureen continued, "why we are here—our raison d'être. That is, to keep Georgiana's wishes and spirit alive. Thank you, John, for being the instigator of that."

John flushed with pleasure. "If I played any part at all that turns out to be good, then I'm pleased beyond . . . and speaking of parts, Ms. Frost, may I say that three years ago, I took Dolly to the theater in Plymouth, and we saw you in an Alan Ayckbourn play. You were wonderful."

Maureen bestowed that smile upon him, the one that softened her usual steely countenance. "I'm glad you enjoyed it."

Charles Henry gave a small cough, and Maureen took a step back. The floor was his.

"As you may know, I am working with Ms. Burke to create an index for the First Edition Society newsletter, a publication that began when my aunt Georgiana sought a way to bring members from around the world into this library to enjoy its unparalleled collection of books from the women authors of the Golden Age of Mystery."

John sank back in his chair. I sidled over to mine and reached for my glass of sherry.

"The index will be a vital tool, of course," Charles Henry continued, "for scholars and enthusiasts alike, to search for topics and people who have influenced the genre through the decades. My aunt created many ways to infuse a sense of camaraderie among the worldwide mystery enthusiasts. One of her methods was to publish short items of news about members, including academic achievements, marriages, births. And deaths."

There was a frisson in the room as Charles Henry reached into his satchel and drew out one of the newsletters. "Only yesterday did I come across this small item from December 1979. If I may, I will read it to you. 'On the passing of Margaret Aubrey, honorary member, who did her part to make Flambeaux come alive and who will be greatly missed by her daughter and others. Be at peace.'"

Charles Henry handed the newsletter across the table to John, who accepted it, blinking rapidly.

"This is my grandmother," he said, his voice thick. "Look, Frances"—he handed the paper to her—"my grandmother." He raised his head. "Thank you, Charles Henry."

Dill stuck his chin out. "You're welcome, John."

I sniffed, Adele wiped a tear off her face, and Mrs. Woolgar rummaged in the sleeve of her dress, drawing out a lace-edged handkerchief.

John took the newsletter over to show the Moons.

"It's just like Georgiana, isn't it, Aud?" Sylvia said. "She never forgot anyone."

"Margaret's name must appear on the early membership roles," Mrs. Woolgar said. "I'll have Duncan bring over those ledgers, and we'll find it. It might be time to create a document that lists all the members over the years to show the vast reach of the Society. Ms. Burke, perhaps this warrants another read through her ladyship's notebooks?"

"I'd be happy to," I said.

This segue from emotion into workaday tasks signaled an end to the gathering. Bunter jumped down from the mantel and went out the door, positioning himself in the Chippendale chair next to Lady Fowling's portrait as if to bid good evening to his guests as they departed. After a round of pleasant good-byes, Mrs. Woolgar saw Maureen and Charles Henry out. The Moons, gathering bags and wraps, voiced a wish for a sherry gathering every Wednesday afternoon.

Audrey reached out a hand to Frances. "We hear you want to start your own publishing house. Georgiana would've loved the idea. She was a great supporter of women in business. Wasn't she, Syl?"

"She was. Remember the time she backed the woman who started her own book and stationery shop," Sylvia said. "And quite success- ful she was—ran it for twenty years and then sold it on. Sort of an upscale newsagent. A place for books and fountain pens—but no chewing gum."

John looked over from talking with Val. "I have an idea about fountain pens."

"Why don't you tell us about it when you bring Frances to dinner?" Audrey said. "Now we must away. Fundraising event at the Roman Baths, and we've booked a taxi."

"I'm off, too," Adele said.

"French conversation class?" I asked.

"In this one, you pick a topic from a hat and start talking," Adele said. "The goal is a one-minute speech. So far, my best is twenty seconds."

Sylvia said something to Adele in French, and the three of them left.

Val came over to me. "John's moving the boat back along the towpath this evening. He asked if I would help out."

"My arm, you see," John said, nodding to the injury. "And there is the cranking of the windlass. That's the handle that fits onto the spindle, and it's turned to raise and lower the paddles that let the water in or out of the locks."

I turned to Val. "Well, lucky for John you're available. Will it take long?"

"Not long," he replied.

"It depends," John said. "Traffic at the locks, finding a forty-eight-hour spot to moor. We may have to bide our time, perhaps travel up past Saltford before we turn round and come back down. Also, we'll need to take care—even after the rain Monday evening, the canal is low this time of year. We could be one hour. Two. Possibly more."

Val did not look unhappy about this.

"Off you go, sailor," I said.

John slipped his free arm round Frances's waist.

"Hayley, perhaps later when Val and I have moored, you and Frances will come out and we four will have drinks?"

I looked at the time. "Sounds lovely. It's seven o'clock now. Let us know when you get there. And where you are."

John glanced round the library. "This has been an amazing time, and I'm so grateful—to you, Hayley, as well as Mrs. Woolgar, the Moons, Adele. And to Maureen and Charles Henry. Everyone is being gracious. But this isn't quite the happy ending, is it? What of Milo's murderer?"

My visit with Celia, pushed to the far back of my mind, returned in a rush. "John," I said, "about Milo. He seemed like a calm person who didn't rile easily—or perhaps I just didn't see it. Did he have a temper?"

John smiled. "A temper? No, Milo had a calm, even nature. Circumspect, you know. He always said it was better to stop and think rather than act in haste. It's what made him a good therapist. He could show you yourself and let you decide how best to proceed, instead of telling you what to do."

Milo had been no Rockingham. I had known it, of course, but it was good to have John's assessment. And if he had not been Rockingham, could Celia have killed him?

Downstairs, Mrs. Woolgar came out from her office. "That was kind of you, John, to mention Maureen's acting career. It's still quite dear to her."

John shrugged and then winced at his shoulder.

"Mrs. Woolgar," I said, "I did drop by to see Celia yesterday. I'm sorry she wasn't here this afternoon. We could've asked for her surname. We could've asked about Milo."

"And any word from the police about her signature?"

"Celia."

That was John talking.

"Yes, Celia," I said with a spark of excitement. "Does her name sound familiar? Did you know her? She's from Plymouth, you see, and she works at the scooter factory. You've seen her. Celia was here the afternoon Charles Henry punched you."

"What does she look like?"

"Heavy eye makeup. Streaky blond hair." No sign of recognition on John's face.

"Tall espadrilles," Mrs. Woolgar added. "And she smokes."

"No, sorry" he said. "I don't recall. I was distracted by Frances." They exchanged smiles.

"It's just that Celia talked about seeing a therapist in Plymouth," I explained. "And how he'd become her boyfriend. This afternoon, I learned that she'd gone to the Larkin."

John's focus sharpened. "Milo was staying at the Larkin."

"Yes, so you see she knew that much."

But how did she know? Had Milo told her? Had she seen him and followed? Did she stab him? Where would she get a filleting knife— her bedsit kitchen certainly didn't look well enough equipped. But then, murderers had their ways.

John stared off into the middle distance. "No, not a client."

"No," I echoed with disappointment. "That's what police said. They didn't see her name in his records."

"Also, the last woman he dated was from St. Austell," John said. "That was early in the year, and she took a job in Canada. Milo would not be in a relationship with a client. He was careful about that—it would've been unprofessional behavior."

The flame that had flared up about Celia being a murderer died back down. Again I asked myself, if she were the murderer, why would she advertise herself at the Larkin?

Val and John left for the marina, and Mrs. Woolgar, with a discreet glance at her watch, bade Frances and me a "good evening."

"Come up for a glass of wine, Frances?" I asked. "We could wait out the narrow-boat journey."

"I would do, but for my paper—I promised an update to the granting agency. If I finish before *La Mouette 2* returns, I'll give you a ring."

I closed the door and turned to find Bunter on the bottom step, his tail wrapped tidily round his legs. "Why doesn't the Society offer grants to women who want to write or edit or publish?" I asked him.

The tip of his tail gave a faint nod. "Well, cat, looks like we're on our own for a while. Come up and keep me company?"

But monitoring the library gathering had apparently exhausted Bunter. He yawned, stretched, and sauntered off toward Mrs. Woolgar's office and his bed.

I headed for my flat, but paused on the first-floor landing to have a word with Lady Fowling.

"He may not be your grandson, but I'd say he knows you as well as anyone," I said. I glanced over the railing to make certain we were alone. "I suppose the solicitor and the secretary are getting ready for dinner. *The Solicitor and the Secretary*—doesn't that sound like a good title for a paperback romance? You could've written that one."

The portrait didn't change—portraits don't, as a rule—but it had always seemed to me that different details of the painting stood out at different times. Now, for example, at my comment about Mrs. Woolgar and Mr. Rennie, my eyes were drawn to Lady Fowling's slightly arched brow.

"A bit cheeky of me?" I asked. "Well, what of the murder, then? The police are running down every bit of information they have on Milo. They're in possession of more clues than I know about it, certainly. I'd prefer to leave it to them and think of other things."

I continued to my flat, returning to my fanciful imaginings of an evening with Mrs. Woolgar and Duncan. Did they always go out or sometimes stay in? If in, who did the cooking? I unlocked my door, tossed the key on the table, and headed for the kitchen.

"Who's the better cook?" I asked no one. "Given a whole sole and a filleting knife, who would be better at . . ."

I stood motionless for I don't know how long, and only the fridge, rattling as its motor switched off, broke my thoughts.

"I should eat something."

But what? I could cook myself an omelet. No, my flat was warm enough as it was, and no cross breeze as yet offered to cool it off. Too early, I suppose. I gathered olives and crackers and poured myself a glass of wine. I stripped off my work togs and pulled on a light linen shift, and stretched out on the sofa, glancing round for reading material. Here, easiest to hand—the stack of François stories on the coffee table.

"François and Evil on a Moonless Night" lay on top of the pile. I reached for it, drew back my hand, and then said aloud, "Go on, Hayley, you know you want to." After all—I glanced out the window—it was still daylight. Barely.

> When the moon was full, she could walk from the house down to the creek without stumbling once, even though the landscape was washed of color, transformed by the orb's luminous glow into white or black or gray. But on a moonless night, although the stars may offer their shimmering sparkle, it came from an icy distance, revealing nothing, but causing a shiver to run down her spine, even in summer. For on a moonless night, there were places for evil to hide.

I read further and realized that Lady Fowling had continued to channel du Maurier's *Frenchman's Creek*. The story took place at a dinner party late in the evening, and from its opening, it was infused with unseen fears and tensions. Flambeaux was expected, but had yet to appear. The reason for his delay remained unknown, but ominous. The woman—that special woman in his life—is forced to entertain a host of shallow, greedy men, every one of them desperate to discover Flambeaux's whereabouts, never realizing that she alone knew, but would not tell.

Late in the story, the dinner guests have all left, and she is alone. Or is she?

The candle she held guttered and failed, dying with a hiss. The dining room fell into an inky blackness. She crept forward, one hand held out in front of her. She heard the scratching of mice in the baseboards, the only sound that existed in the world until she reached the door and pushed it open. It creaked, and the sound magnified in the vast cavern of the entry. There, on the far wall near the library, a single flame burned. It flickered, then it danced, caught in a current of wind that came from some unseen source. Her eyes were drawn inexorably up the stairs to the gallery. There he stood, looking down at her and blinking slowly, with one hand on the railing, the other holding a knife.

When my phone rang, I shrieked, then gasped, and then burst out laughing at myself. I caught my breath before answering.

"Hello."

"Hello, Hayley, this is Celia. You wouldn't have time for a drink, would you?"

21

❦

"Celia, where are you?"

"What? Oh, I'm in the garden where we had our picnic that day. By the weir. Lovely out, it really is. Drink? There's a pub just here."

"The Boater?"

"Hang on," she said, and came back a moment later. "Yeah, that's the one."

I looked out the window—a summer evening nearing nine o'clock and that lovely washed-blue twilight in the sky.

Celia rushed on. "It's only that I want to talk with you. There's something I need to do, see, and a bit of Dutch courage wouldn't go amiss, I can tell you that."

Good. I was more than ready to hear her entire story—while sitting in a crowded pub. Why not have a drink with her and clear up these assumptions that she had anything to do with the enquiry.

"Yeah, sure. I'll meet you in, say, twenty minutes?"

"Good. Yeah. Because, if I can explain it to you, then it'll make sense."

I was out the door and walking down toward the Pulteney Bridge in five minutes, pulling out my phone as I went and texting Val.

How's the cruise?

In only a moment, he replied.

Managed two locks so far.

Don't get lost.

And then, for good measure—and because I am not stupid—I added:

Meeting Celia for a drink at the Boater. Will report back.

Text Kenny? he asked.

Sure.

When I had something to tell him.

Celia stood outside the pub waiting and smoking. When she saw me, she put out the cigarette and dropped it into a bin.

"How are you, Celia? We missed you this afternoon," I said.

"Oh yeah," she said over her shoulder as we worked our way inside. "I really wanted to stop, but there was this other thing."

We held up at the bar.

"I'll get this," I said. "What will you have?"

"Thanks, Hayley. Gin and tonic, please," she said to the barman. He looked at me.

What would I have? Wine? Orange squash? It was stuffy inside and still warm outdoors. I noticed a chalkboard with the summer drinks on offer. "Pimm's," I said.

Out in the garden overlooking the weir, we found a recently vacated table and handed the empty glasses left behind to a passing young man with a tray.

Celia deposited her bag on the table and, after a sip or two, lit a cigarette and sighed.

"Well, what was it you wanted to talk with me about?" I asked.

She sat back in her chair and crossed her legs, the dangling espadrilled foot quiet. "Don't you love all those stories in your library?" she asked. "Don't you wonder what those women were really like—the ones who wrote the books? And your Lady Fowling, she wrote her own books. Have you read them?"

"Not all of them," I said, "but even what little I've read, you can tell she loved to write."

"I can't find her books to buy, and so I've only glanced at them in your library. Who do you think her detective is most like?" Celia asked. "Sayers's Wimsey, Marsh's Alleyn, or Tey's Grant?"

I entered the discussion with caution. Celia knew more than I did about those women authors and their male detectives, and so I let her take the lead, making only the occasional comment. She lit another cigarette, and as the conversation progressed, her foot began to bob in a slow cadence. She was stalling—that was obvious—

and would either come to the point of this meeting, or I would begin to ask my own questions.

"I'll get this round," she said. Her G-and-T was long gone, and I'd finally got down to fishing the cucumber slice and strawberry out of my glass.

"Celia, there's something you wanted to tell me. Is it about Milo?"

She froze halfway from sitting to standing. "You've figured it out," she whispered. "Of course you have. All right, all right—I'll tell you. I want to . . . I'll just go get the drinks." She pulled her wallet from her bag, grabbed our empty glasses, and fought her way indoors as more people spilled out into the garden to enjoy the evening.

I attempted to put together a few interview questions in my mind before she returned, but by the time she did appear with drinks as well as two packets of crisps, I'd decided to let her tell her story first.

She seemed charged up and out of breath.

"Okay," I said, calmly and confidently, "tell me about it."

Celia fidgeted with her drink and then dived into her shapeless bag, rummaging round, dragging out lipsticks, mascara tubes, a hairbrush, old bus tickets, and cigarette packets. She checked each one of those, peering inside with one eye, and once assured it was truly empty, she crumpled it and tossed it aside. All the while, she talked.

"Yeah, okay. But I don't want you to think that I . . . I may have assumed that . . . but, this is not my fault, because that bloody man . . . no, I mean the thing is, you see—" But at the third empty cigarette packet, she leapt up and shouted, "Oh, sod it! Look, Hayley, I'll just nip across the road to that newsagent's for fags. I swear I'll be right back and I'll explain. And then"—she gulped—"will you go with me to the police? I'll need a friend. All right? Won't be two ticks."

Celia swallowed half her G-and-T, grabbed her purse from her bag, and hurried back into the pub as more people streamed out.

I should've followed, but her words had left me immobile. The police? I couldn't believe it of her—murder. And yet both Detective Sergeant Hopgood and Detective Constable Kenny Pye had said more than once that a person could snap and . . .

When Celia returned, I would ring Kenny. I hoped the police wouldn't make a scene here at the Boater. No, instead I could walk with Celia to the station. It wasn't as if she would turn and stab me along the way. It wasn't as if she carried a filleting knife about with her at all times. I eyed her bag, left in a heap on the table.

I waited, sipping on my Pimm's. I watched the other people in the garden. Finally, I opened one of the packets of crisps. I looked down to the weir and across the river and noticed the sky had darkened. Every time someone came out of the pub, I looked up. No Celia. She might've stopped at the bar for another round. I shook my glass, trying to loosen the strawberry at the bottom, and then tipped it up. The strawberry slid down into my mouth, and the sprig of mint lodged in a nostril.

I would get a text ready to send to Kenny.

With Celia at the Boater. She wants to confess.

But I couldn't hit send before I heard her out. Then I noticed the time—ten thirty. Celia had been gone for at least a half hour. I sent her a text instead.

Long queue at the bar?

A muffled *ping* came from her bag. I reached in and pulled out her phone, the screen aglow with the notification of my message.

Then my own phone pinged with a text from Val.

We're at the deep lock, but two boats ahead of us.

That spurred me into action.

I'll come meet you.

I crammed everything back into Celia's bag—being careful to check for long knives first—picked it up along with my own, and left.

22

As I made my way through the pub to the door, I inspected every face. The oddest things can go through your head when you're trying to make sense of a situation. She had her purse, but not her phone. She'd sworn she would come back, and we would go to the police together. She could've changed her mind and scarpered, or she could've decided to drink indoors to see how long she could go without a cigarette.

Celia wasn't in the pub, and so, before I started off for the towpath, I checked the other pub on the bridge and the newsagent. I eyed every cluster of smokers I came upon. I took off down Great Pulteney Street, and as I walked, I called up the unsent message to Kenny Pye. Surely he wasn't on duty now—wouldn't it be better to ring the station?

But when the night-duty desk sergeant answered, I found it difficult to give a coherent account from the jumble in my head.

"Celia, she's a witness . . . no, not a witness, possibly a suspect. That is, she knew the victim in a recent murder. Milo Overton's murder, and DC Pye and DS Hopgood are looking for her, and I was just with her, but she went off to a newsagent to buy cigarettes and she hasn't returned."

"Is this an emergency?"

"No, I don't think so. But it's odd, don't you think? It's got me worried."

"Are you in any danger?"

I looked round—the street was well lit, and there were still people out walking.

"No, it isn't that, but . . . she left her bag behind. And her phone."

"I'll send a car out. Give me your location."

"No, she didn't come this way," I said. "Or, at least, I don't know she did. You see, I'm going off to the towpath, but she might've gone anywhere. Back to her flat. Or to the Crystal Palace—she likes that pub."

The desk sergeant asked again where I was, and I told him. He instructed me to stay and keep to a well-lighted area. I disobeyed. When I ended the call, I continued toward Sydney Gardens and the towpath. I wanted to get to *La Mouette 2* to meet Val and John. They would help. We could all look for Celia.

I circled round to the right of the museum to walk through the gardens. This was the way John had walked me out that first day I saw his narrow boat. The day after Milo was murdered. The path through the garden was tarmac, broad and with light posts spaced widely apart, but bright enough. But there were fewer people out here. I passed a couple strolling hand in hand and felt glad of it. It was a lovely evening, really—it smelled green and, if not cool, then not as warm as it had been.

Before I went any farther, I sent Kenny the text.

She wants to confess.

When my phone rang, my heart pounded. Not Kenny—it was John.

"Arrived?" I asked with relief. "I'm almost at the towpath."

"I've remembered," he said.

"Remembered what?"

"Celia Jelley."

"Jelley?" I asked, unable to do more than echo the last word John had said. "Jelley?"

I had stopped dead next to the stone folly—Minerva's Temple— set back from the path. Ahead of me was the bridge that spanned the rail lines below.

"Celia Jelley," John repeated. "She was neither a client nor girl-friend. Milo mentioned her only once or twice that I can remember. She met him at the factory and developed what he called 'attach-ment issues.' She had become rather a nuisance—almost as if she were stalking him."

"She's Celia Jelley? But Jelley is that fellow who was here in Bath looking for Milo."

Silence. "The owl?" John asked. "Yes, of course—that's why the name was familiar."

Two pieces of the puzzle dropped, but into the same slot, vying for position.

"Did Milo feel as if he were in danger from Celia?" I asked.

"He didn't speak of danger, only of her actions. I believe he encouraged her to see someone to work out these issues. Someone else."

Celia hadn't done it. She hadn't murdered Milo. The rambling story she had told me over our several visits began to make sense. "He's her ex," I said. "That must be it. This Jelley is Celia's exhusband. She mentioned him. Actually, now I see that she talked about him a lot, only without naming him. Jelley must have followed Milo here. Or, did he follow Celia, who followed Milo? Did he think Celia and Milo were—"

"Hayley?" It was Val.

"He liked the countryside," I said, coming up with any snippet I could remember. "He liked to camp. He liked to fish—to catch his own dinner. He would have a filleting knife."

"Hayley," Val repeated. "Ring the police."

"Have done, will do again. Where are you?"

"We are at the Wash House lock   not far now, but someone ahead has managed to get himself stuck in the lock, and now we're in a queue, waiting. Are you safe where you are?"

"Yes. I'm in Sydney Gardens near the railway bridge. I'm almost to the towpath. I'll head your way and see you soon."

I ended the call and glanced round. It had grown quiet. A breeze had come up. The trees rustled and branches swayed lazily, throwing odd shadows on the ground. I started off and had reached midspan of the railway bridge when my phone rang again.

"Kenny?" I answered.

"Are you with her?" he asked.

It took me a moment to understand his question, because my mind had taken another direction. "Celia? No, she left—I believe she may have cold feet."

"She confessed to you she killed Milo?"

"No, she didn't do it," I said.

"But your text."

"Yes, sorry, but then I heard from John. He remembered hearing Milo talking about her. She's Celia Jelley." I ran through the latest with him. "It all makes sense now—the things she said to me. But I'm worried because she's missing."

That was it—not just that Celia had wandered off in search of cigarettes or that she'd bought a drink in another pub and forgot. She was missing.

Kenny was quiet for a moment and then said, "That abandoned campsite at the marina. It looked as if someone had been gutting fish there. I sent a sample in to be analyzed, and we've got the results. It wasn't all fish guts. They found Milo Overton's blood."

My stomach flip-flopped. The wound may not have bled much, but there had been blood left on the knife.

"That's where he was," I said. "And so, he attacked John, too."

"Hayley, where are you?"

"I'm walking out to the towpath," I said. "I'm in public and in full view of everyone." But, I admitted to myself, this was the quiet end of the towpath, away from shops and locks and moorings. I'd seen no one the last few minutes. "I'm going out to John and Val on the narrow boat."

"Are you alone?"

I wish he hadn't asked that.

"I'm all right," I said. "I'm moving now. But you should search for

Celia. Have you tried her flat again? She could've gone back there. Or, try at the Crystal Palace pub. The thing is, now I know what all her talk of Rockingham meant."

"Rockingham?" Kenny asked.

"Daphne du Maurier. *Frenchman's Creek*. She was talking about her ex. I believe she knows that Jelley did it—Jelley murdered Milo. And she thinks it's her fault."

"Can you stay where you are and we'll find you?"

What is all this "stay where you are" business?

"No, it would be better for me to keep going, get to the towpath and down to the narrow boat. I'll ring you from there. I'm fine."

I ended the call and hurried over the railway bridge, veering off to the white ironwork gate and the stairs down to the canal. At the bottom, I stopped. The towpath led through a tunnel. The tunnel wasn't a narrow, worrisome thing—it was low but broad, spanning the canal. There was light on both sides, but shadow beneath, and within that darkness, I saw someone waiting.

Then she spoke, her voice low and furtive.

"Hayley."

"Celia? What are you doing here? Where did you go?"

She came out from the shadows, breathing heavily. She held one arm close to her chest, and I saw a dark bloom of a stain on her dress. "Come out of the light," she said.

I followed her back into the shadow of the tunnel. "Jelley? Is he your ex?"

"Thinks he owns me, does he? Thinks if he can't have me, no one will?"

The world round us was still. "Is he following you?"

Celia shook her head. "No, it's all right. He's gone now."

I touched her arm. "What's he done?"

"I was only going for cigarettes," she said, her whispered voice shaking. "But then I saw him, and my only thought was that I've had all I can take. He's going to pay, and so I went after him. He was heading this way, but I lost him in the garden and then I remembered about you and thought I'd text you, but—"

"But you didn't have your phone. I've got it—it's here in your bag."

She looked at her bag, but didn't attempt to take it. "I'd just walked into the garden when he grabbed me."

"Didn't anyone see?" I glanced up and down the towpath and up the steps I'd just come down. We seemed to be in an empty, forlorn spot.

Celia shook her head and then nodded. "But he had the knife in my side, and I know what he can do—look what happened to poor Milo—so I walked along like he said."

"And he stabbed you?"

"Just a nick," she said, looking down at it. "Made a mess, though, didn't it? Up there in the garden, he stumbled and I tried to get away, see. I yelled, and that's when he ran off. That'll be the end of him for the night. That's his way. Coward," she called out to the darkness.

"But what are you doing on the towpath?"

"I needed to rest a minute, and I came down here. I know the place because I followed Milo out when he went to visit that fellow, the one he said he worked for."

"John?"

Celia nodded, her face screwed up in misery. "I followed Milo and Jelley followed me. It's all my fault."

As we talked, I'd pulled my phone out to send a quick text to Kenny, but my thumbs weren't working well and *towpath* came out as *turbo*. I kept trying and then hit send, not knowing how it would read.

"Right, let's go."

"No, please, Hayley, I can't seem to catch my breath."

She was wheezing now. The result of her cigarette habit or a panic attack? I scanned the towpath, the stairs, the footbridge overhead. Quiet.

"All right, just another minute. Don't you want to sit down?"

She shook her head.

"Milo wasn't your therapist, was he, Celia?"

A sob escaped. "I'd seen him round, see, and so I tried to make an appointment through the company, but they fobbed me off on someone else. I wouldn't go. I knew Milo was the one who could help me—I just felt it. I tried to ask him about it, and he was ever so nice explaining why he couldn't be my therapist. But I . . . I felt this connection to him."

"Celia, you saw John in the library. Did you not think he and Milo looked alike?"

She squinted at me. "Not much. When you love someone, Hayley, you couldn't make a mistake like that. But Jelley cottoned on to it, of course—that some people thought they looked alike. He heard you and me at the pub that evening—little sneak. He was sitting the other side of that ivy lattice. Then he made me tell him more."

"You've talked to Jelley while you've been in Bath?"

"Not after I found out what he'd done," Celia said. "He's evil, Hayley."

"Yes, yes, Rockingham. Look, all this can be sorted out by the police. They are on their way." I spoke with as much confidence as I could muster, not knowing how my last text had read. "It's a good thing Jelley ran off, but you and I still need to get out of here. We'll continue down the towpath to the narrow boat. Come on, now—let's shift ourselves."

"No!" She jerked her good arm out of my grasp. "I can't, I tell you. I'm not going to run any longer. That's what got me into this, thinking if I got far enough away, everything would be all right. Well, it wasn't. And now I'm going to find him."

"Celia, the police will find Jelley."

"You don't know, Hayley, you don't know what it's like, you . . ." Her voice petered out. She didn't move, but instead looked up and over my shoulder. Her eyes grew large.

I whirled round and saw, at the top of the white ironwork stairs, Jelley, owl eyes wide and dark behind his glasses. He had one hand on the railing, and in the other hand, a knife.

23

※❦※

R un!" I whispered fiercely.

I pushed Celia ahead, but she fought back with more strength than I gave her credit for. Flailing wildly with her one good arm, she struggled, choking out, "No, this is enough." I raised my arm to ward off her blows and she came down hard, knocking my phone out of my hand. It skittered to the other end of the tunnel.

"I've had enough of you!" Celia shouted at Jelley.

I grabbed her again, but she shook loose, throwing her arm back and landing a hard blow near my left eye.

"Ah!" I reeled and slammed into the wall of the tunnel, hoping the world would stop spinning. Through the sparkly light show of my vision, I saw Jelley start slowly down the stairs.

He moved as if he had all the time in the world, and as he advanced, he spoke. "You ruin everything you touch, don't you, Celia? Look now, you've dragged someone else into this. Another person damaged by your crazy brain." He lifted the knife and I saw a glint as he pointed its tip at his own temple. "I'm the only one understands you, you know that."

Celia pointed a shaking finger at him. "This is it, Jelley."

Jelley paid no heed. "Do you know what he told me, this fellow of yours? He told me he wasn't the one who would fix you. That you were a strong woman and would work this out yourself and I should leave you to it. You, strong! You buckle at the thought of making a cup of tea."

"Celia," I said, pushing away from the tunnel wall and reaching for her, but she shook me off. "You go on, Hayley," she said. "You go. I'll take care of this."

Jelley had paused only ten feet away. If we ran the other direction and I picked up my phone on the way, I could set off the self-defense alarm app—downloaded but never used. Did I remember how?

I grabbed her wrist. "You will not take care of it. We're getting out of here."

When I yanked on her arm, Celia yanked back, pulling me off balance. Then she shoved me away. I'd been clutching both our bags in one hand, and they now went flying through the air as I stumbled backward, waving my arms like windmills. One step, two steps, and then, there was nothing underfoot and I felt myself tipping back, falling in slow motion. I crashed into the water, bottom first.

Down, down I don't know how far into a murky world. The broken light far above me rocked. How deep was the canal? I righted myself but felt no bottom to push off from, and so I swam, pulling myself up and up with broad strokes and frog kicks.

I broke the surface, sputtering and coughing.

"Stop it!" I yelled, but my voice was weak and watery. Also, I couldn't quite tell what was happening. I pushed the hair from my face, swam to the edge of the canal, and reached up to the edge—two feet above me. How was I to get out?

I could see them now. They were near the white ironwork gate and the stairs that led up to the garden. Jelley had both of Celia's arms pinned with one of his. With the other he held the filleting knife against her throat.

"Don't, Jelley," I gasped.

Jelley glanced over his shoulder at me and barked a laugh. "You'll drown before you get out of that," he said, and turned away. "Now, Celia, what am I to do with you?"

I tried to scream for attention, but couldn't make noise and, at the same time, work at getting out of the water. My arms hurt and I was quickly losing energy, clinging to tufts of grass while my feet scrabbled and danced against the wall of the canal trying to catch hold of something, anything that would help me climb out.

At last, my bare foot—I'd lost my shoes—hit on a thick loop. A tree root, like a little shelf. I stood on it, and it took me halfway out of the water, my waist nearly level with the towpath. With one huge effort I flung my body up, the edge of the canal hitting right in my tummy and knocking the wind out of me. I crawled the rest of the way out combat-style and lay panting, my face in the grass.

They hadn't got far, and Jelley took no notice of me.

"This was your fault from the start," Jelley said in Celia's ear, his voice louder now and menacing. "You know that. I had to set things straight. Lucky you told me that Overton and that other bloke looked alike. This is all on you. You gave me the idea to lay the blame on that big fellow, even though you didn't know it. That's about all you're good for, Celia, as a snitch."

I opened my mouth to shout again, but coughed instead. Jelley looked my way and Celia must've felt his grip slacken, because she stomped on his foot and then sent a sharp elbow into his stomach.

He grunted and doubled over. She broke away, shouting, "You go, Hayley!"

But Jelley was quick to recover. He raised the knife. I heard Celia roar as she charged him, lowering her head and butting him. He fell hard against the white iron railing and flipped over it into the brush. I heard the knife clatter to the path and saw Celia dive for it.

I got as far as my hands and knees, and looked up as Jelley fought his way out of the brush. He vaulted himself at Celia—the very moment she raised the knife, blade up.

He as much as stabbed himself. The blade went in just under the arm that he had raised to attack her, and he screamed. Celia screamed, too. Pulling the knife out, she dropped it and backed away.

Jelley staggered toward it, blood streaming down his side. Celia didn't move. I scrambled to my feet and grabbed the nearest thing to hand—her bag. I ran, stumbling forward, and hurled it. It hit him in the chest, and he fell back flat onto the towpath and lay still.

Footsteps—there were footsteps from behind, and I spun round to see someone running through the tunnel toward us. It was Val.

24

I laughed when I saw him. He certainly didn't look like laughing.
"You're soaking," he said, panting and pulling me close.
"Were you in the canal?"

"I lost my shoes." Another giggle escaped before I sobered up.
"Celia?" She stood next to me, quiet, head bowed. I kept hold of Val's
hand, but put my arm round her. "Celia, it's all right now."

"Yeah," she said, barely making a sound.

"We're all right," I said to Val.

"Good thing you told me, because you don't look it." Val glanced
over to the still figure on the towpath. "Is that Jelley?"

All at once there was a great deal of light—white lights, flashing
blue lights—and people everywhere. Three or four uniforms came
running down the ironwork stairs followed by Detective Sergeant
Hopgood and then three ambulance workers.

"There's Jelley," I said, and nodded. The EMTs immediately started to work on him. "And this is Celia."

She squinted in all the light. "Is he . . ." she whispered.

I heard chatter about BP and respiration. "Alive, I think," I said.

"And the two of you?" Hopgood asked.

"Celia needs to be seen to," I said. "Jelley stabbed her in the arm."

"Did he do that to you?" Val asked, bringing one hand up to my face.

I touched the spot. That's why my vision was so odd—my eye had swelled.

"No, he didn't. That was an accident."

"Ms. Burke," Hopgood said, "both of you need to go to A&E. You can ride along in the ambulance."

"No!" Celia had found her voice at last, although it had a crack in it. "Not if he's in it, I won't." She shook and swayed.

"Nor will I," I said. "Come over here and sit down, Celia." I guided her to the edge of the towpath, and we sat in the grass where we were out of the way. "You can't expect us to ride along with a murderer, can you, Sergeant? He killed Milo. He attacked John. And tonight, he attacked Celia. He stabbed her, then he followed her here. He had that knife, and if it weren't for Celia's quick actions, we'd both be dead. She saved our lives."

Hopgood nodded. "We'll see to your statements later, why don't we? In the meantime, I'll get a uniform to drive you to A&E."

There was a face missing. "Where is Kenny?" I asked.

"He's with John on the boat," Val said. "He met us as we got to the Pulteney Gardens lock and told us police were starting at this end to look for you. It seemed quicker for me to come on foot. I wouldn't say I broke any land records, but I know for certain that's the fastest I've run in a lot of years."

I pulled him down beside me. "I'm glad you did."

A PC appeared with two cups, handing one off to Celia and one to me. Sugary, milky tea never tasted so good.

"Thanks, love," Celia said to the PC. "I don't suppose you'd have a fag on you?"

The PC shot a glance round at the busy scene. "Hang on a mo," she whispered.

La Mouette 2 came chugging up the canal with Kenny in the bow and John at the rear—is that the stern?—driving the boat.

I stood up and waved as they approached, but the action seemed to knock me off balance. Val stood, too, and put his arm round me. "You're shivering," he said.

"Am I?" As soon as he said the words, I felt light-headed as if I were vibrating. I took hold of his arm and held tight.

"Hayley, are you all right?" John called.

"Yes, fine. Well, not fine." I looked back to see the EMTs carrying Jelley off.

"Is that the man?" John asked. "The one Constable Pye tells me killed Milo. Killed him on purpose, not as a mistake."

"That's him," I said.

John looked up into the sky. "You know what this is, don't you?"

"I do," I said, "'Evil on a Moonless Night.'"

K enny told his guv he would stay on board *La Mouette 2* as far as the next winding hole on the canal in order to help John turn the boat round and come back for one of those precious forty-eight-hour mooring spots. We waved them off. Celia and I were driven to the hospital by a PC in a blue-and-yellow-checkered car, and Val followed in a taxi. At first, I worried about my damp clothes on police upholstery, but then thought they probably had worse. I told the driver the blue lights weren't necessary, but she did put them on at the last minute when we pulled up to A&E. "Better service," she told us.

A nurse took Celia back.

"I don't really have anything that needs tending to," I told the nurse at the desk.

"Your eye," Val said.

"It was an accident," I assured them both.

"And you're in shock," he added.

"But I've already had a cup of tea." Nonetheless, I leaned on the counter for support and kept a firm hold on Val's hand.

An orderly took me back, and on the way, I caught a glimpse of myself in a mirror. Unfortunately, my vision had cleared, and I could see every detail.

I sat on the examining table, and everything began to hurt. The left side of my face throbbed, my arms felt as if they'd been stretched to twice their length, and my shoulder was sore from where I'd slammed against the side of the tunnel. My feet were an awful fright. But I could hear moaning in the cubicle next to me, so I told myself it could be worse.

The doctor came in, asked questions, looked into my eye, and prodded my face. No X-ray necessary. The nurse applied a cold compress and told me to take an over-the-counter pain reliever. I was released wearing paper booties and with a tinfoil blanket over my shoulders to keep me warm.

Val and I waited for Celia, and while we did, I filled him in, in a disjointed sort of way. He, in turn, gave me what he could.

"Kenny rang after you'd talked to him. He says the manager of the caravan park recognized Jelley's E-FIT."

"It didn't occur to Jelley that could happen?"

"Not the sharpest knife in the drawer, is he?" Val asked, then frowned. "Sorry."

Celia had more than just the one cut from Jelley—he'd caught her twice more when I had been in the canal, once on her shoulder and once on her other arm. But her injuries were not severe, and they soon released her. Val and I were waiting.

She came out of the ward, paperwork in hand, bandages showing from under her sleeveless dress, and her eye makeup smeared across her face, possibly in an attempt to wipe it off. She looked round the waiting area in a daze. I went to her.

"Are you still here?" she asked.

"Yeah, although I could just do with a long, hot shower." My hair had dried stiff, and I detected an odd odor about myself. "Look, Celia, I want you to come back to my flat for the night. I don't think you should be alone in your bedsit. Not after all this."

Tears flooded her eyes and streamed down her cheeks, carrying what was left of her mascara with them.

"I wouldn't want to put you out," she managed to squeak.

"You won't be putting me out—although you'll be on the sofa. Is that all right?"

"I don't mind a sofa," she said.

"And also—you won't be able to smoke. Sorry."

That gave her pause, but only for a moment.

"Ah well, I've been meaning to quit."

25

The next morning, I awoke to the sun streaming in the windows, traffic on the street below, and the shrieking of the gulls on the roof. I took a deep breath and let it out slowly as I recalled the end of the night before. Val had stayed long enough to have a brandy with us—I'd taken the bottle from Middlebank's liquor cabinet, which was actually a cupboard in the kitchenette. I would be sure to replace it.

While Celia had a bath, Val and I had said our good nights.

"You sure you don't want me to stay?" he asked.

"I very much want you to stay," I replied, "but it'll be better just Celia and me."

"Then I'll see you first thing," he promised.

After he'd gone, I had locked Middlebank's front door and set the alarm and wondered what sort of note I should leave Mrs. Woolgar.

I'd got as far as turning the light on in her office—Bunter didn't even look up—and picking up a pen, but nothing coherent came to mind. I decided it would be better to explain in the morning.

By the time I had got back upstairs, Celia was snoring on the sofa. I took what I admit to be one of the longest showers in history and stayed up after that only long enough to dry my hair.

Now, on this bright morning, I reached for my phone to check the time, but my phone wasn't there. The police, I remembered, had gathered up everything at the scene, and both Celia and I would need to retrieve our property when we gave and signed our statements.

Well, there's my day planned. What day was it? Thursday, I thought.

I ventured out of bed, stopped in the bathroom, and then continued to the kitchen to switch the kettle on, bent on not disturbing Celia. But when I looked into the living room, I saw the sofa was empty.

That's when the door opened.

"'Morning," Celia said, slipping in. She had on clean clothes, but the most notable difference in her appearance was her makeup—she wore none, and without her usual heavy application, I could see she had sparkly brown eyes.

"Where have you been?"

"I didn't want to disturb you," she said, "so first thing, I went downstairs, thinking I'd go and try to get into my flat. Your Mrs. Woolgar was in her office, and she didn't seem at all surprised to see me. She rang the police, and a nice woman PC came and took me over to my flat for clothes. I came straight back."

Not straight back, I thought as I caught a whiff of fresh cigarette smoke about her.

"What time is it?"

"Quarter past eleven," Celia said. "But Mrs. Woolgar said to tell you not to hurry."

The kettle switched off. "Well, then," I said, "tea?"

And toast and scrambled eggs. We made quite a job of it, and I saw that Celia had a hearty appetite when she put her mind to it.

"The PC let me use her phone, and I rang my sister in Exeter," Celia said. "She's coming up to collect me. Says I need to quit my job and stay with her while I heal from my inner wounds."

"You have a sister, that's good."

"I've got three of them—this one in Exeter, plus one in Norwich and one in Chester. We're sort of spread out."

Celia appeared a new woman—calm, unsquinting. I hoped it wasn't denial. "How are you feeling this morning, Celia, in yourself?"

She took another slice of toast and scraped butter over it before she answered. "I'm all right, really. Sad, but calm, like, at the same time. The PC told me Jelley's alive, and they expect him to recover." She bit into her toast and chewed and chewed and chewed.

"I meant what I said to Sergeant Hopgood last night. You saved both our lives."

"Yeah," Celia said. "But I couldn't save Milo's, could I?"

Just before one o'clock, Celia and I said our good-byes. Her sister would meet her at the police station. She promised to return for the winter salon series. We headed downstairs, and Bunter, who had been loitering on the library landing, followed. I'd no more closed the front door before Mrs. Woolgar popped out of her office.

"Well," she said brightly, but clenching her hands at her waist. "Here you are. You're all right?" She peered at my black eye.

"Yes," I said. "Fine, really." I touched my cheek—a thick but carefully applied coat of face powder did nothing to cover the purple and blue. "I'm sorry I didn't come down first thing to explain."

"Nonsense," the secretary said. "There was no need. I had a text from John early this morning—something about 'Evil on a Moonless Night.' I rang him immediately, and he told me what had happened. Then, not long after, Mr. Moffatt rang, too. Then I saw Ms. . . . Celia, and I knew you wouldn't be down. I don't believe you should even think about work today."

I was stuck on the fact that John had texted Mrs. Woolgar early in the morning, and she immediately rang him. My goodness, things move quickly when the dam bursts.

"Just as well—I'm sure my afternoon will be full as it is."

"I hope you don't mind," Mrs. Woolgar said, "but I thought it best to let the board know—at least in brief—what occurred, as they would most likely see it on the local news. Mr. Moffatt offered to tell Ms. Babbage, and I've talked with Audrey and Sylvia Moon, Jane Arbuthnot, and Maureen."

"Thank you, that's a relief."

The secretary's face soured. "Not long after, Charles Henry rang."

"Oh?"

"This indexing business has gone to his head. He suggested that it become a permanent position and that we refurbish the kitchenette as an office for him."

"He what?" There you are then, the leopard doesn't . . . "What did you tell him?"

The secretary arched an eyebrow. "I told him that wouldn't be possible, as we were considering turning the kitchenette into a tea-room."

I burst out laughing, and Bunter skittered back up the stairs.

"That should put him off long enough for him to lose interest," Mrs. Woolgar said.

V al showed up not long after, and my afternoon was as I had predicted—full of all manner of tasks mostly unrelated to the First Edition Society. We went to the police station, where I gave my statement, and Kenny Pye reported that he would return my bag and phone later that afternoon. Val and I stopped at Waitrose and bought sandwiches and a bottle of prosecco and ate lunch on *La Mouette 2* with John and Frances. While Val and Frances discussed how the color scheme on a book cover affects sales, I pulled John aside for a quiet talk.

When I'd explained, he said, "Yes, of course. I'll do anything I can to help."

"Ready?" Val called. "We'd best be on our way."

John gave me a nod and tapped his finger aside his nose.

"Are we in a hurry?" I asked Val as we climbed up onto the tow-path. "Do we have an appointment? I thought I was off work this afternoon."

"Oh yeah, well, you are, of course, it's only that . . . didn't Kenny say he'd be dropping by Middlebank this afternoon?" He checked the time and walked faster.

"Are you feeling all right?" I asked.

"Me? Yeah, fine. Why?"

"No reason."

When we got near Middlebank, I noticed a car parked across the road with its flashers on. I didn't recogize the car, but I certainly knew the driver who got out.

"Dinah, sweetie?"

"Hiya, Mum!" She stretched out her arms in greeting. "God, you've been the busy one, haven't you? Val's told us all about what's happened. It's no wonder you didn't remember we were coming."

Remember? No, I didn't remember.

"We? Is your gran in there, too?"

"She is," Dinah said, and with a flourish opened the passenger door.

I ran up. "Mum?"

She smiled at me, held out a hand, and clucked. "Look at your face, poor sausage."

"Oh, it's nothing," I said as I helped her out. "Or at least, not much of a thing."

"More than not much, according to Val," Mum said.

"Lenore rang me this morning when they couldn't get hold of you," he said. "The three Burke women on the road—apparently it's this weekend."

We shared hugs all round as we stood on the pavement, and then crossed the road in a cluster, and were met in the entry by Mrs. Woolgar, who had also been alerted to the arrival of my mother and daughter.

After that confusing time of greeting—talking about the journey and all else—Val took Mum up to the library, and Mrs. Woolgar went to the kitchenette to put the kettle on.

"I'll go get our bags," Dinah said.

"I'll follow you," I called. "Mrs. Woolgar, do we have enough biscuits? I could nip down to the—"

The secretary nodded to a pink bakery box on the counter. "Sorted."

The problem with being a single mother is that you become imbued with the idea that you are the only one who can get anything done. It can be difficult to cede power, but once done, it's quite exhilarating.

"Lovely, thanks," I said. "I'll go out and help Dinah."

I came out onto the pavement in time to see Dinah across the road and Kenny Pye approaching her. He glanced at the car as she slammed a door.

"Sorry," he said, "you've left your flashers on."

"Yeah, I know," she replied.

"And you're parked on a double yellow," he said. "Flashers don't give you permission, you know."

"It's only for a minute," she said.

"This isn't a good place for a stop, even temporary."

"I'll be right back," she snapped.

"There's a reason it's painted double yellow," Kenny said, his usual mild manner edged with annoyance.

"And who are you to tell me how to park my car—the police?"

I couldn't get across the road fast enough—too much traffic. At last, I made it and took hold of her arm. "Yes, sweetie, as a matter of fact, he is. I'd like you to meet Detective Constable Kenny Pye. Kenny, this is my daughter, Dinah."

"Oh," she said, her nose in the air. "Hello."

"Nice to meet you," Kenny replied, sounding as if it was anything but. "Hayley, just stopped by to return your phone and bag."

"Won't you stay for tea?" I asked. "Wouldn't that be lovely, Dinah?"

Dinah had her head in the boot of the car and didn't reply. Kenny glanced at her and said, "No, I've got to be on my way."

So much for my matchmaking.

By the time we were back inside, tea was going in the library. We caught up on all the news, and Mum and Dinah told us of their journey from Liverpool and their arrival in Bath, which prompted Dinah to recount her exchange with Kenny.

"The cheek of that detective to tell me not to park on a double yellow. He isn't in traffic." She reached for another scone, and as she did so, she said, "What did you say his name was, Mum?"

The three Burke women had a holiday that suited all of us—one night away in Salisbury, which was little more than an hour away, and so limited my anxiety. Not that Dinah wasn't a careful driver, she was. Still, I needed tea and a nap by the time we arrived at our hotel. Dinah had the car for only three days, and so she and my mum left on Saturday. I worked the rest of the weekend because a board meeting had been called for Tuesday afternoon.

By Monday morning, I'd written an agenda and a report of my first year as curator, emphasizing the Society's accomplishments and leaving out anything that didn't actually need to be there. Milo's murder, for example—what did that have to do with us?

On Monday, Mrs. Woolgar met Charles Henry at his usual time and escorted him up the stairs while I stayed in the kitchenette and polished the silver. After that, I went out and bought more sherry.

At Tuesday afternoon's board meeting, the library table resplendent with a gleaming tea set and tray of enticing pastries, I took a moment to look round at those present—Mrs. Woolgar, Duncan Rennie, Audrey and Sylvia Moon, Jane Arbuthnot, Maureen Frost, and Adele. I hadn't known any of them a year ago, except Adele, who'd put me on to the post at a desperate time for both the Society and me. But now I daresay they'd each of them become a friend of sorts. Still emotional over recent events, I found a lump in my throat and gave a little cough.

"Good afternoon," I began. "First on the agenda . . ." And we were off. The year review was much more fun than I imagined it would be. We discussed the salons and favorite speakers, the exhibition, and the lovely gown I wore to the opening gala. I had Mrs. Woolgar and her dressmaking skills to thank for that, and I did so—for about the thousandth time. Then I came to new business.

"We have an incredible opportunity before us," I said. "Lady Fowling's early short stories are such a treasure, and I believe, with a small amount of sympathetic editing, they could be published. They would not only take a proud place beside the Flambeaux series, but also they would stand by themselves—perhaps in a more affordable format so that all readers of mystery could experience her ladyship's creativity. And, I believe we should put the proceeds from sales toward a fund that would offer grants to women mystery writers."

There was silence round the table except for the titter from Sylvia Moon. Everyone looked to Maureen Frost.

"Well, Hayley," she said, "this is either fortuitous, or some unseen hand is at work. Those of us here had a brief meeting yesterday afternoon. I hope you don't mind, but we did need to go over a detail or two, as this marks the end of your year at the Society." I felt a stab of apprehension. "That is, the end of your *first* year." There, I could breathe again. "The board has voted to offer you a pay rise as curator of the First Edition Society and its library—on the condition you will also oversee the publication of Georgiana's short stories."

"I vote to include Hayley's idea about the grant," Audrey said.

"Audrey," Jane said, "that isn't the proper procedure. First you must—"

"I second it," Sylvia said.

"You can't second a—"

"Can we can settle the details later?" Maureen asked over them. "For now, I'm sure we can agree that this is a brilliant idea."

A brilliant idea and a pay rise. Not bad.

On Tuesday and Thursday afternoons, I was away from Middlebank learning new skills, shopping for our upcoming holiday, and avoiding Val and his questions.

"Lunch?" he would ask.

"Sorry, I can't today—this thing with an article I promised to write."

"Dinner?"

"If I don't leave my office straight, I'll regret it when I return from our holiday."

"Which seaside?" he asked. "Shouldn't I plan our route?"

"Don't worry, I know how to get there."

On Friday morning, I rang John three times.

"Yes, don't worry," he said each time. "You need only be there and wait. Everything is ready."

It had not been easy to keep quiet—also, Val had almost caught me on *La Mouette 2* at the top lock, working the windlass. But now the waiting was over.

At four o'clock, I had positioned myself at the back of the boat under the parasol, feet propped up on the edge of the boat. It wasn't *La Mouette 2*, but *Pride of Bath* had a good ring to it—for a rented narrow boat.

The water lapped gently against the side of the boat. I opened a paperback copy of *Frenchman's Creek* in front of my face, occasionally, peering over the top, looking for familiar faces amid the walkers on the towpath. At last, I caught sight of John's white pirate shirt up ahead and hid behind the book once again.

As they drew closer, I heard their exchange.

"I don't see your boat, John," Val said.

"It isn't my narrow boat we seek," John replied. "Ah, here we are, Val. Your home for the next fortnight."

I peeked over the top of my shield. The two men stood just off the back of the boat, John with hands on his hips and Val looking both suspicious and flummoxed.

Val's gaze took in the boat and came back to me. I put down the book and gave him a smile.

"Hello, sailor."

ACKNOWLEDGMENTS

Thanks to the host of people for their help through all phases of this, the third book in the First Edition Library Mysteries: my agent, Christina Hogrebe, from the Jane Rotrosen Agency; my editor at Berkley, Michelle Vega, and assistant editor, Jenn Snyder; and my writing group—Kara Pomeroy, Louise Creighton, Sarah Niebuhr Rubin, Tracey Hatton, and Meghana Padakandla. *The Librarian Always Rings Twice* is a better book because of you.

Thanks to friends and family (especially my sister, Carolyn Lockhart, and my brother, Ed Polk!) for showing such great support and interest in my books.

And thanks to the generous mystery-writing community—we may write about murder, but we're good folk at heart.

About the story.

You may not expect to find Daphne du Maurier in a collection of books from the Golden Age of Mystery, but you will find her on the shelves of the First Edition Library at Middlebank House, because she was one of Lady Fowling's favorite authors. (It's always nice to be able to blame one of your characters.) So, I was able to choose *Frenchman's Creek* as the springboard for *The Librarian Always Rings Twice*, and I wove threads of Dona and pirate Jean Benoit-Aubéry's story into that of Lady Fowling and her pirate turned sleuth, François Flambeaux. I hope you enjoyed reading it as much as I enjoyed writing it.